DOES LOVE ALWAYS WIN?

DOES LOVE ALWAYS WIN?

DIANE BILLAS

Published in the United States by Creative James Media.

www.creativejamesmedia.com

978-1-956183-70-2 (trade paperback)

First U.S. Edition 2023

To Matt,
Love you, always and forever.

CHAPTER ONE

I was a happy person, well, for the most part. I usually had a smile plastered on my face but every now and then, there was a little voice in my head whispering that something didn't add up. Like right now. I should've been enjoying the moment, but instead I was daydreaming about what jaw-dropping dress I'd wear for the first day of school tomorrow.

Bryan's roaming hands snapped me out of my train of thought. I couldn't take it anymore. Even if he was the best kisser and hottest guy in the world, I still wouldn't want to be here with him. The feelings that fueled my flirting last school year disappeared once we became serious.

I pulled away from his grasp, stretched my arms above my head, and let out an exaggerated yawn. "I really should get ready for tomorrow. Big day, right?"

"Shorty, I just got here!" Bryan ran his hands through his dark brown hair. His muscles threatened to escape through his tight gray T-shirt.

Did he purposely buy his shirts skintight to show-off his ripped body?

I glanced at my silver watch. "Maybe some other night. Besides, my parents will probably be home soon. You'd better leave before they know you were here."

A sick part of me wanted my mom to come home earlier than usual and find us alone in the basement. If I was lucky, she'd ban me from seeing him.

I was running out of excuses not to be with him.

Bryan didn't make a move to leave. Instead, he tightened his grip around my waist and pulled me closer, a glint of mischief in his eye. "Let's keep going until we get caught."

Before he could act on his impulse, I escaped from his clutches and leaped off the couch. I tripped over one of the discarded throw pillows, landing in a disheveled heap on the floor. I quickly stood and adjusted my flowery sundress. "Stop! I'm waiting, remember?"

Didn't no mean no? This was the billionth time I had turned him down.

Bryan threw his hands in the air. "You know what Shorty, I don't care. I'm so done. You're a big freaking tease."

"Excuse me?"

Bryan stood. "You heard me. You're all talk." His expression was cold, and for a fleeting second, I thought I saw a sinister flash in his eye.

I positioned my hands on my hips. "What do you mean?"

Bryan pointed at me. "You flirted with me all last year, and then after we got together, you freak out if I touch you. Paul told me you did this to him, too." His voice raised with each accusation.

My jaw dropped. "Wait, what? You talked to Paul?"

"We're both on the football team. You don't think we talk?"

"I didn't think you were friends, that's all."

What was Bryan's problem? Why was he freaking out so much?

Bryan's face reddened. "I thought maybe things would be different because Paul's the kicker, and I'm the quarterback, but nope. You're acting just like he warned me you would."

"Bryan, I'm not ready to have sex with you or anyone. You've known that!" I blew a loose piece of long, blond hair out of my face.

"It's not just that, but whatever. I'm done. Find someone else you can string along." Bryan slung his navy-blue backpack over his shoulder and sulked up the steps from my basement.

Once he was gone, I sat frozen on the couch. After a deep breath I felt all the way down to my toes, a small grin crept across my face. *Oh, thank God. I wouldn't have to deal with his excessive handsy-ness and ego anymore. Shouldn't I be more upset, or run after him? Was it weird that instead I felt like a weight had been lifted off my chest?*

Why did this always happen? Sure, my fling with Bryan lasted longer than the others, but it ended the same way: me dreading to be around the guy a single second longer. All they wanted to do was fool around or talk about sports. Wasn't a relationship supposed to be deeper than that? I had never felt a connection. Maybe it was because I had a deep-rooted crush on someone else? He was the reason I wanted to wear a sexy dress tomorrow, one that complimented my short frame and pin-straight blond hair.

I'd harbored a crush on Zack Hurley ever since middle school when almost every girl in our grade shared a similar obsession. He had rumpled, sandy blond hair, dimples, and he always knew the right thing to say to make me smile. He was the type of person that was always there to help someone in need. I still remembered the day he paid for a random girl's lunch when she burst into tears because her wallet was missing. When I told him how cool it was, he brushed it off.

"Oh that? I was super hungry and next in line. Everyone

should be able to eat, and I had the money," he'd said, shrugging.

I had an inkling he liked me, but the stars never seemed to align. We had always dated other people. Last I had heard, he and his girlfriend Zoe were on the rocks; coincidentally that had happened right after band camp where Zack and I began to move past the fake flirting stage with each other and into *dangerous territory.*

In reality, Bryan actually did me a favor by breaking up with me. Every time Bryan came over, I would've rather been texting Zack. I'd put off the inevitable because who really wanted to break up with a person? It was literally the worst.

I picked up my iPhone from the ground where it had fallen during my non-erotic make out session with Bryan and noticed I had a couple of missed texts from my best friend, Hannah Greer. I usually responded to her ASAP, so she was probably worried.

> Is Bryan still there?

> R u alive?

> Text 911 if you need me!!

I smiled and texted back.

> I'm alive, but Bryan broke up with me! The nerve.

> What? He broke up with u? No one breaks up with u! R u ok? Tyler can punch Bryan in his stupid face.

Hannah was dating my ex-boyfriend, Tyler. I had realized after a couple of months that it was more like dating a friend, so I ended that relationship. That breakup hurt the most because I had liked hanging out with him. We had talked about anything and everything, but I couldn't get into his kissing. When Hannah had confided in me that she had a crush on Tyler, I told her to go for it. Just because I dated him didn't mean it should ruin her chance at happiness.

> Yea, I'll get over it. I mean, I was pretty much done anyways. He beat me to it. Btw do you know how Zack is? We haven't talked since band camp.

> OMG, guess what?! Zack broke up with Zoe b cuz he liked someone else. 99% sure it's u.

My heart beat rapidly, and my stomach fluttered.

> What!? I mean we did almost make out at band camp a month ago, but I didn't think he'd break up with her so fast!

> YES! Txt him to see how he's doing! Zoe's gone so there's an opening at our lunch table.

Hannah, Tyler, and Zack's lunch table was *couples only.* The only way I could secure a seat was if Zack asked me out; this was my golden opportunity.

> YESSSS. About freaking time! I'm going to text him now and see how he's doing.

> Good luck

> Thanks!!!

I took a deep breath. The time had finally come; I was finally going to be happy! My hands shook as I typed in Zack's name.

> Hey there. Sorry to hear about your breakup with Zoe. Are you ok? Let me know if you need anything.

Almost immediately a reply appeared.

> She's got a new guy already.

> No way!? That's SO rude. Probs to make you jealous.

> Thanks.

After a couple of seconds another text came in.

> How's Bryanland?

> That's so over. Now when I play the trumpet at football games, I don't have to pretend to care about the game.

> Really? I would have texted. You ok?

> Yea I'm fine. We weren't right together anyways.

> True. Ur too good for him.

> I'm blushing... 😉

A couple of minutes passed without any word from Zack, and I started to panic. Did I scare him with the wink? What if

I misinterpreted our random flirty texts throughout the summer?

I thought back to a few weeks ago at band camp when we were inches away from each other's lips in the empty practice room. He had run his hand through my hair, and I had lost track of how many minutes we stared into each other's eyes. Right when I thought he would go in for the kiss, he re-directed it to my forehead instead. Maybe the forehead kiss wasn't him being respectful, but showing he only liked me as a friend. Maybe ...

Then the typing bubble appeared.

You should sit with me at lunch.

YES! Just according to plan. I couldn't believe this was happening. There really was a god! I texted back.

Can't wait!

Shorty for the win. I smiled and sent a screenshot of the conversation to Hannah. She congratulated me on my mad skills, and I headed to bed after saying a quick goodnight to my parents after they arrived home. I laid out my flowery pink and blue dress for tomorrow.

When I got straight A's at the end of last year, I could pick any dress I wanted in the store. I ran around Macy's in a flurry until I found the perfect one. I had been waiting to wear this since I saw it on the rack. I was *blessed* with a four feet, ten inch stature, hence my nickname. Pants didn't fit me, and my mom didn't want to pay to get them tailored, so I was forced to wear dresses, skirts, or shorts every day. Not that I was complaining, dresses were super cute, but it would be nice to be a normal teenager occasionally and wear a pair of skinny jeans.

After I finished my prep for tomorrow, I tucked myself into my pink flowered sheets, and tried to fall asleep. Thoughts of my whirlwind night rolled around in my head, and I couldn't wait for school. Hopefully, everything with Zack would work out and all the pieces of the puzzle would finally fall into place.

CHAPTER TWO

My school parking spot, number two, was a well-earned accomplishment. Anyone on the junior honor roll could enter the parking lottery to receive a prime spot rather than be stuck with one behind the school. At the end of school last year when my name was pulled for a spot, I let out a whoop of joy. No more lugging my trumpet case around the building!

I stole a quick glance in the car mirror to inspect my make-up and was ready to take on the world. I stepped from my vehicle when I heard, "Shorty! Wait up!"

I whirled around toward the sound of the voice. Zack strode toward me, his dirty blond hair slightly wet. He wore a Pink Floyd T-shirt, khaki shorts, and Chuck Taylor shoes. I wanted to ruffle his wet hair; he was so adorable. I felt a rush of warmth reach my cheeks. Who knew I'd fall for a true band nerd?

"Hey! It's so nice to see you," I said, flashing him my million-watt smile. That smile had been absent around Bryan for at least a month. *Thank God he was out of the picture.*

"You too," Zack said, running his hands through his hair

while his eyes scanned the length of my body. I swear they dilated while doing so.

I stole a whiff of his shampoo as we hugged. It smelled insanely good—suave and earthy—enough to drive any girl wild.

We pulled away and Zack said, "You look amazing."

"You don't look too bad yourself."

"I'm glad you texted. I'd been hoping to hear from you."

I twirled a piece of my hair with my index finger.

"Oh, were you?"

This was happening just like I fantasized. Finally, we're both on the same page.

"Yeah, band camp was intense."

"It really was. Not going to lie, I've thought about that a lot," I said.

He raised his right eyebrow. "Oh really? What exactly were you thinking about?"

I cocked my head. "Are you going to make me spell it out?"

He pulled me toward him again. "I think I remember being this close to each other."

"Your memory is correct," I said, very aware that my body was pressed up against his. My hands began to sweat. *Was our first kiss finally about to happen, already?*

I could still smell the exhaust from my car, and I heard my classmates greeting each other in the background. *I'd hoped our first kiss would be somewhere more romantic and private, not in a school parking lot full of loud people.*

He tipped my face up toward him, and I looked expectantly in his eyes.

"But at band camp I couldn't do this," he said, closing the gap between us. His lips brushed against my own.

I waited for my heart to burst, fireworks to explode, and birds to flock around us harmonizing melodious songs of love, but there was none of that. I didn't feel a single ounce of excitement when his lips locked with mine, nor when he kissed me a second time with his tongue slightly slipping into my mouth. I ran my fingers through his hair to pull him closer to me, trying to feel some kind of emotion, anything. But none arose. Zack let out a small groan as he plowed ahead.

What was going on? I'd been dreaming of Zack since forever. Shouldn't I be feeling something?

I tried not to venture into full-blown panic mode, but everything seemed wrong; kissing Zack was just like everyone else.

How could this be happening? What was wrong with me? Was I doomed to never have a love story of my own?

I kept my composure to prevent Zack from realizing that anything was awry. I even rubbed his back and prolonged the kiss to keep up the charade. Meanwhile, he was still going full steam ahead, oblivious to my inner meltdown and the unsolicited catcalls in the background that could only be for us.

I thought Zack was the answer to all my problems. How could I have a crush on him for so long and then be this disappointed?

After what seemed like forever, he pulled away, out of breath.

"It's like I always imagined it would be," he said.

At least that made one of us.

"We had to wait how many years for this moment?" I asked.

"Too long." He came in for a third kiss when I put up my fingers to his mouth.

"We should probably get to class. Walk me to my locker?"

"Sure. Here, I can carry your lunch bag and iPad."

I handed over my stuff that had landed on the trunk of my car during our impromptu make out session. I should've tried dating nice guys sooner. Paul and Bryan would never have carried my bags. As we were walking through the school's front door, I felt my phone vibrating. I rooted around for it, stepping off to the side to let my classmates go around me. My heart sank as I scanned the text from Bryan.

> I didn't mean what I said last night. Let's try again. Sit with me at lunch. I'll make it up to u.

Why did Bryan have to break up with me first? I really wanted to be the one to end it on my terms.

"Who's that from? Hannah?" Zack asked.

"No, I wish. It's Bryan. I guess he's regretting breaking up with me. He wants to get back together, but that's so not going to happen," I said, walking toward my locker.

Dale High seemed the same, as if I never left. Hallways devoid of color supplemented by that musty odor of old textbooks and a labyrinth of rows upon rows of gray, rusted lockers.

"He broke up with you?"

"Before I got the chance to end it with him. Guess I'll have to tell him we're done."

Zack wrapped his arm around me. "What if you don't respond? He can figure it out himself when you sit with me at lunch."

I spun the dial to enter my combination to my locker. "That's true. Speaking of lunch, thanks for carrying my stuff." I tried rattling the lock when my locker didn't open.

Great. Well, now I looked stupid. Would this washed-up school ever get new things? Or maybe Zack's lingering arm was making me nervous.

"Here, let me try."

"That'd be great. God, I hate these things."

After one try, the locker popped open. Zack placed my

lunch bag onto the gray, dusty shelf, and I slammed the door shut. I took the iPad from Zack and slipped it under my arm.

"Thanks! You're a lifesaver."

"No problem." His lopsided smile should've made my heart flutter. *He's doing all the right things. I don't get it. Why don't I feel anything?*

"I guess I better get to homeroom. See you at lunch!" I kissed Zack on the cheek but slipped away before he could return the favor. *Shouldn't I want to be kissing him every chance I could get?* I shook my head. *No time to figure this out now, I can't be late for homeroom on my first day.*

Most days I really didn't mind being short; I loved my nickname, but when I needed to get somewhere fast, not having long legs was a pain, especially when your homeroom class was at the opposite end of school. With only a couple of minutes to spare, I slid into the desk with my predetermined paper name tent. Our degenerate public school never seemed to have any money. We still had the type of desks that were physically bolted to the chair. During open house last year, my mom commented how she remembered sitting in the same exact desk at Dale. Maybe by the time I had a child the school would invest in a desk and chair that were detached from each other. *A girl can only dream.*

Homeroom was a glorified attendance tracker, PSA for school updates, and a holding cell for dreaded standardized tests. I always questioned the need for a homeroom period, but today it at least gave me some downtime to process what happened with Zack before having to pay attention at an actual class.

As soon as I sat down, the teacher, Mrs. Jacobs, called my actual name.

"Sam Daniels, can I see you?"

I sighed, reluctantly rising from my seat.

"As Student Council President, I thought it might be nice

if you could show a new student around today. Her name is Kristy Davis, and she should be here shortly. It would be most appreciated."

"Oh, uh sure. No problem." *So much for having time for myself.*

Being voted Student Council President was once again biting me in the butt. I knew that random responsibilities would arise, but I didn't think much of it when I ran for the job. I only signed up because my parents thought it would look good on my future resume. The election quickly morphed into a battle between myself and my sole competitor and former friend-turned-frenemy, Cashi. When I ultimately won, I thought victory would be sweeter, but not only did I lose my friendship with Cashi, I realized I had the added responsibility to schedule and run the meetings. One more thing to worry about and now, even before senior year officially started, *other duties as assigned* entailed serving as a glorified tour guide to the new girl.

As the bell rang, a girl with short, auburn hair cut asymmetrically strolled in. She was wearing a leather jacket, a form-fitting maroon T-shirt, and the tightest black jeans I'd ever seen. You could trace every curve of her body. Her leather jacket strained against her toned arms. I couldn't look away, even if I tried.

"I take it you're Kristy Davis. I'm Mrs. Jacobs. Your seat is right behind Sam Daniels. She'll be showing you around today."

Kristy nodded her head and sat down behind me.

I took a deep breath and turned around with an award-winning smile. "Hi, I'm Sam, but most people call me Shorty, because, well, I'm stupidly short. Happy to help you out today and tell you about all the great things Dale High has to offer!"

Kristy slowly looked me up and down.

Was she checking me out? I blushed and picked a hair nervously off my dress.

"You obviously know who I am."

My grin wavered. *What kind of reply was that?* I contemplated what to say back, when Mrs. Jacobs handed out paper copies of our class schedules. I grabbed mine from Mrs. Jacobs' hands. I already knew it by heart and was about to place it in my purse when Kristy tapped the back of my dress. I turned around.

"Shouldn't we compare schedules, so you know where you're guiding me?"

"Oh right, for sure!" I laid my schedule out in front of her. After comparing the two, it appeared we had creative writing and lunch together.

"This should be easy. Dale High is simple to navigate so it shouldn't take you long to figure it all out."

She arched a brow. "Already planning on how to ditch me?"

"No, of course not!"

Lie. I was trying to figure out what the heck to do with her during lunch. It was highly unlikely she could sit at my new lunch table; I secured the last seat there and she wasn't a part of a couple.

Lunch at our high school was cutthroat. If you didn't secure a seat by the first day of school, you ran the risk of being stuck at the rejects table for the rest of the semester or even worse, a table by yourself. A few years back a popular cheerleader broke up with her boyfriend on the football team mid semester and clearly didn't think of the ramifications. She had to sit by herself for the remainder of the year. She ended up dropping out of cheerleading because no one ever let her participate in the routine. Last I heard, she moved out of town.

I didn't break up with the other guy I dated last year, Paul, for fear of having nowhere to sit and losing all my friends. Cowardly and perhaps selfish, I know, but I hadn't been ready to be a table of one, and I didn't want to make Hannah leave her table to prevent my misery. Sure, she'd have done it in a heartbeat, but I didn't want her to be put out just because I couldn't find anyone that made me happy.

After school was over for the year, I finally got the courage to break up with Paul. That night Bryan showed up on my doorstep, asking me out. Still not sure how he found my address, but at the time, I thought it was romantic and couldn't refuse, especially since we'd started to text and flirt more before the end of the school year.

I needed to make sure I maintained this new lunch seat and relationship with Zack the rest of the semester to avoid any table drama, especially now that I had secured a coveted seat at Hannah's table. Introducing a random new girl to the table I'd only recently been invited to wouldn't help me float under the radar.

The bell rang signaling the rush to first period. I grabbed my iPad and on my way out, a guy touched my shoulder and said, "See you at lunch!"

I looked over; it was one of Bryan's jock friends. *Guess Bryan forgot to mention our breakup. Maybe Bryan was still holding out hope that I would want to get back with him.*

"Hey Trev, see you around," I said avoiding his stare and went the other way with Kristy trailing me.

"Our creative writing teacher is pretty fantastic. I had him for Honors English last year, and he's a lot of fun. I heard he lets you write about anything you want!"

I rattled off a couple more fun facts about Mr. T when Kristy interrupted me to say, "Are you always like this?"

"Like what?"

"So full of energy for a Monday. You do realize it's not even eight in the morning."

"She really is. Sometimes I get texts from her at five a.m., and I have no idea why she's up," a voice behind us interjected.

I turned around and squealed, then gave her a huge hug. "Hannah! Where've you been hiding?"

"Tyler was running late today so I sprinted to homeroom."

"I was wondering. But guess what? Zack walked me to homeroom and was waiting by my parking spot."

"That's so exciting!"

Hannah turned to look at Kristy.

"Hey, are you new? I don't think we've met," Hannah said.

"Oh! My bad, Hannah, this is Kristy. Kristy, this is my BFF Hannah. Kristy recently moved here and I'm showing her around."

Kristy's eyes flicked up and down, giving Hannah the once over, but Hannah didn't even notice. Hannah never thought she warranted any attention, but she was cute, with her long, wavy dark-brown hair and a few freckles dotting her nose; she was super skinny, and at least six inches taller than me. Hannah was wearing her typical skinny jeans, a light-purple tee, and white Adidas sneakers complemented with blue stripes.

"That's amazing about Zack," Hannah said.

"Right? It's what I've always wanted! I wish you were in creative writing with me so we could talk about it more. You're going to miss out on Mr. T's awesomeness!" I exclaimed.

"I know. You've gushed about Mr. T for the past year, but I wanted to take Honors Calc during that time."

"Why do you have to be all math smart?" I asked.

Hannah laughed. "I better be or else I'd need to switch my actuarial science major next year."

"If you switched majors then you could come to my

university, which has regular math degrees, not the fancy pants ones."

Hannah gave me a small smile. "Too bad it doesn't, I'm going to miss you." She glanced down at her phone. "I better get to class, see you at lunch."

Kristy and I approached creative writing. "Let's grab a seat near the front." Not waiting for an answer, I took my place front and center.

Kristy sat in the chair behind me.

"Sorry, I'm not the front seat kind of girl."

Huh. Maybe she was shy? At least I was short enough, she could easily see the whiteboard over my head.

Mr. T, who wore a perfectly ironed, white dress shirt and red tie walked in the classroom as the bell was ringing. "Welcome, welcome! I see some familiar faces from the Honors English class I taught last year. Sam! Did you write anything over the summer?"

"Of course. I'm always in the middle of writing a couple of stories. My newest novel is about how all the guys my heroine dates are never good enough for her."

"Looking forward to reading it." Mr. T walked to the middle of the classroom. "That leads perfectly to our first writing project of the year, which is all about collaboration. Usually writing is an individual task, but novelists these days are always looking for new perspectives, so co-writing is becoming more and more popular. Look at Bill Clinton's and James Patterson's books, a very unlikely duo. In a similar fashion, everyone's first assignment is co-writing a paper; I want you to pair up with the person behind slash in front of your seat! You can pick any genre or subject matter."

I have to write with someone else? Group projects were always the worst. I'd always get stuck with all the work.

"You also have to read at least two books that are co-authored, and I'll pass out a list of acceptable books. Once you've made your selections, I'll give you the code to download them to your school iPad. Reading these will help you write your twenty-page short story, due in a month. The outline for the story is due by the end of the week."

Everyone groaned. *You've got to be kidding me. I thought this class was going to be easy.*

I turned around to face Kristy. "Since you aren't a front row kind of girl, guess you're stuck working with me."

"Isn't it my lucky day?" Kristy said, leaning back with a slight smirk on her face.

Was she being sarcastic? I hoped writing this paper together would work out.

"What are these school iPads?" she asked.

"Some rich guy gave the school a boatload of money a couple years ago to provide each student a school-issued iPad. They didn't give you one last week?"

"No, this is the first I've heard of it."

"Last Thursday we all had to come in and check one out, because at the end of each school year, we're forced to return it. That's how I do all my non-school reading, so thank God I got it back. You might have to ask the library for one, because we get all of our textbooks that way."

Kristy's face brightened for the first time. "That's pretty sweet."

"It's a really awesome deal, but sadly you have to give it back the day before graduation."

Kristy scrunched her eyebrows. "That's stupid."

"It works out for those of us who could at least have it for all four years. You, not so much."

"Sounds like my life."

I wasn't sure how to respond to such a depressing statement. *How bad could her life be?* I did what I usually did when I wasn't sure what to say, pivot. "What do you like to write?"

"I hate writing for school. I'd rather write what I want. I took this because it was one of the only classes that had openings left."

This didn't bode well for us. Writing this paper together was going to be a nightmare.

Kristy studied my face. "What about you?"

"I love writing, especially fiction. I got into it freshman year and try to write stories not for school when I have time. Mr. T suggested this class to really help my writing grow."

"What kind of stuff do you write?"

"I write about things that've happened to me but change it a little bit so I can call it fiction. Write what you know, right?" *My next story should be based on Bryan. I could see it now, the future New York Times Best Seller,* Devil Boy.

"Like your current book?"

I coughed. "Yeah, kinda."

"What guy is it based on, so I know who to watch out for?"

"A combination of all the guys I've ever dated."

"That sounds like the title right there, *All the Guys I've Ever Dated.*"

I laughed. "That's a pretty good title to be honest. The guys here aren't bad, but they are super immature. My ex, Bryan, played pranks all the time on his football friends and other classmates. I didn't realize how annoying he was until we started dating and I really got to know him. I kept apologizing for his stupidity to everyone."

"What's his deal?"

"God knows. He's also super privileged. If something didn't go his way, he'd freak out. Like last night, he broke up with me for not putting out, but then lo and behold today he wanted to get back together."

"What a tool."

"For sure, and now I'm finally with my dream guy!" I said.

But was Zack really my dream guy? Would his kisses get better in time?

"Oh?" Kristy said, her face emotionless.

"Yeah, I've been in love with Zack since forever, but our timing was always wrong. But I think we have it right this time." *It had better be. I'd been waiting too long to find the right guy.*

Kristy grunted. "How does Bryan feel about that?"

"I don't think he knows yet."

Kristy raised an eyebrow.

"This just happened. I'm sure it's fine. He's the one that broke up with me." I opened my iPad and looked away from Kristy. "I think we should figure out what books we want to read and maybe they can help us figure out what to write?"

Kristy's emerald green eyes were scrutinizing my face. After a moment she replied, "Talk about change in topic."

I shrugged. "What can I say, I hate talking about my ex."

"Fair enough. How about I'll read one you pick, and you have to read one I choose."

"Works for me. I've been wanting to read the second James Patterson and Bill Clinton book, *The President's Daughter.*"

Kristy's eyebrows raised. "Didn't take you for liking thrillers."

"What do you mean?" I asked.

"From the book you're writing, I'd thought you'd read more romances."

"I've tried, but they're pretty dumb and all have the same plot. Girl meets boy. Girl falls for boy, but he's with someone else. Girl tries to make him love her but falls in love with the best friend in the process, and they live happily ever after. Like that actually happens. I prefer murder and treason." *You don't end up disappointed when your happily ever after doesn't happen.*

"You win, we'll go with the cheesy thriller by the two

famous people, but I guarantee it's going to be as stupid as those romances."

"Whatever, I can't wait to prove you wrong," I said, happy I was able to read something I've had on my overflowing TBR list.

I went to retrieve the download code from Mr. T with an extra bounce in my step. *Even though Kristy and I didn't seem to agree on books, it was fun talking with her. I wasn't used to having discussions that were so engaging.* I also explained Kristy's iPad situation and Mr. T agreed to let us see the librarian, Ms. Weir.

I grabbed my iPad off the desk. "Come on, we're going to get your iPad now. Mr. T said it's okay."

Kristy shrugged and followed me out the door. The library was close by and as soon as we came in, Ms. Weir greeted us.

"Hello girls, I've been expecting you. Sam, nice to see you again. And Mr. T said you're Kristy Davis?" she asked, turning to look at Kristy.

Kristy nodded.

Ms. Weir's fingers hit a few buttons on her keyboard.

"Ah, yes. I remember now," she said. "We received your technology paperwork late last week, completed incorrectly. I re-sent the paperwork to the address of your legal guardians. Do you have it signed by them?"

"I don't live with my parents. That's the whole reason I started going here; I live with my aunt. I even put that on the paperwork. Why can't my aunt sign it?" Kristy asked, raising her voice.

"I'm sorry Kristy, your legal guardians have to be the ones to sign the paperwork, otherwise we aren't allowed to provide one. Can you call them and have them mail it in?"

Kristy slapped her hand on the desk. "That isn't going to happen. I'm sure they threw the papers away as soon as they saw it was something for me. What if my aunt becomes my legal guardian?"

Ms. Weir looked around the room and lowered her voice. "That could work, but changing your legal guardian takes quite a bit of time. I'm sorry, I wish I could help more. That's why it's better to get paperwork filled out earlier rather than later."

Kristy gripped the side of the desk. "I didn't even know I was coming here until last week. I filled out the paperwork as soon as I could."

A girl sitting alone reading her iPad, turned around and shot Kristy daggers.

"Young lady, please lower your voice, this is the library," Ms. Weir said, giving Kristy a stern look.

I needed to help Kristy out somehow. This wasn't fair.

"How's she supposed to do her homework? I can clearly see all the extras you have back there!" I pointed to an overstuffed shelf of iPads behind Ms. Weir.

"Sam, I'm sorry, the school board voted that each student's legal guardian must sign off on an iPad. I can bring it up with the principal, but that might take a couple of days. I can't promise anything."

I sighed. "Come on Kristy, we aren't going to get anywhere here."

"But what am I going to do?" Kristy asked, her eyes filled with concern.

Ms. Weir pointed to a bookshelf filled with hardback books.

"You can find older copies of the textbooks over there."

I walked over to the shelf and opened the first biology book I found; dust flew up into my face. I gave a loud sneeze.

"Bless you," Kristy said, picking up a monster-sized math book.

I opened to the first page and saw the copyright was 1988. "These are way over thirty years old!"

"And really heavy," Kristy said, putting the huge math book back on the shelf. She rubbed her hand.

"You can't use these books. They probably say Pluto's a planet. Let's go. We can figure something else out."

We turned to leave and didn't say another word to Ms. Weir.

What the heck was this school's problem? Why couldn't they bend the rules a little to help Kristy out? She just moved here and already had to deal with this crap?

Outside the library I said, "I'm really sorry. I didn't think getting one would be such a big deal. You could always borrow mine or something while I try and figure out a way for you to get your own."

Kristy gave me a small smile. "Thanks. I used to have one, but it's at my parents with the rest of my stuff, and no way I'm going back there."

The bell rang, which only meant one thing, math class, my least favorite subject in the world. I changed course and walked Kristy toward her next class. "I'll come get you after class so we can walk to lunch together."

"Alright, see you then."

CHAPTER THREE

The entire class I couldn't focus, and it wasn't because math was boring.

What should I do with Kristy at lunch? I couldn't leave her alone to fend for herself in the cafeteria, especially after that awful experience. It blew my mind she only found out last week she was moving here. I'd be freaking out too, and Ms. Weir certainly didn't help make Kristy feel welcome.

When the bell rang, I quickly gathered my stuff and shot out the door to Kristy's class.

"Hey! Hope you didn't have to wait too long," I panted.

"You really take this showing me around seriously. You didn't have to run."

"We need to get to the lunchroom ASAP. Need to stake out our seat." I was still gasping for breath.

I wasn't kidding, the lunchroom was already filling up by the time we arrived. Some lunch tables only had one or two seats left, including the table where Zack stood waving at me. There was that sheepish smile of his again that used to make me weak in the knees. Sitting next to him at lunch had been a recurring daydream, but now that I could, I wanted to find a different table to sit at with Kristy where there were no rules, but then I wouldn't be able to sit with Hannah because I didn't see her leaving Tyler's side anytime soon.

This table couldn't be too bad, right?

"Come on, I see Zack."

I weaved between the tables and masses of people attempting to grab a seat. I gave Zack a quick kiss on the cheek. "Hey! So, this is Kristy. She's new here and doesn't know anyone. Is it cool if we pull up a chair for her until she gets to know more people?"

"Hey Kristy. Sure, no problem," he responded. He was about to grab a chair from the table behind us that only consisted of a girl burrowed in her iPad, when at the last minute he said to her, "This okay to borrow?"

She looked up and gave him a smile. "Sure, no problem, Zack." *How did she know him? I'd never even seen her around before.*

"I owe you, um," Zack said, scratching his head.

"Maggie," she said, turning back to her iPad.

Maggie didn't flinch when the chair made an awful scraping sound as Zack moved it to our table.

Everyone else including Hannah, Tyler, and some other band guy Dylan, eyed Kristy curiously and mumbled hello.

Hannah stared at me and raised one of her eyebrows.

I shook my head and mouthed, *later.*

After Zack, Kristy, and I sat down, I reached into my lunch bag to pull out my peanut butter and jelly sandwich when I heard, "Shorty! What. The. Hell."

I whipped around. Bryan elbowed people out of his way as he barreled towards my seat. There was fire in his eyes as he towered over me.

Oh my god. I forgot about that freaking text. Maybe I

shouldn't have taken Zack's advice and told Bryan in person we were actually over.

Zack shot up from the table. He looked up at Bryan. "Sorry man, she made her choice. She's with me now."

Bryan puffed out his chest. "The hell she is!"

Zack straightened. "Go back to your table, Bryan."

"Why would she pick you over me? I'm on the Varsity football team! You're just a band nerd!"

Zack gritted his teeth. "I'm more than that. I'm also president of the robotics club. And Shorty's a musician too."

"Robotics? Talk about nerd alert," Bryan cackled.

My mouth dropped. I was used to Bryan making fun of people when we were together, but it had never been one of my friends.

Bryan got closer to Zack, looking at him with an expression that scared the crap out of me.

"Shorty's smoking hot and mine," Bryan threatened.

"You don't think I can get someone that's hot?" Zack asked. His eyes were stone cold.

This was not how I expected my first day of senior year to play out. I glanced over at Kristy, who was munching on crackers with a bemused expression.

"This is more entertaining than a trashy TV show on Bravo," Kristy said.

I covered my face with my hands. "My life isn't a TV show."

"That's why it's more entertaining; it's so real."

Bryan glared at Zack. "Let's ask Shorty." He faced me. "Are you with Zack?"

My legs trembled as I stood. I took a deep breath and looked up at Bryan's gaze. "Yes. We're never getting back together. You broke up with me, so I've moved on and am with Zack now. I like that he's a musician!"

I turned to Zack and planted a kiss on his lips for an added effect. *I needed to show Bryan I wasn't playing around because he didn't seem to get the hint.*

Zack kissed me back and tried to add a little tongue. I struggled not to gag and continued to kiss him as seductively as possible. I finally pulled away and snuck a quick glance at Bryan. His face was fire engine red.

"Is this why you wouldn't have anything to do with me? Were you with Zack the whole time?"

"N-no, this just happened," I said.

"The hell it did. You two look mighty comfortable together."

"We weren't together until today," I said. *Except for when we flirted all the time at band camp.*

"Whatever. You're exactly like Cate. A cheater and a liar."

I opened my mouth, but I couldn't think of anything to say back.

"I'll never forget this. Both of you need to watch your back." Bryan glared at us and then stalked off to the jock table where they all were doubled over with laughter. Bryan shouted something indistinguishable at them and the laughter stopped. The jocks traded concerned looks and began eating their lunch in silence.

How did Bryan have that much control over them? And how did I never notice this before?

Zack and I slunk into our respective seats. After a beat, Zack turned to me, puzzled. "Who's Cate?"

"That's his ex who graduated last year. They were together for like six months. Bryan found her in a dark hallway sucking on some guy's neck at prom."

Zack's eyes grew wide. "Woah, I don't remember that."

"Yeah, Paul had to pull Bryan off the guy," I said.

"Was that near the end of prom?" Zack asked.

"I think so, why?"

"Zoe and I left early."

My face flushed. *Did they sneak out early to go have sex?* I knew there was a real possibility that Zack was more experienced than me in that department but hearing it from his mouth made it even more real.

"Right ... yea, that's when the fight happened."

"What went down?"

"Once Bryan found Cate making out with this senior, he punched the guy in the jaw. I guess it wasn't hard enough because the guy also got a few punches in before Paul pulled them apart."

"Geez. I missed all the good stuff. What happened to them?"

"They both got in trouble for fighting. Bryan was suspended from school for a couple of days."

"When did you start dating Bryan?" Kristy asked, as she chewed on more cheese crackers.

"Oh, maybe a couple weeks later, as soon as summer vacation started."

"I've always wondered, how did that even happen?" Tyler asked.

"What, you didn't think I was popular enough to date him?" I asked defensively. Tyler and I were never the same ever since I broke up with him. Now on the off chance we talked, it was usually making fun of each other.

"No, he's an ass. I didn't think you would go for someone like him, although I guess you did date Paul and he's not much better," Tyler said coldly.

I gave Tyler a look. "Paul's in both band and football though, you can't hate him that much."

"He's only in concert band, not marching band. That's completely different."

"Sorry he's not a diehard marching band person like you. He can't march when he's on the football team," I said.

"The cheerleaders in band do both at the same time, why

can't he? Paul and Bryan wanted to get in your pants," Tyler said, glaring at me.

Did I sense some bitterness? I guess I did dump him, and then date two guys that were popular and ripped. Tyler needed to get over it. It had been almost two freaking years.

"How did you start dating Bryan?" Zack asked.

Could we PLEASE get off the topic of my ex-boyfriends?

"After the whole prom debacle, I felt bad for him, so we started texting. Texting turned into talking and then flirting. After I broke up with Paul on the last day of school, Bryan asked me out and the rest is history."

"Didn't Paul get pissed you moved onto Bryan so fast?" Kristy asked.

"I don't know. School was over by that point, and I didn't have to see him anymore. Maybe he didn't even know," I said.

"Doubt that, your Instagram stories were all of you and Bryan," Dylan said. He popped a chip in his mouth.

I didn't even realize Dylan followed me. I really needed to check out my followers list.

Zack opened his lunch bag. "Do I need to worry about him killing me?"

"I don't think so, although he did seem pretty mad."

"I'd be too if my ex made out with her new guy in front of me and the entire cafeteria," Tyler said under his breath.

I gave him a please shut up look.

He rolled his eyes and stuck his usual bologna, cheese, and cracker lunchable in his mouth. He's packed the same lunch every day since middle school. You'd think he would want to eat something not made for children, but Tyler isn't a fan of change.

"Sorry I'm late guys! Can't wait for senior year. It's going to be amazing! Wait, who's this?" A brunette girl with bleached blond highlights pointed at Kristy. She was sporting a lavender billowy tank with flips flops to match and a short black skirt.

Erin. I completely forgot she sat here with Dylan, her boyfriend. I only knew her as the stick thin guard member that screamed at the highest decibel whenever a bug flew near her at marching band practice. I also heard from Bryan she had tried out for the cheerleading squad every year but never made the cut. Her hair was always flawless unlike Dylan who desperately needed a haircut; his bangs were currently covering his eyes. He was a crass, blunt kind of guy who really wore whatever he found in the closet. It was baffling how they ended up together.

"Erin, this is Kristy. She's new here and I'm helping show her around."

"Oh. Okayyyy," she said. "Dylan, O-M-G, I haven't seen you since this morning. Missed you babe." Erin kissed him on the cheek before she flounced in the last empty chair. I averted my eyes as she sat. How could she get away with wearing a skirt that short? She knew how to rock it for sure but now I had her bright-orange panties imprinted in my mind. At least she was wearing some. I flushed at the thought of Erin going commando. *Why would I even think about that? It's not like I'm thinking about Zack's underwear, although I probably should. But I don't want to.*

"So, Kristy, where were you before Dale?" Tyler asked, pulling me out of my thoughts.

"On the other side of town at Archfield Academy," Kristy said.

Everyone grew quiet. Archfield was *the* school to attend—the rich kid school. Everyone enrolled lived in McMansions with their doctor and lawyer parents.

"Why are you here then? If I were at Archfield, I would never leave!" Erin exclaimed.

"My parents kicked me out and I moved in with my aunt.

Didn't realize that also meant they weren't paying for my school until I showed up last Monday and was told I wasn't enrolled at Archfield anymore."

That explained the last-minute paperwork.

Everyone stopped eating for a second and were silent until Erin broke it by asking, "What's Archfield like?" She moved closer to Kristy, leaning her elbows on the cafeteria table while propping her head in her hands. Her sharp gaze zeroed in on Kristy.

"Awful. Almost everyone was spoiled and hated me. The school itself was ridiculous and had a ton of useless extracurricular activities like water polo. Everyone was so freaking fake."

Erin's mouth dropped and her eyes widened. "Are you kidding?"

"Not at all. Guess it's not the worst thing that my parents stopped paying my tuition," Kristy said.

At least she was honest, it just wasn't the answer anyone expected or wanted. Archfield was always thought of as the classier, sexier version of Dale High. Even at football games, Archfield fans didn't boo or try and distract our offense. I always assumed they were too sophisticated but maybe they thought they were too good to sink to our level? Or Kristy could be bitter because she clearly didn't fit in.

"How could you hate Archfield? My dream was for my parents to win the lottery, buy the house on the corner of Fourth and Pine, and attend Archfield," Erin shared.

"That would be hard to do since that's my parents' house and I'm guessing they aren't selling it anytime soon," Kristy said, looking sideways at Erin.

"What? That's so insane. I wish I had your life!" Erin exclaimed, throwing her hands in the air.

"No, trust me, you don't. But I'm sure my parents are in search of a new daughter they aren't ashamed of, so go right ahead and introduce yourself. Thanks Sam for inviting me to lunch but I can find my next class myself." Kristy gathered her belongings and walked out of the cafeteria.

I glared at Erin.

"What did I do?" she asked, eyes wide, blowing a piece of her perfect hair out of her face.

"Are you kidding? Couldn't you tell she has issues with her parents? You kept asking her more questions." I pushed my chair back and stood up. "I'm going to find her." I sprinted out of the cafeteria without thinking twice.

CHAPTER FOUR

I searched for Kristy where I typically hid from bad situations: the girl's bathroom. I crouched down to inspect under the stalls and was greeted by a pair of worn leather combat boots under the last one. *Bingo.*

"Kristy?" My voice echoed.

"Go away. Your friend sucks," Kristy replied, her voice muffled.

"Erin isn't my friend."

Kristy opened the stall and walked to the sink. I caught a glimpse of excess mascara running down her cheeks. She ripped off a piece of paper towel and dabbed it under her eyes. Still not looking at me, she inspected herself in the mirror, wet the paper towel, and cleaned off a couple of remaining black spots.

"I was hoping I could erase my past, and on my first day, I've already had to explain myself. I was an outcast at Archfield and now it already seems like I'm going to have the same problem here," she said.

"Everyone's curious because Archfield seems like the best

school ever, so for someone to say otherwise only makes us curious. Too bad you didn't say you were from Kansas."

Kristy sighed. "I'm not going to lie about where I'm from or who I am. If that were the case, I wouldn't be here in the first place."

"What do you mean?" I asked.

"I'll tell you later. Isn't your boyfriend going to wonder where you went?"

I was impressed, she took a play out of my book by changing the topic when she didn't want to talk about something, but I didn't want to press her, especially after Erin's probing questions.

"Zack's not my boyfriend, yet. I don't care if he's looking for me. I can do what I want."

"For the record, that kiss in the lunchroom was one of the least sexy things I've ever seen." Kristy finished dabbing her eyes and threw the paper towel in the trash can.

"It was only our second kiss. It can only get better, right?"

"You keep telling yourself that. What happened to the peppy Sam I first met in homeroom?"

I shrugged. Man, this girl was a quick study. Or was I too easy to read?

"I don't do well with change of plans. After that lunch scene with Bryan, my day really went downhill."

"If it's worth anything, that fight at lunch was still the highlight of my day."

"At least it was helpful for someone." The bell rang. "I can walk you to your next class if you want and then tell you how to get to your final one since we aren't in them together. That work?"

Kristy nodded. Luckily her class was only three rooms away from mine so I wouldn't run the risk of being late.

"Good luck with this one. I heard Mr. Paul is rough. I

have him next period. Make sure you tell him you don't have an iPad yet and see what he can do for you."

"Thanks, but I should be okay. I actually like science."

I gave her instructions on how to find her last class, said goodbye, and headed to history. Showing her around wasn't as bad as I thought, she kept things interesting. Oddly enough I wasn't feeling the same way about seeing Zack. *What the heck did that mean?* He was my dream guy. Maybe I needed to kiss him alone and not in front of a million people. Having an audience would give anyone performance anxiety. Plus having my ex and him fight the moment before kissing Zack couldn't have been good for my nerves. Next time Zack and I kissed it was bound to be better.

I stepped into history class and recoiled. Bryan was lounging in the back row with his feet propped up on the desk in front of him, a smirk aimed right at me. My heart started to race. *Great. Would I ever get away from him? He wasn't supposed to be here.*

Hannah and Zack slipped in at the last moment and sat by me.

"I thought I was going to be late, it's so hard to get away from Tyler," Hannah said with a sly grin.

"You mean it's so hard to stop making out with him?"

Zack nodded. "I had to pull her off him so they wouldn't be late to class on our first day."

"We're making up for not seeing each other much this summer," Hannah said, not meeting my eye.

I must have broken Tyler in for Hannah because when we made out, he had been hands down the worst kisser ever and believe me, I've had many terrible kisses. His teeth somehow scraped the inside of my mouth during each kiss, and I had to wipe my face off with a towel to get off all the excess saliva. The memory of his kissing made me shutter. *At least Zack wasn't that bad.*

"Shorty, you never came back to lunch. Everything okay?" Zack asked, his forehead creasing.

I shrugged and didn't meet his eyes. I didn't have to expand further because the bell rang. A very young dark-haired man with deep brown eyes, khaki pants, a navy-blue button-down shirt, and powder-blue floral tie walked to the front of the class.

"Hi everyone, I'm Mr. Ricardo, your history teacher for the semester. This is my first year here so be easy on me."

Hannah and I glanced at each other with raised eyebrows. This guy was our teacher? He looked like he stepped out of the cover of a J Crew catalogue. I was betting all of the girls would have a crush on him.

Since he was new, he made us each introduce ourselves and say two sentences that were true and one that was a lie and we had to guess which was the lie. Hannah preemptively began to blush. She hated attention, especially when she had to talk about herself. Lucky for her, I went first so she had more time to plan. I had mine all mapped out. Other people said sentences that had no thought behind them; I knew I could do better than that.

Finally, it was my turn. I took a deep breath and looked Mr. Ricardo in the eye. "I'm Sam, also known as Shorty. I am going to Temple University in the fall for Communications, I was born in California, and I've been to Europe."

Bryan yelled from the back. "And she's a bitch!"

The classroom erupted, half with laughter and half with gasps.

My cheeks were on fire. *Are you kidding me?* I tried to hold in my tears. Instead of saying I was going to Temple and that I was born in California, I should have said one of my truths was Bryan's kisses were worse than my period cramps.

"Quiet down please. What's your name?" Mr. Ricardo asked.

"I'm Zack," Bryan said, smirking.

"No, he isn't, I'm Zack. Bryan's pissed because Shorty's done with him." Zack glared at Bryan.

Mr. Ricardo crossed his arms. "Bryan, this is a warning. Next outburst, especially with a swear word, is going to land you at the principal's office."

"Yeah, okay," Bryan said under his breath.

It must haven't been quiet enough.

"You know what, this game's over. It's apparent we need to learn history immediately, so Bryan isn't doomed to repeat the same mistakes as many men throughout history."

I glanced at Hannah, and she gave me a small smile. At least the disruption saved her from having to give her two truths and a lie, but now Bryan seemed to be my mortal enemy.

Mr. Ricardo passed out our iPad history book code and started the lesson talking about how many conflicts throughout history had started over love and breakups. Did he come up with this on the fly and if so, what did he originally have planned? He even discussed how the future of England changed all because Henry VIII wanted to get a divorce and marry Anne Boleyn.

At the end of class, Mr. Ricardo assigned us pages to read about Henry VIII and after that, to write a one-page paper on how history could've been changed if Anne Boleyn didn't exist, due the next day. Everyone groaned. Usually, the first day of school was so easy. *What was with all this homework?*

Mr. Ricardo approached my desk and asked, "Can you stay after class really quick?"

"Sure."

The bell rang and I stood. "Hey guys, I need to talk with Mr. Ricardo so don't wait for me."

Zack placed his hand on my shoulder. "Shorty, I'm sorry Bryan called you the *b* word. I should've done more but I was trying to make sure Mr. Ricardo knew Bryan wasn't actually me." Zack's lips were pursed in a straight line.

"You did more than enough. I'm glad I'm with you now," I said, squeezing his free hand.

"Want to watch a movie at my place after school tonight?" Zack asked, his hand still casually resting on my shoulder.

"I'd love to."

Maybe being alone with him will help my feelings come back.

Hannah winked. "You two have fun, but not too much fun."

"Like you should talk," I said.

Mr. Ricardo looked up as I approached his desk. "Thanks for staying. I wanted to check in with you to see if you were okay after that comment."

"Oh, thanks. Yeah, I'm fine."

"Let me know if he continues to bother you and I'll take it to the principal's office, okay?"

"Sure, thanks. And good luck with the rest of your first day. Hope it isn't as bad as this class."

"It could have been worse. At least no one threw anything at me."

"Not yet, you mean."

He chuckled. "I'll let you know tomorrow if any rogue objects fly my way. Have a good rest of your day, and here's a note in case you're late."

I slipped into biology as the bell rang.

Hannah patted the seat beside her, and I attempted to discreetly sit in the spot. No such luck.

Mr. Paul cleared his throat while he coldly stared. "Nice to see you could make it. Next time be here before the bell rings."

"So sorry, Mr. Paul. Mr. Ricardo kept me late because of an issue. Here's my note," I said sweetly.

Mr. Paul grabbed the note out of my hand, quickly

scanned the contents and legit rolled his eyes. "Sam gets a one-time pass. Everyone else, do not be late or else I'll give you a week of after-school detention."

Everyone groaned. *The rumors really were true, Mr. Paul was a jerk.*

"As you should know, this is biology class, and it isn't for the faint of heart. We'll be cutting open animals and learning about body parts. If you feel sick, I don't care, get over it. Real life is gritty, and no one gives you a pass then, do they? I'm going to hand out the class syllabus. Make sure you take note when assignments are due because I won't be reminding you."

As Mr. Paul passed out the syllabus, I turned to Hannah and whispered, "This is going to suck. Can we ..." I trailed off when I saw Mr. Paul standing in front of me, glaring.

"I see being next to this young lady is going to be a problem. Time to switch seats. Whomever I pick for you to sit next to will be your lab partner. Everyone up!"

I kept my head down after I noticed many evil glares being shot my way.

"You, first. Sam Daniels, right?" Mr. Paul asked.

"Yes, but most people call me Shorty."

"I don't care if your friends call you the Queen, I will only call you by the name the school office gave me. You're sitting upfront with Kristy Davis. You shouldn't have much to discuss since she's new."

Kristy stood in the back, leaning against a slate black counter. *How did that happen? Didn't I walk her here last period?*

Kristy sauntered to the front and sat next to me. As Mr. Paul called out other names and as my other classmates got settled into their seats, I whispered to her as quietly as I could, "What are you doing here?"

I looked at Mr. Paul and my decibel level must have been on point because he didn't glance my way. He was too focused on an argument with a girl not wanting to pair with her ex-boyfriend.

"My last class of the day was wrong. I was supposed to take Latin this semester, but I somehow was enrolled in Spanish One, which I've already taken at my old school. I talked to Mr. Paul last period before class started and he let me go to the guidance counselor's office to work everything out. The only way to change to Latin was take biology last period."

"You're lucky Latin wasn't full. I heard that class fills up as soon as we can pick our classes."

"Some jock dropped out right as I was coming in the guidance office. He found out the class was more than watching the movie *Troy*," Kristy said, shaking her head.

"Sounds about right. Kids at Dale love doing the bare minimum to get by," I said. "Guess this means we're stuck together again as partners."

Hannah and I were supposed to be lab partners so we could spend the evenings together saying we were doing homework. Her parents were overprotective and the only way she could hang out with me, or anyone, was by proving we had a project together. I gave a large sigh and stared down at my hands. *Why was everything going wrong today?*

"I'm not that bad, am I?" Kristy asked.

"No. My day just wasn't what I expected. I thought this year was going to be amazing."

"Join the club. Today wasn't great for me either."

Before I could respond, Mr. Paul clapped his hands together. "Now that we're all arranged, I'm going to make note where everyone is sitting, so I have our seating pattern written in stone. No changes now!" He started furiously typing away on his computer.

I forced myself not to groan aloud. I looked for Hannah and gave her a sad puppy dog look. She returned my facial expression and gestured her head toward the person sitting next to her, which happened to be my evil nemesis of the moment, Bryan. *Are you kidding me? How could that be possible?* Before Bryan and I broke up, I memorized his classes by heart so I knew I would only have to face him in lunch after I dumped him. *He wasn't supposed to be in history class or this one.* At least he wasn't my lab partner, but poor Hannah. I hoped he wouldn't take his anger for me out on her.

Kristy saw me staring in Hannah's direction. "Can you have another fight with your ex? I really could use something to brighten my day."

"Last period he called me the *b* word in front of the entire class. That's enough drama for me today."

"Wait what? Is that why you were late?"

"Not late, fashionably on time. But my history teacher wanted to make sure I was okay. Guess Bryan's going to hold a grudge for eternity."

Kristy was about to respond when she was interrupted by Mr. Paul.

"Okay class, now that the paperwork is out of the way, let's begin by taking a look at the instruments we'll be using this semester."

"Shorty knows all about instruments since she loves a band NERD," Bryan shouted.

Couldn't he just leave me alone? I sighed and looked straight ahead at the whiteboard.

Mr. Paul glanced at his seating assignments. "Mr. Rickter, I don't know if you received the memo, but I'm the teacher and you're the student. That means you don't talk unless you are called upon. Your comment landed you in after-school detention today and guess what? I'm the proctor!"

"Sounds like you got the short end of the stick in the teacher's lounge," Bryan said, looking around to see if anyone else would join him in laughing. The silence was deafening.

"I chose to proctor detention. I'll see you there after school," Mr. Paul said, crossing his arms.

"I have practice after school. Coach won't allow it," Bryan said while leaning back in his chair.

"You should've thought of that before you interrupted class. I'll talk to Coach and explain why you won't be there this afternoon. Keep talking back to me and you'll earn a whole week of detention."

Bryan groaned. "This majorly sucks." He put his head on the desk.

I had to keep from chuckling. I knew how important practice was to Bryan.

Mr. Paul turned away and showed us the tools we would be using. I tried to pay attention, but my mind kept thinking about what happened. *Would Bryan ever stop harassing me? What if he kept saying these terrible comments all year? My senior year could be ruined. Maybe I should have stayed with him, especially since everything with Zack isn't as good as I'd hoped.*

Later in class, Mr. Paul allowed us to discuss our worm dissection lab project with our partner. He instructed us to list the dissection process and write down what tools we would use.

As soon as Mr. Paul stopped talking, Kristy said, "You weren't kidding when you said Bryan had it out for you."

"He could get any other girl he wants. Why does he care so much about me?"

"I bet it's because he can't get you. Now that you're with someone else, it probably makes you seem even more irresistible."

"Or he thought I'd been cheating on him, like Cate did."

"He might be mad that you didn't get back with him."

"I don't know but there is something going on. He was

never this mean to anyone before. He used to play pranks and stupid stuff like that but was never blatantly rude."

"Breakups bring out the worst in people. Maybe he'll forget about you soon?"

"God, I hope so."

Kristy stared at me, a small smile on her face. A few strands of her red hair escaped from behind her ear and my hand began to reach out to tuck them back. My hand was in mid-air when my brain realized what was going on. I abruptly dropped my arm.

What was I doing? My face burned with embarrassment. To defuse the situation, I blurted out, "Okay, so this project sucks. I hate science to begin with and cutting things open sounds even worse. I barely even eat meat. I tried being a vegetarian, but my dad said if I'm under their roof I have to eat what they make me. Most of the time my mom is understanding and makes something more vegetarian friendly."

Phew crisis averted, right? Maybe she didn't even notice.

"I'm vegetarian and my aunt doesn't seem to care. I don't mind cutting things open that are already dead; I don't want something to die for me to eat."

"You're lucky you can do what you want."

"Trust me, I'm not that lucky," Kristy said.

I scrunched my face. "It sounds like you've had a rough time. I know we just met, but if you need to talk, I'm happy to listen."

"Thanks. Sometimes I'm better off not thinking about it all."

"In that case, should we get started on this project?" I asked.

Kristy nodded in response. She arranged our tools and suggested we make notes about which one would be used for what part of the process. I pulled out my iPad and notated our plan of attack.

"Any big plans tonight after the first day of school?" Kristy asked casually.

"Not really. Just going to Zack's place to watch a movie."

Kristy raised an eyebrow. "Don't you mean *watch* a movie," Kristy said, making air quotes with her hands at the word watch.

"What do you mean?"

"In my experience, movie night is never about watching the movie."

"It's technically our first date. I'm sure we'll see most of the movie." I bit my lip. *At least I'd hoped so.*

"If you say so."

I'd forgotten that movie nights meant sweaty make out sessions that lasted for hours. With Tyler we watched the entire movie, but that could be why we lasted longer than everyone else. We had fun together and enjoyed each other's company. In the beginning with Bryan and Paul we would watch a movie the whole way through, but eventually it turned into one big make out session. *Why can't a guy just want to see a movie? Why does it have to be some secret lingo to getting into my dress?*

"You can't fault them for wanting to go after a hot girl."

I stopped typing on my iPad for a second. *Did she call me hot?* Hannah and I called each other sexy all the time, but I just met Kristy. I adjusted my dress and averted my eyes from her intruding gaze.

"Uh, thanks! What about you, what are you doing tonight?"

"Oh, you know the usual, nothing. Reading or Netflix. Maybe I'll talk to my aunt about getting my parents to sign those stupid iPad release forms."

As soon as the bell rang, Hannah appeared beside me.

"I'm sorry you have to partner with Bryan. That's awful!"

"I'd rather him being stuck with me than you. He was sweet and told me I had nice eyes," Hannah said blushing.

"What? Of course, he starts hitting on my best friend when he can't get me. Good luck with him as a lab partner. He's a meathead jock!" I said loudly, hoping he'd hear me.

Bryan whipped his head around and stood next to Hannah. "What was that Shorty? Did you say you miss my meat? I'm starting to think that I should've dated your friend Hannah instead of you, she's hotter and not as uptight. See you tomorrow," Bryan said rubbing Hannah's shoulder before he left.

"Ugh! He's the worst. Hannah, if he's too horrible to you, please report him to Mr. Paul."

"It's okay, Shorty. I'll be fine, I promise! If not, we can sick our guys on him!"

Kristy laughed. "You mean Tyler and Zack? The guys that look like they binge watch *Game of Thrones* after they've finished their Calculus homework? I'd love to see that."

"Oh, whatever. Zack can bludgeon Bryan in the eye with his percussion stick."

"That I would pay to see!" Kristy said.

I rolled my eyes. "Speaking of, Zack's probably waiting for me."

"Have fun with your make out session, I mean movie with Zack," Kristy said smirking.

I crossed my arms. "Very funny."

I diverted my attention back to Hannah as Kristy sauntered away.

"Excited for Zack's tonight?" Hannah asked.

"Of course." I forced a smile, even though my stomach churned, as if I ate bad fish.

"You're so lucky he invited you over to his house. Only Tyler and Zoe have been there, and they never talk about it.

Every time I ask, they get quiet and completely avoid the topic."

"That's weird. Do you know why?"

"I've been wondering that myself. He must really like you to invite you over!"

I didn't realize being invited to his house was going to be such a big deal. I'd thought we would take this slower.

"I guess he does," I said. My stomach flipped. *Was I going to mess up another relationship already? I should've gone to somewhere more public instead of his house.*

"Try and sneak a picture so I can see what's up with it and let me know if he's any good at making out. He has to be better than Paul and Bryan!"

"God, I hope so," I replied. I didn't have the heart to tell her that so far Zack's kisses today were as disappointing as all the other guys I've ever kissed. Maybe they will feel different once we were alone?

CHAPTER FIVE

As Zack and I parted ways in the school parking lot, he slid into his BMW. *Who gives a seventeen-year-old a BMW?* I opened the door to my electric blue ten-year-old Toyota Corolla, Thor. Thor had a ton of miles on him, but he hadn't let me down yet.

I checked my watch; it was three fifty. My parents didn't know I was going to Zack's, but they wouldn't be home until at least seven. I could make this work. My eyes flicked to my rear-view mirror.

Zack backed out of his spot, so I put my car in reverse and followed him down the road. We drove by the normal three-bedroom houses, very similar to mine and Hannah's, and then we arrived into richy, rich land, near the vicinity of Bryan's house. Zack turned right and we entered a wooded area. After about ten minutes, the wooded area cleared and a long, windy driveway with a wrought iron gate protecting the property appeared. Zack pulled into his driveway, leaned out the window, swiped a card, and the gate swung open. He motioned for me to follow him through. As I inched up in my car, the biggest house I had ever witnessed in my seventeen years of being alive came into my view.

One of three garage doors opened, and Zack slid his car effortlessly into the space. Yep. A three-car garage. I'd only witnessed those on TV shows; who knew they existed not too far from my humble home. I didn't know where to park my car, but it wasn't from lack of space, no, quite the opposite.

Zack appeared and called out, "Park in the roundabout!" I veered left onto the roundabout and stopped right in front of the doorway. Once I put the car in park, I could ogle the house before me. I grabbed my purse and slammed my car door shut.

"Woah, you live here?"

"Yea I know, it's ridiculous. I never really want to talk about it."

"It's huge!"

"Sometimes too big. My brother and sister are both in college so it's only my parents and me in this freaking huge place."

I stood gaping at his house. I couldn't tear my eyes away from the stark white columns, huge bay windows, and the Rodin style sculpture by his front door. *I knew Zack was rich, but not this rich. Why would he want to be with me? My parents were barely scraping by.*

"Do you mind showing me around? I've never seen anything like it," I said breathlessly.

Zack shrugged. "Yeah, no problem. Just don't tell many people. I don't want anyone to think about me differently."

"I mean, people kinda assume you're rich. You drive a BMW to school."

"That thing? It's like over twelve years old and was my dad's old car. My parents were going to get me a new one for my birthday this year, but I told them I didn't need it."

Guess he didn't realize that not everyone could receive luxury hand-me-downs from their parents. The Corolla was my dad's old car, and it didn't even have a working air conditioner.

"I won't tell anyone about your place, I promise." I didn't mention that excluded Hannah. I couldn't NOT tell her. I'd already promised her I'd send her pics, but I wasn't sure how to take them without looking creepy.

I followed him to the backyard, which had a humongous pool. Someone could comfortably swim laps in that thing. There was a cabana surrounding it, palm trees, and a waterfall. How did palm trees even survive in Pennsylvania weather? Behind that was a tennis court and a gazebo.

"Oh my god."

"The backyard is my favorite. I spend hours out here. You should bring your swimsuit sometime."

"Totally!"

Swimsuit meant he would see me half naked since all I had was my itty-bitty pink bikini that I had begged my mom to buy me. Now I was wishing I had gone for the classier option. I didn't want to ask for another swimsuit because it was the end of summer, and I knew money was tight enough as it was.

We moved inside and I tried to keep my mouth from dropping. The entrance chandelier looked more expensive than my entire house, with crystals cascading down like the pool's waterfall. A grand staircase led to, what I guessed contained ginormous bedrooms. There had to be at least six bedrooms and I guessed it had several rooms that were never used but just for show, such as a sitting room and dining room. We walked room to room, and they were more elaborate than the next, except Zack's bedroom. It was a typical boy room with framed *Star Wars* and *Lord of the Ring* movie posters, but it was at least double the size of mine with a large navy-blue couch.

"I can't believe you live here!"

"I don't talk about it much because you saw what

happened to Kristy today. I don't want to get a million questions or have people be friends with me because of where I live, although, we do have a sweet set up. Here, I'll take you to the movie theater room."

"Movie theater room? Are you kidding?"

Zack chuckled. "Not in the slightest."

We bounded down a couple levels of stairs to the basement. I stopped in awe before entering the room. There had to be at least fifteen plush red seats in three different rows complete with a movie theater sized screen.

"Wow." *How did he live here?* I could see why he didn't want to tell anyone.

People would be trying to take advantage of him all the time, even to use this room.

"What movie do you want to watch?"

"What are the options?"

Zack showed me a computer attached to the projector. Was there really a computer dedicated for streaming movies? There were a million options to choose from. I selected one of my favorite movies of all-time, *Thor Ragnarok.* I was such a sucker for anything Marvel.

Zack picked seats for us right in the middle and grabbed my hand as the title credits began. His hand was already drenched in sweat. *Gross.* I resisted the urge to pull away and wipe my hand on my dress.

As Thor appeared locked in chains Zack whispered in my ear. "I've been dreaming about this since band camp."

"Oh yea?" I highly doubted he had dreams of watching a half-naked Norse God while sweatily clutching my hand.

"I've been wanting to do this so bad."

He moved his mouth close to mine and his lips enveloped my own. *So soon? The movie just started! Couldn't I watch at least the first fifteen minutes?*

His kisses at least weren't as wet like Tyler's smooches, but true to form, I still felt nothing. As we continued to make out, I noticed his breath had a minty fresh taste. He even prepared for this, unlike Paul; I still distinctly remembered his fishy breath.

In the background I heard Thor talking with his brother Loki and it took all my power not to stop and watch the actual movie. Maybe I shouldn't have picked a favorite flick to *not* watch.

After five minutes my brain wandered. Guess Kristy was right about this being used for a make out session.

What was she doing? What should we write about for our collaborative project?

At least fifteen minutes later, I was so done. How much of this could a girl take? At that moment I noticed Zack's left hand reaching for the bottom of my dress.

No way. That wasn't happening. Especially on a first date.

Maybe Zoe allowed his hand to wander but I wasn't her. I wasn't ready.

This wasn't the Zack I fell for. Why was he being so forward? At school he had always been so sweet.

I began to scheme a way to break apart when Zack quickly pulled away and sneezed. "Bless you!"

"Sorry, that was nasty," Zack said, turning the color of the movie theater seats.

"It's fine. I need to get home because I never told my parents I was coming over here. My mom will flip if I'm not home when she gets there."

Zack frowned. "Oh, okay. Maybe we can finish the movie some other night?"

"Sure." *Not if I could help it.*

As he walked me to my car, I saw a movement in his stainless-steel kitchen. I gave a small yelp. A lady with short brown hair and all black clothes waved and went back to cleaning the granite counters.

"Who's that?" I whispered.

"Oh, that's Rose, our housekeeper. She's awesome."

A housekeeper? Wouldn't that be nice? It really did feel like Zack lived in a whole different world. I stood beside my car. "What do your parents do for work?"

"My mom is a lawyer, and my dad is a doctor. They aren't home much. But Rose is always around."

That explained everything. I'd have to remember about Rose. She'd be a good excuse to not have anything go further between us at his place.

"Well, see you tomorrow!" I said as I leaned in for a quick kiss. As I neared his face, Zack stated, "I actually wanted to ask you something."

Zack rubbed his hands together and beads of sweat appeared on his brow. "Shorty, I really like you. I've liked you on and off for a while now, but you were always dating some other guy and then I started dating Zoe. You're finally single and I don't want to miss my chance again. So um, do you want to be my girlfriend?"

A smile froze on my face. The words spewing out of Zack's mouth were what I've always wanted him to say. After a memorable slow dance together in middle school, there have been many daydreams of Zack confessing his undying love to me.

So why did this all feel so wrong?

If Zack had asked me earlier in the day or even last night to be his girlfriend, I would have said yes without overthinking but after tonight's kisses, I was torn.

Tonight confirmed that being intimate with Zack was the same as all the other guys I've ever dated. I'd rather be at home, curled up with a steaming cup of peppermint tea reading the James Patterson/Bill Clinton thriller. I enjoyed when we flirted and hung out but as soon as kissing came into play, I wanted it to return to how things were before his face was all up in mine.

Maybe it would get better, and I need to give it a chance. Plus, he's the guy of my dreams. I had always been a firm believer in taking risks and leaping into the unknown, which prompted me to say, "Yes sir!"

Facepalm. *Did I really say those words aloud?*

"Awesome!" he said, kissing my lips. *Did I seal my fate with this kiss?*

I pulled away. "Okay, I really have to go. See you tomorrow!" I opened the car door and sped away before Zack uttered another word.

As I raced down the street, I blinked back the tears that threatened to be released. Any girl would be lucky to have a guy like Zack. *Why couldn't I be satisfied with what I had?*

The driveway attached to my rancher style home was empty. I breathed a sigh of relief as I parked on the street. I made it home before my mom.

After changing into my comfy plaid pink sleep shorts and matching ribbed tank, my stomach gurgled. Guess I should eat something other than Zack's spit.

In the kitchen, there was a note from my mom.

Sam,

There's veggie lasagna thawing in the fridge. I'll be home around 7. Hope you had a good first day!

Love,

Mom

The clock on the microwave read six thirty. I had to eat fast before she arrived so she didn't realize I just arrived home. I didn't have to worry about my dad. He owned the corner grocery store downtown, where I worked on occasion, and the earliest he locked up on a weekday was around eight.

I threw the vegetarian lasagna that was chock full of peppers, onions, mushrooms, and broccoli in the microwave and flipped on Disney+. I scrolled through the movies until I found *Thor Ragnarok*. After being forced to not see it, I now yearned to re-watch the movie in hopes it would help me forget all about my day.

At seven p.m. sharp, my mother walked through the door.

"Sam! How was your day? Good, you found the lasagna," she said motioning to my plate on the end table. It was empty except for the remnants of tomato sauce.

"It was okay. Bryan and I broke up last night and then today he wanted me back. I said no because Zack and I are together now and then Bryan became super rude to me. Oh, and because I'm Student Council President, I was asked to show a new girl named Kristy around."

"That's a lot of things to happen in the past twenty-four hours. Who is Zack?"

"He's a percussionist in band with me."

"Oh, Zack Hurly! Dr. Hurley is a cardiologist at the hospital. I see him on occasion in the halls."

As much as Mom talked about the doctors she worked with as a nurse, she had never talked about Dr. Hurley.

"Zack's mom has quite the reputation as a lawyer. She's what they call an ambulance chaser," my mom added.

"Wait, what's that?"

"It means whenever there is an accident, she's there trying to represent the victim. It's a shameless way to make money off someone else's problems. Look on the billboards sometime, you're bound to see one of her ads."

Remind me to never introduce my parents to Zack's unless I'm ready for us to break up. My mother was never one for knowing when to keep her opinions to herself.

"What happened with Bryan?" she asked.

"He broke up with me because I didn't seem interested in him."

"Oh baby, I'm so sorry. Maybe you should take a break from dating instead of rushing into something else so soon?"

And there it was. Another one of her opinions my mom really didn't have to tell me. I should've learned to never confide in her about my love life.

"Mom, this is how I grieve. Besides, he was right, I wasn't into him anymore. I liked Zack while I was with Bryan, so it all works out."

My mom's concerned look was still plastered on her face. She sighed and walked into the kitchen. After a couple of minutes, she returned with a slice of lasagna and a side spinach salad. She placed herself next to me on the couch.

"When I was your age I wasn't interested in dating. I had more fun shopping with friends and playing tennis. Your dad was my first and last boyfriend junior year of college. Wouldn't change a thing."

"Well, I'm not you," I said as I turned up the volume on the TV.

"I know, but I don't want you to miss out on the high school experience because you're focused on dating."

I wasn't focused on just dating. I was the Student Council President, hung out with Hannah, wrote stories, and lots of other things.

I ignored her and kept watching the movie.

"I know you can hear me. Just follow your gut. But enough heavy talk for one day. What are we watching?"

"*Thor Ragnarok,*" I mumbled.

"Again? Haven't you seen that at least five times?"

"It never gets old," I replied. *And it helps me forget my real life.*

My mom took a large scoop of her lasagna and chuckled at something Loki said. I sat back to enjoy the rest of the movie.

A little later my dad arrived home with a white takeout box. He usually brought his dinner from the store. It saved my mom the trouble of making something all three of us would like. He saw us watching a movie, said hello, and headed into the kitchen. He was a man of few words, but we got along pretty well, as long as I stayed out of trouble. He came back in with a beer and the takeout container. My dad eased himself into his well-worn easy chair and didn't even bother asking what we were watching.

He turned to me, after taking a swig of his beer. "No homework?"

"I've started on some assignments that we have due in the coming weeks."

That wasn't a complete lie, I mean, Kristy and I began discussing our papers, so that counted right?

"Good," he said. He opened the container and took a large bite out of a meat-filled hoagie and pieces of lettuce and tomato spilled out into the container in the process.

We sat in silence the rest of the night as we finished the movie. After it was over I hid in my room before my mom could give any more of her unsolicited advice. I started to read my history assignment when my phone dinged.

It was a text from Hannah:

> Where are the house pics??? I want deets!

> His house was crazy! I didn't get any pics, didn't want to be a creeper, sorry. Next time.

> Awwww ok. Anything at all you can tell me???

> He had a movie theater room.

> WTF!? Movie theater room?

Yea, but he made me promise not to tell anyone.

I won't!! Did you have fun?

Uh. Not really.

Wait what? I thought this is what you wanted.

Me too. He was different tho. He already tried to put his hand up my dress.

RU kidding? He doesn't seem like that!

Yeah, he was very different at his place. Maybe he was used to doing it with Zoe?

Can you say ur waiting until marriage?

I don't know. Bryan and Paul freaked out when I told them.

Zack's different. You should tell him ASAP.

Yea, I guess. How's your night?

I hate being trapped here. My parents made me watch TV with them. We need to make a fake study date.

Works for me. Oh, btw, I'm Zack's gf now.

What!? Ur just telling me that now!?

I don't feel as happy as I thought I would.

Maybe ur not over Bryan …

I set my phone down and picked up my iPad to finish reading. My phone vibrated indicating that another text message arrived, but I ignored it and tried to read about King Henry VIII, but I couldn't focus.

In all my daydreams after Zack asked me out, I had been all smiles and the happiest person ever. In real life happy wasn't even close to the emotion I was feeling. Yet again, I was stuck in another relationship where I had to fend someone off me which would inevitably lead to me telling Zack I was saving myself until marriage. That excuse was a load of crap because I wasn't, but it was the only one that worked. Hannah gave me that idea when I was with Tyler and the excuse stuck ever since. She was a genius and never pried into why I didn't want to have sex. Good thing she never asked because I had no clue what I would tell her.

Would I ever want it?

Tossing my iPad on the floor, I sunk under my flowery pink comforter and closed my eyes. Maybe in my dreams I could find happiness.

CHAPTER SIX

I pulled into the parking lot at school the next morning and noticed Zack waiting next to my spot, wearing his typical ensemble: black T-shirt with the Beatles logo, cargo shorts, and Chuck Taylor shoes. His sandy blond hair was ruffled as usual. He wasn't the sharpest dresser, but in the past I'd always found his style cute. It matched his laid-back personality perfectly.

Today I wasn't in the mood to see him. His style irritated me even more. *Couldn't he find the time to comb his hair?*

I parked, grabbed my stuff, and stepped out of my car. Before I could even utter a word, Zack stated, "I didn't hear from you last night. Did you get my text?" He rubbed his hands up and down his shorts as he spoke, avoiding my gaze.

I looked down at my phone and saw two unread messages. *How did I not see these after my alarm went off this morning?* One was from Zack and one was from Hannah.

You home? Had fun tonight 😊

Oh no.

"Sorry I didn't see your message. I had to hang out with my parents and must have missed it."

"That's okay. I wasn't sure if you had fun," he said, eyes darting around the parking lot.

"No, I did." I gave him a quick kiss to emphasize I meant it.

How bad could it be with him? It was nice he was worried that I didn't respond. Bryan wouldn't have cared if I made it home at all. Now that I thought about it, after we started dating, the only time I received texts from him was when his parents weren't home.

"Want to walk me to homeroom?"

"Sure!"

Crisis averted. I really was off my game. Normally I would text a guy as soon as I was parked in front of my house that I had such a great time and couldn't wait to see him again. Last night I didn't even want to think about seeing Zack again.

We reached homeroom and Zack said goodbye and that he would see me at lunch. We kissed and I walked inside. Kristy was already in her seat, her eyes following me as I sat down. I went to turn on my iPad when I heard, "So, how was the movie?"

I sighed. *I really didn't feel like reliving last night.*

"You were right, we didn't watch it." I turned around to glare at Kristy.

She sported a forest-green low-cut T-shirt with a leather jacket over top, tight black jeans, and combat boots. She was dressed as if she was going to stylishly rob a bank. Her angular red hair was tucked behind one of her ears. My inspection of Kristy's outfit took longer than was probably socially acceptable. Heat crept up my neck as I quickly looked away.

"With all your boyfriends I would have thought you would have figured out by now that *watch a movie* meant make out."

"I thought maybe it would be different since it was a first date, but no such luck. Oh, and he's officially my boyfriend now."

Kristy silently assessed me. "If you don't want to kiss him, then why are you his girlfriend?"

"You don't understand. I know I like him. Almost my entire life I've always wanted to date him and now I finally am," I said exasperated.

Before she could say anything else, Mrs. Jacobs started taking attendance. I stared off into space and wished I could crawl back into bed and never have to face Zack or Kristy again. *Why was I so worried about Kristy and what she thought?*

After homeroom was finished, I gathered my belongings and tried to quickly scoot out, when Kristy placed her hand on my shoulder. "We're both in Mr. T's class so we might as well walk together."

"Okay, yea, sure."

After a few steps down the hallway, Kristy broke the silence. "What's really going on? You're like a completely different person today."

"I woke up in a bad mood. I don't feel like being here and dealing with life. This school year already isn't going the way I expected."

"I get that. I've for sure had those mornings when nothing seems to be okay."

"That's exactly how I feel."

After a second, I added, "Sorry I bit your head off earlier, but I keep getting a ton of unsolicited advice. I thought once Zack asked me out, I'd be happy and have everything I ever wanted. But Zack is like all the rest of the guys and just wants to make out. I don't get it. Why is everyone so obsessed with kissing when it's so boring?" I said, throwing my hands in the air.

"It's only boring when you haven't found the right person to kiss." Kristy gave me a side glance and quickly looked ahead when I met her eyes.

"I mean I had fun with all of them before we dated but then as soon as they asked me out, BOOM, it changes and all we're doing is locking lips. Has that happened to you? I've asked Hannah and she has no clue what I'm talking about. She said she really enjoys kissing."

"Yeah, sometimes," Kristy said, sitting down in her seat in Mr. T's class.

I was about to ask her to elaborate when the bell rang. Mr. T announced that we would work with our partners during class for our outline and long-term writing project.

I turned around. "I take it you probably still don't have an iPad."

"No and my aunt won't call my parents. She doesn't want to start anything. I can read the hardcopies the librarian showed me, it's fine."

"For bio you're going to want the most up-to-date book and not have to lug something that heavy around."

Kristy shrugged her shoulders. "I don't know what else to do."

I thought a second. "I have an idea. Zack might have an extra iPad laying around somewhere. If so, maybe you can come to his house with me to get it, although he's not a fan of people coming over."

I didn't add that it would also help me out, because I would have a legit excuse to not *finish* the movie.

"Why doesn't he like people over?" Kristy asked.

"I think his family is pretty private."

"If it's a big deal, don't worry about it. I can put up with the musty biology book."

"No way. You'll probably die from inhaling mold from reading it. I'll ask him at lunch and see what he says."

Kristy gave me a long look and eventually shrugged. "Okay, you win."

"Good. Now what collaborative book do you want to read? We still need one more book and I picked the first one."

After a small debate, I agreed to read the Stephen and Owen King book, *Sleeping Beauties*. It wasn't at all my first choice, but Kristy convinced me to try reading something new.

"I love reading and writing horror books, but I've never worked on one with another person. It could add a new spin to my writing," Kristy mused.

I cracked a small smile. "That's true. I better not get any nightmares from reading my first ever Stephen King novel."

"They aren't that bad. I promise. Some are more thrillers than horror."

As I retrieved the code from Mr. T for my iPad, he said, "I heard from Mr. Ricardo that Bryan Rickter has been giving you problems."

"Do all teachers talk to each other?"

"Shorty, don't forget we're people too," Mr. T said, smiling.

"Right." I took a breath. "Bryan's pissed at me, but whatever. Maybe I'll create an evil monster named after him in my collaborative story."

"There you go."

The rest of class, Kristy and I brainstormed ideas and started the story outline, especially since it was due Friday. But we didn't make much progress. We couldn't even agree on the name of the main character. How did Bill Clinton and James Patterson make it work? They were clearly two different people. At the end of class, Kristy and I decided to first try and read some of the books and maybe they would spark an idea we both could agree on.

When the bell rang, Kristy asked, "Okay if I sit with you again at lunch?"

"Oh yeah, sure! I'll also try to talk to Zack before lunch about getting you an iPad."

Kristy nodded and headed the other way.

As I walked to math, I found myself looking forward to lunch and seeing Kristy again. I'd have to see what other kind of books she liked to read and take notes. Maybe I could broaden my horizons and try something new.

CHAPTER SEVEN

Before lunch, Zack caught up with me as I exited math class. He eagerly agreed to give Kristy an iPad he had lying around, although he looked dejected when I suggested that Kristy come with me to get it. Zack frowned. "I was hoping we could finish that movie tonight."

"Oh, I actually finished watching it last night with my parents." Zack still had a frown on his face. "If you're worried Kristy will say something about your house, she won't say anything, especially since she doesn't know anyone yet."

Zack thought for a second and nodded.

By the time we finished talking, we found ourselves in the cafeteria. I sat in the same seat as yesterday and whispered in Kristy's ear that we were on track for our evening plans. Her hair smelled like a field of lavender flowers.

Kristy gave me a smile. "Thanks for all you're doing."

I felt myself blush. "Oh, it's no problem."

"Kristy, are you sitting with us from now on?" Erin asked as she flounced into her chair. Even though her teal sundress was only an inch longer than yesterday, I didn't get a show of her underwear this time.

Heat crept to my neck recalling that memory.

"Uh, maybe? I don't know anyone else yet," Kristy said. Her face became unreadable.

"Not sure if Shorty informed you, but this is a couple's only lunch table and I doubt you have a boyfriend. You either need to find one that we approve of or have to find another table to sit at for the rest of the semester," Erin stated.

The table was silent, and my anger started to rise. Who died and made Erin queen? Did I somehow wake up in the movie *Mean Girls*? Hannah was my only close friend that was a girl, and she was amazing. *Were other girls really this awful?*

I took a deep breath and was about to utter a retort when Kristy said, "Sam, it's okay. I got this."

She turned to Erin. "I've only been here for a day, and I can tell you think your ridiculous rules make you important. But guess what, you aren't. You wanted to know what Archfield was like? Everyone there was head to toe in real designer clothes with legit salon highlights, unlike you, with your Old Navy dress and failed dye job. And they even pretend to be nice."

Erin's mouth dropped as Kristy stalked out of the cafeteria.

I stared at Hannah, and she refused to look me in the eyes. Why didn't she warn me that Erin was the spawn of Satan? At least Kristy knew how to stand up for herself.

"Way to not be welcoming, Erin. What's wrong with you?" I asked, glaring at her.

"I was nice enough to let you in, do you really want to question me? If she ever sits here again, you're out!" Erin said, her voice growing louder after each word.

I took a deep breath and slowly let it out to calm myself. *How could Hannah stand to hang out with this menace?*

I sat in a brooding silence and took a bite out of my peanut butter and jelly sandwich. Being an almost vegetarian at Dale High was hard, so I packed the same thing every day. My mom always worried I wasn't getting enough protein, but I emphasized peanut butter is not only chock full of nuts, but also protein.

Zack looked over at me, his eyebrows furrowed. "Are you okay?"

"Yea," I said, staring down at my lunch. I wasn't, really, but he was the last person I wanted to talk to. The person who *should* be asking if I was okay was too caught up with her boyfriend, aka my ex-boyfriend. Speaking of being okay, I really should check on Kristy.

I scarfed down my sandwich and gathered my belongings. "I gotta go. I'll see you tonight," I said to Zack giving him a quick kiss on the cheek.

Before he could respond, I walked toward the cafeteria's exit. I couldn't believe I was leaving lunch early two days in a row, but I felt responsible for Kristy's departure and wanted to make sure she was okay.

On my way out, I heard, "Shorty!"

I turned toward the voice. It was my frenemy in the flesh, Cashi. He wore his typical plaid button down, jeans, and black wire-rimmed glasses. His dark brown eyes studied me. I had been avoiding him ever since I beat him for Student Council President because I didn't know what to say, but I couldn't ignore him forever.

"When is our first Student Council meeting of the year?"
Oh right.

"Um, I still have to figure that out with Mrs. Jacobs but thanks for the reminder."

"Let me know as soon as you find out. I want to make sure I'm pulling my weight as your number two. I think the two of us can really plan some cool things for Dale High," he said while pushing up his glasses.

I felt a pang of guilt; he clearly cared more about Student

Council than me. At least he was granted the role of Vice President, mainly because there was no contender in that slot. Last year's VP graduated, and no one decided to run this year, so when I won President, Cashi automatically became VP.

"Yeah, sure," I said as my eyes darted to the exit in hopes he would get the hint I had places to be.

"Do you still have my number?" he asked.

"Yep. Plus, you live across the street, so I know where to find you," I said.

"Don't wait too long, we have a lot to talk about."

I nodded. *Why did I listen to my parents and run for President? I should've planned an easier senior year.*

In the bathroom, I bent down and saw Kristy's combat boots peeking out of the same stall as yesterday. "Kristy, it's Sam. I'm so sorry. I had no idea Erin was like that. I never really talked to her before yesterday." My voice echoed throughout the room.

"This place is worse than Archfield. At least everyone there left me alone. I'd rather go back to sitting by myself than dealing with a girl like Erin."

The stall door opened, and Kristy's steely gaze struck me. "Look, I appreciate everything you've done for me, but you don't have to pretend to be my friend. I can find my own way around. I don't want your reputation here to be screwed up because of me."

"First off, I'm not dating a football player anymore so I doubt people will like me as much. It's not like they really knew who I was anyways. Don't worry about me, I'll be fine," I said, giving her a reassuring smile. "Second off, I'm not pretending to be your friend. I like hanging out with you."

Kristy gave me a half-smile. "Sometimes it's hard to tell. Everyone at Archfield pretended to be nice to me, so now that's screwed up the way I think."

I shook my head. "People there sound pretty awful," I

said. "Do you still want to come with me to Zack's tonight to get your iPad?"

"You sure? He's okay with it?"

I smiled. "He didn't seem to care too much, so you're in!"

Kristy returned my smile. "Guess I should cancel my hot date with Netflix."

"Just don't tell many people about his house. He doesn't like people knowing he's rich."

Kristy chuckled. "Who would I tell anyways?" Her hair shone underneath the bathroom's bright light.

I wished she smiled more; it lit up her entire face. My gaze held hers beyond the normal amount of time as I was watching her. I was the first to break the staring contest and I could feel my cheeks on fire. *Why did I feel so embarrassed to look at her? I've never had that issue talking with Hannah.*

Luckily, before things got even more awkward, the bell rang, and it was time for Mr. Ricardo's class. Kristy and I parted ways and I walked to my seat, trying to avoid any contact with Bryan.

This proved to be difficult since he came up to my desk and whispered in my ear, "No one embarrasses me. I'm going to make your life a living hell and if you tell anyone, I'm going to ruin Hannah."

By the time I looked up he was already headed to the back of the room. *Who said things like that?* However, I did notice Mr. Ricardo staring at me with his brows scrunched.

He approached my desk. "Sam, is everything alright?"

"Oh yea, I'm fine. Bryan told me that I left something of mine at his house," I said, lying through my teeth.

I didn't care one bit if Bryan threatened to ruin my life but bringing Hannah into my problems was what worried me. She shouldn't be affected because of something I caused.

Mr. Ricardo looked at me skeptically and I thought I

would have to make up more lies but instead, he left when Zack sat next to me.

He leaned over toward me. "Where did you go?"

"To see if Kristy was okay after Erin kicked her out of the lunch table." I was about ready to say more when Hannah stepped in the room and as she sat, I heard from the back, "Hey hottie, Hannah! You should come sit back here with us instead of Zack and his ho."

That comment could only be from Bryan. Hannah's face reddened and she shot me an alarmed look.

I hated seeing Hannah uncomfortable. I could feel my face also flush, and my hands started shaking uncontrollably. I leapt up out of my chair and turned around to face Bryan head-on. "Leave her alone Bryan! Why would she want to be with you? You're literally the worst."

I sat, and it started to sink in what I did. Not only did I make things much worse for myself, but I probably also did for Hannah. *Why couldn't I learn to keep my mouth shut?* I squeezed my eyes closed so tears wouldn't escape.

"And don't call my girlfriend a ho!"

I opened one of my eyes to find Zack sprinting to the back towards Bryan. *Oh no. Did I wake up in the high school version of Jerry Springer?*

"Zack, it's not worth it," I called out too late.

Zack swung his right fist toward Bryan's face, but Bryan must have been anticipating this reaction. Before Zack's fist could connect, Bryan grabbed his arm and twisted him around and roughly pushed Zack's face against the desk.

Hannah and I gasped aloud at the exact same moment. The panic in her eyes matched my own.

Why did Zack have to do that? This was only going to make things worse. In no scenario would Zack win in a physical fight against Bryan.

Mr. Ricardo flew to the back of the class and demanded that Bryan take his hands off Zack.

Bryan dropped his hands, but only after he pushed Zack's face into the desk a little harder.

Zack made a muffled sound against the desk.

At this point I didn't care that tears were falling down my face.

Hannah stared at me horrified.

I gathered my stuff and sprinted out the door. I found myself in the girl's bathroom where I locked the door to the stall and sunk to the ground. What did I do to deserve this? Zack liked me enough to defend my honor and here I was wondering if I even made the right choice going out with him.

"Sam? I know you're in here. Please talk to me," Hannah whispered.

I unlocked the bathroom stall and ran to Hannah for a hug. "I don't know what to do," I said between sobs. "Why can't he leave me alone?"

"I know, I'm sorry. He's being such a jerk."

I pulled away and reached for a paper towel. "I wish I had never dated him." I dabbed my eyes to clean up the large black streak of mascara off my cheek.

"I know, but you can't change that now."

I sniffled and turned to Hannah. "Thanks for coming after me."

"Always. Mr. Ricardo marched Zack and Bryan down to the principal's office so it's safe to come back to class."

"Poor Zack. I didn't mean to involve him. My life is such a train wreck right now." I let out a large breath of air.

"Come on, let's go back to class. It will be okay once we figure out how to get through to Bryan."

We walked back to class in silence. As soon as I entered, the busy chatter ended abruptly. Everyone's eyes were glued on me. I took a deep breath and said with the fakest smile I could muster, "Show's over, get back to work class!"

A few people chuckled but one of Bryan's friends yelled, "Shorty, you're going to regret rejecting Bryan!"

At that moment Mr. Ricardo strode in the door and looked Bryan's friend straight in the eye. "If anyone else decides to speak up today, you saw I'm not shy to take you to Principal Jergens's office." Mr. Ricardo turned to me and lowered his voice. "Sam, please no more outbursts. If you have something to say to someone, do it after class."

"Sorry," I said looking at my bright pink fingernails.

"It's okay. It is important for people to stick up for themselves, just be more aware of where and how you are doing it," Mr. Ricardo said with a small smile.

"Okay, no problem." *I wasn't used to being reprimanded in class. Everything was so awful right now; I wanted to go home and have a do-over.*

Mr. Ricardo made us pair off to discuss last night's homework. Naturally Hannah and I worked together. After we hurriedly read our essays to each other, Hannah asked, "Are you doing any better?"

I sighed. "Not really. Clearly Zack really likes me, and I thought I felt the same way about him, too. But, like always, things changed after we started kissing. We don't have fun together anymore and it's all about *seeing a movie*," I said making air quotes.

Hannah chewed on her bottom lip. "It seemed so promising this time. At band camp you two were flirty and couldn't get enough of each other. And you've been crushing on him since forever. What happened?"

"I don't know. I'd rather go to the dentist than kiss him! At least there I can open my mouth and not have to pretend I'm having a good time." Despite feeling awful, I couldn't help but crack a smile while I was joking around with Hannah.

Hannah snickered. "You know that's a bad sign, right? What are you going to do?"

"I honestly have no clue. I don't want to give up yet. Maybe we need to get into this new groove and figure out how to make it work for both of us?" I looked down and my hands were in fists. I unclenched them but couldn't stop more words from spewing out of my mouth. "I also don't want to lose him as a friend like I did Tyler. And then there is our lunch table. I'd be kicked out if we broke up." I blew a loose piece of blond hair out of my face and stared at Hannah, praying she'd have the answers to all my problems.

Hannah blinked and reached over to grab my hand. "Who cares? Your happiness is more important. We could find our own table together!"

"What about Tyler?"

"He could come too, and we can make our own rules at the table. Maybe he'd talk to me more that way." Hannah released my hand but kept her eyes trained on me.

"What do you mean?"

Hannah shrugged. "We just haven't been as connected these days. Tyler doesn't text me as much and whenever Zack is around, Tyler always talks to him about some stupid video game."

"Kristy does need a new place to sit now that Erin kicked her out and I don't want her sitting all by herself so that could work." I took a deep breath. "I feel bad though that Zack and I just started dating. Maybe I'll give it a week and see how that goes."

"Make sure you stick with that. Don't hang onto him forever if you don't like him. That's not fair to him."

I chewed on my lip. "I know. Why does dating have to be so confusing?"

"Dating all these guys that aren't a fit should help you figure out when you find the right one."

"How did you know with Tyler though? He's only your first boyfriend and you seem pretty happy."

Hannah shrugged. "It feels right. I wish I could see him more actually, but my mom is so overprotective, so we really don't get to see each other all that much."

"I have no idea what that's like. I was counting down the minutes until I could leave Zack's house. When we were watching *Thor Ragnarok*, I had to do everything in my power to not stop kissing him and enjoy the movie."

"*Thor Ragnarok* is awesome, but it sounds like you don't like him that much."

"Wait, so you and Tyler aren't connecting as much anymore? I thought he was FaceTiming you every day in the summer before you went to sleep. And you guys have been making out so much in the hallways." I was the master at deflecting questions I didn't want to answer.

Hannah didn't even blink an eye. "The beginning of summer started like that, but near the end I would only get a text from him here or there. It's like he forgets about me until he sees me in person."

"Have you asked him?"

Hannah knitted her eyebrows. "He said he's been busy. I just get lonely in the house with my parents and his FaceTiming helped me forget how they never let me do anything."

"Busy? It was summer and he didn't even have a job. He was probably busy playing video games all the time," I said rolling my eyes.

Hannah shrugged. "Maybe it will get back to normal now that we're back at school and can see each other more. I just wish my parents would let me have people over without needing it to be for school."

"I hope so. You guys are the cutest. Maybe we can figure something out."

The rest of class was spent sharing our essays with everyone, but my mind couldn't focus. What if I never found the person I wanted to make out with all the time?

CHAPTER EIGHT

M r. Paul was in a great mood again. And when I say great mood, I mean snapping at anyone that uttered a single word unless they were called on kind of mood. Kristy slipped in right as the bell rang and I was about to say hi when Mr. Paul came up to her. "You got lucky, you made it right on time." *Was he always this strict?*

She ignored him and slouched in her seat.

I opened my mouth to say hi when Mr. Paul strode over to us, eyebrows scrunched. "Sam, no talking after the bell rings. At least you aren't late today."

As Mr. Paul stalked back up to the whiteboard, Kristy and I stared at each other, trying to speak without words but failing miserably. At times like this, Hannah and I would attempt to text each other or pass a journal that we kept exclusively for notes. That would be difficult in this situation because all I had on me was my iPad and that wasn't as discreet as a journal. Plus I couldn't text Kristy because I didn't have her number.

I should get her number in case she gets lost on the way to Zack's or for our partner projects. Should I casually mention to her we should have each other's numbers for the purpose of projects? Or did that sound too weird?

My stomach churned at the thought of asking for her phone number and my hands were clammy. I wiped them on my dress while I was thinking about next steps.

Why was I overthinking this? It's only a phone number for god's sake. I wasn't asking for her Instagram password.

I didn't have to be stuck in my mind too long because Mr. Paul announced it was time to start the worm dissection.

I shuddered.

"Don't worry, we've got this. Anything that grosses you out, turn away," Kristy said. "I'll go get the tools we need."

"Thanks. I don't mean to be such a baby but cutting things open really isn't my jam," I said wrinkling my nose.

As Kristy stood, I craned my neck to see what she was getting, but I quickly turned away when I saw her pull two pairs of itty-bitty scissors out of a drawer. *Is cutting up animals even legal?* My stomach was massively twisting. I held back the urge to vomit. *Was it from the impending dissection or asking for Kristy's phone number?*

When Kristy returned, I purposely didn't look down at all the supplies she dropped in front of us. I took a deep breath. I needed to get this over with. "We should probably exchange numbers since we're partners in two classes," I said, avoiding looking Kristy in the eye. I settled my gaze on a poster with a rainbow pyramid of the biological classifications. I began saying them like a mantra in my head while I awaited Kristy's reply. *Kingdom, Phylum, Class, Order...*

"Give me your number and I'll text you mine," Kristy said.

I forced myself to meet her penetrating gaze.

She gave me a tentative smile.

That wasn't so hard, now was it? I rattled off my digits and Kristy stealthily moved her fingers across her iPhone under the desk. I felt my phone vibrate in my purse.

"Now if I have a burning idea about our creative writing paper, I can text you," I said. I grinned thinking of what kind of snarky texts Kristy might send.

"Or you can text me about non-school related topics too," Kristy said. She tucked a loose strand of hair behind her ear.

"Great," I said a little too loudly.

I haven't had a new friend that was a girl in a long time. Is that why I still feel nervous chatting with Kristy?

"Or if you need me to save you from a bad date," Kristy said. A smirk appeared on her face.

She brought up that I didn't like Zack enough. I didn't need the constant reminder.

"Speaking of, thanks for coming with me to Zack's tonight. That saves me from having to *watch* another movie." The memory of his tongue sneaking in my mouth made me wince.

"It's the least I could do," Kristy replied.

I felt my phone vibrate again. It was a text from Hannah.

> Bryan isn't back yet.

I turned toward Hannah. The chair next to her didn't hold Bryan's imposing figure. Did that also mean Zack was still stuck in the principal's office?

Kristy saw me gazing at the empty chair and asked, "What happened to your ex?"

"Don't get me started," I said, rolling my eyes. "He was being a jerk to me in history again, so I blew up at him. Zack tried to throw a punch at Bryan but like you predicted, was very unsuccessful. Mr. Ricardo dragged them both to the principal's office."

"Where was I? I'm starting to think that being your friend comes with so much entertainment and drama. But props to

Zack for trying to hit him. I really didn't think that he had it in him."

Is this what my life has become, a bad angsty teen sitcom? At least I knew that Kristy considered me a friend and wasn't creeped out by me asking for her number.

"Me either. I've never had anyone get into a fight for me."

"Is that what you've been thinking about?"

"What do you mean?"

"You don't seem with it, like your mind is a million miles away. Do you even realize you've been playing with those scissors that grossed you out a minute ago?"

Was I acting that weird? I looked down and my right hand was grasping a pair of the itty-bitty scissors. *When did that even happen?*

"I feel bad Zack got in trouble for my mess. I'm also thinking that if the tables were turned, I don't think I would do the same thing for him."

"The real truth arises," Kristy said leaning back in her chair.

"Hannah thinks I don't actually like him."

That can't be the case though, right? He's been my forever crush.

"That's obvious."

"You just met me. How would you even know that?" I asked, releasing my hold on the scissors. They clinked on the desk as they fell out of my hand.

Kristy's lips pursed. "I can see the signs."

"Really? Care to explain more?"

"Not in bio, maybe later."

"Okay, but I want to know. I've had a crush on Zack since I can remember so this makes no sense. How can that feeling disappear?"

Kristy crossed her arms. "It's easy to confuse friendship and crushes."

What did she mean? Before I could ask her to explain further, my favorite person sauntered into the room.

"The prodigal child has returned!" Bryan said in his booming voice.

I rolled my eyes. "Asshole," I said under my breath before I could stop myself. Luckily Mr. Paul must have been too busy running towards Bryan's seat that he missed my dig.

"Mr. Rickter, I've been waiting for this moment," Mr. Paul stated, blinking fast.

"Hold on a second, Mr. Paul. I have an excuse note explaining that Shorty's boyfriend tried to hit me but couldn't execute on the delivery, although I enjoyed yesterday's detention. I had a great nap."

"You've interrupted the whole class with your nonsense. I could easily give you more detention," Mr. Paul replied, putting his hands on his hips.

Bryan wiped the smug grin from his face. "Mr. Paul, I can't have detention again, Coach will flip out!"

I'd never heard Bryan use a pleading tone before. *Mr. Paul was my new hero.*

"If that's the case, sit down and stop talking," Mr. Paul said.

Bryan slunk to his chair and crossed his arms.

I wanted to high-five Mr. Paul, but I was afraid he'd throw *me* in detention.

"Please help your partner with this dissection. She looks green around the gills," Mr. Paul said, gesturing toward Hannah.

Hannah did have a green hue to her face, but perhaps that was because Bryan arrived. Either way, I wished I could've rescued her.

Kristy and I went back to our analysis of the worm. After a couple of minutes, I heard Hannah's distinct high pitch laughter. I whipped around and saw Bryan whispering in her ear. Hannah's cheeks had turned from green to rosy pink. I knew that her deep red blush meant she was embarrassed, but I rarely saw her cheeks turn pink except when she had flirted with Tyler in the beginning of their relationship. Did she like the attention Bryan gave her? How could anything that Bryan says make Hannah want to flirt back? Every time he spoke to me, I wanted to poke my eyes out with a sharp object, like the lab scissors I had moments ago desperately been clutching for dear life.

I sat back into my lab chair and stared dumbfounded at Kristy. She shrugged her shoulders. "Sam, this isn't on you to fix. Hannah can take care of herself."

"Doesn't she realize Bryan's trying to make me jealous?" I said, my eyes narrowing.

Kristy shook her head. "I bet Hannah doesn't even realize she's flirting back."

Luckily Tyler wasn't in bio with us or Bryan would have become a punching bag twice in one day. At the end of class as Kristy and I gathered up our stuff, Bryan stalked over to our table. "Tell your pathetic boyfriend that if he ever tries to come after me again, I won't let him off so easy next time."

"Did you guys get in trouble?" I asked.

"Just a warning, for both of us. If you ask me, he should've been suspended like I was last year but for some reason Zack is the golden child and gets away with murder." Bryan rolled his eyes. "If I ended up getting more than your boyfriend, you both would be in deep shit. Just remember that. See you, Hannah!" Bryan said, giving a backward wave as he walked out the door.

Kristy rested her hand on my shoulder. "That makes *me* even want to punch him. Are you okay?"

"Yeah. I'm so over him. He sucks, but I need to talk to Hannah to see what the heck is going on. Want to meet by my car to go to Zack's? I'm at spot two."

"Works for me, thanks," Kristy said, slinging her messenger bag over her shoulder before exiting.

"What was that?" I asked more sharply than I intended.

"What are you talking about?" Hannah replied, gathering up her belongings and avoiding my eyes.

"You were flirting with Bryan." *How did she not realize that?*

"I was not! He said something funny, and I laughed. That's it. Why are you getting so upset?" Hannah asked in a defensive tone.

My stomach sank. "I'm not. I'm worried about you. He's awful and I don't want you getting hurt. You should've heard what he said to me!"

Hannah's face reddened. After a second, she raised her gaze to meet mine. "It seems like you're jealous, but I don't get it. You never liked him anyway." Hannah pushed past me to the door.

I jogged to catch up with her. "Don't you think it's convenient that he starts flirting with you right after we break up? He's trying to make me jealous!"

"Thanks for thinking Bryan wouldn't like me," Hannah said, her face flushed.

"That's not what I meant."

"Sure sounded like it." Hannah walked in another direction. "I have to say goodbye to Tyler before I'm banished back to my house with Bryan."

My eyed widened. "Wait, Bryan's coming over to your house?"

"Might as well have someone over so I'm not so bored since I'm sure Tyler won't call me. At least with Bryan I can prove he's my lab partner. I have to go," Hannah said. Right before she walked away, the cold stare she gave me made my heart drop to my feet.

CHAPTER NINE

After an awkward iPad exchange at Zack's, Kristy followed me to my house in her black Jeep so I could help her set up the school apps. The whole time we were at Zack's my mind focused on the fight with Hannah. Normally if we got in a tiff, it blew over and didn't amount to any confrontation, unlike today.

When I stepped out of my car, Kristy said, "Your house is cute."

"It's nothing like Zack's place, but it's comfortable."

I unlocked the door and a grumbling erupted from Kristy's stomach.

"Oh sorry. Skipping lunch two days in a row is catching up to me."

You and me both. I was starving.

"My mom usually leaves something vegetarian friendly in the fridge for me if you're hungry."

"That'd be awesome," Kristy said.

"Skipping lunch isn't going to happen anymore. I'll ask Zack if it's okay if you sit with us. I'm sure he'll be fine with it."

"Honestly, I'm better off sitting alone. Nothing against you, but I'm done defending myself. I can catch up with my homework," Kristy said, scuffing her boot on the fake hardwood floor.

That would be social suicide but there wasn't much I could do if she didn't want to stay.

I shrugged. "Okay. If you're sure."

Another thought popped into my head. *I didn't want her to go.* Even though Kristy just arrived, I liked having her around, especially since Hannah was mad at me. Kristy made life more interesting with her sarcastic comments and I wanted to know more about her.

I reached to open the fridge and peered inside. My mom did not disappoint. I pulled out a large Rubbermaid container and opened the red lid. A waft of spice reached my nose. The container held a red Thai curry concoction with brown rice, tofu, broccoli, peppers, onions, carrots, and mushrooms.

Kristy sniffed the air. "That smells good."

"I hope you like spice. My mom sometimes gets heavy handed with it." I opened the microwave and hit the reheat button for two minutes.

"Fine by me. The spicier the better."

As the leftovers reheated, I moved all the junk off the kitchen table so Kristy and I would have a place to sit. I couldn't remember the last time it was used, except to collect mail and other random items, like my mom's coupon book. Once the microwave dinged, I grabbed the food and parceled it between two plates. I placed the meal and silverware in front of Kristy and then took a seat directly opposite her.

Kristy inspected the dish. She scooped a modest size on her fork, blew on it, and placed it in her mouth. After a second, she licked her lips. "Your mom can really cook. I never get homemade meals. My aunt and I mainly order takeout." She took another heaping bite.

"I'm really lucky." I savored the food I placed in my mouth. I was going to miss this when I was at college next year.

After we chewed for a minute in silence, I took a deep breath and asked Kristy, "What happened with your parents?"

Kristy's fork stopped moving. She raised her eyes to meet mine. "Are you sure you want to know?"

"You know a lot about my life already. I can't have you always asking me all the questions."

"That's fair. If you don't want to be my friend after I tell you, I get it." She fiddled with her fork.

"It can't be that bad," I said, my eyes wide. *What was she about to tell me? Did she actually get kicked out of Archfield and that's why she ended up at Dale?*

"I haven't told anyone this story besides my aunt, so I'll let you judge." She was still twirling the fork, oblivious of the food sitting in front of her.

"I used to date around a lot, like you. It first started out with a bunch of guys, but I went through the half-decent ones at Archfield, and they still were rich, self-centered, and dull. Some of the action wasn't bad, but I never wanted anything long-term with them. After I got bored of the guys, I started moving onto girls," Kristy said quietly. She stared down at her half-eaten plate of food.

She liked girls? "Oh really? How was that?" I asked, leaning forward, my face warm.

"It was more exciting, especially since most girls weren't looking for anything serious or even out yet, so we had to do a lot of sneaking around. I fooled around with a couple I met online because I didn't know of any openly bi or gay girls at Archfield but then one of them, Talia, wouldn't let me go. She thought I was the love of her life and pressured me into being her girlfriend."

"Pressuring someone doesn't sound like a good way to

start a relationship." I frowned. *At least Zack didn't do that to me.*

"You're telling me. Fast forward a couple months to when my parents came back early from an event this summer and found Talia in my bed in only a bra and panties. They completely lost it," Kristy said. She recited this information without any emotion in her voice, as if she was Amazon's Alexa reciting the weather.

My mouth dropped and I gripped the end of the table. "Holy crap. What did they do?"

I couldn't even imagine what my parents would do if they found me in a similar position.

Kristy's shoulders moved up and down from her large sigh. "They threw Talia out of the house and told me I had to move out by the end of the week," she said flatly.

"Wait, you mean like forever?" My face was frozen solid.

How could her parents even think of doing that to her? She's their daughter!

"Yep. They said if I want to, and I quote, *participate in homosexual behavior* I couldn't do it under their roof."

I shook my head, and my anger rose. *I want to punch her parents so bad.*

"Didn't they even try to see your side of things?" I asked, my voice raising.

"It would take an act of God for that to happen. Trust me, I tried to explain, but my parents, especially my mother, were never good at listening. I called up my aunt. She's always had my back. She was so mad at my mom and offered to let me stay with her until I graduated so here I am." Her voice was still robot-like, and her eyes were dull.

I wanted to do anything I could to help her. I couldn't believe everything Kristy went through. Was she gay? Or bi? A feeling in my stomach was growing, but I couldn't identify the feeling. *Was it excitement? That'd be weird since Kristy just told me a terrible story.*

I realized I was silent for too long. "I'm so sorry all of that happened to you. I don't understand how your parents could be like that. You can't help that you like girls."

"According to them I chose to be this way and they wanted no part in it."

I shook my head. "What's wrong with people? How can people still think that?"

Kristy shrugged her shoulders. "I don't know. I never would've chosen this lifestyle. It's so confusing but I can't change who I am."

"I can't even imagine."

The feeling in my stomach grew more pronounced and an urge to grab Kristy's hand to comfort her flitted in my head.

I tried to put both out of my mind and focus on the moment. "What happened with Talia?"

"I broke up with her once I moved in with my aunt. I said we were in different stages of our life, but in reality, I didn't want her to find out where I moved to. She was getting really clingy and jealous."

"She sounds desperate."

"Something like that."

I picked at the curry. I had so many questions racing through my head, but I wasn't sure what was okay to ask. *How did she know she liked girls? When did she know she liked girls? What was it like to have a girlfriend?*

I settled on the least intrusive one. "Do you miss her?" I leaned closer to the table.

Kristy looked off in the distance. "Sometimes. I couldn't wait to see her after school, and I felt like she was the only person who really got me. But that was on her good days. On her bad days, she had serious jealousy issues. If I didn't text her right away, she'd flip out and accuse me of cheating on her with some person at Archfield. I know I'm better off without her but I really wish she'd been around the past couple of days. It takes a lot for me not to text her."

"That has to be hard," I said, having no idea what she was feeling. *I couldn't remember a time I missed texting an ex that much.*

"If I'm ever tempted, I think about all the bad times. She would've lost her mind that I started hanging out with you."

My eyes widened. "But we're only friends," I said, my voice taking on a screechy tone.

Kristy shrugged her shoulders. "Reason doesn't make sense to someone looking for excuses to be jealous."

"You said earlier you only found out last week you were coming to Dale. How's that possible?"

"Even though I've been with my aunt the rest of summer, I still assumed I was going to finish my senior year at Archfield. I'd thought my parents already paid the tuition bill before the incident. I never heard otherwise."

I sucked in some air. "I don't like the way this story is heading."

"I was turned away on the first day of school because my freaking parents had canceled my enrollment and were reimbursed my tuition costs. It would've been nice if someone warned me. Archfield wasn't the best, but I still had some friends there. Now I have no one." Kristy's voice broke as she talked, and she turned away right as I saw a single tear slip down her cheek.

"Sorry. I thought I had myself under control."

"It's okay to be upset."

"I was forcing myself to not really think about what I was saying, otherwise I wouldn't be able to get through it." She faced me, her black eyeliner was smudged under her eyes.

Screw it. I jumped up and gave her a hug.

She patted one of her hands lightly on my back. It was as if she was afraid to touch me.

After a moment, I pulled away and sat in the chair across from her. "I'm so sorry about all that's happened to you. Your parents are real jerks."

"You aren't scared of me now? Or worried I'm going to hit on you?" Her right boot tapped the linoleum floor while she waited for an answer.

"No. I don't know any girls that are bi or gay, but it doesn't scare me." I pointedly looked in her eyes to send her a reassuring look.

She returned my gaze and gave a half smile. "Okay," Kristy said, her voice neutral.

I couldn't tell if she trusted me or not, but I'd have to prove it to her that I could not care less about her sexuality. If anything, it made her more intriguing. "Thanks for telling me all of that. I won't tell anyone."

"I don't care if you do. I'm not shy about dating guys and girls. It's a part of me. I just don't go out of my way to tell people, especially since I already have enough trouble fitting in."

"Can I ask you more questions?" *This was all so new to me.*

"Shoot," Kristy responded, leaning back in her chair.

"Are you bi?"

"I'm not a fan of labels but if I had to choose, I'd say pansexual. I'm attracted to people, doesn't matter their gender, sexual orientation, or fluidity. It makes no sense to me that I'm this way and is confusing as hell but that's what I am."

"That sounds super confusing. How do you know you like both?"

"I've been excited by both guys and girls." She was silent for a moment and then said, "But I have dark days when I wish I was straight. Things would be so much easier. I'd still be living with my parents with some boyfriend that I could boss around, and ready to go to Columbia in the fall. But nope, I had to mess around with girls and ruin my life."

Oh god that sounded awful. I couldn't believe just because she'd been with someone she liked, the consequences were so bad.

"You couldn't help it that you liked Talia."

"I should've known. My parents always said stupid homophobic comments."

I thought about my parents' church and how the pastor was very clear in his sermons that homosexuality was a sin. I heard from Hannah he wouldn't marry a gay couple at the church. Is that what my parents thought, too? My mom never missed a Sunday service.

"Even when I begin to think that another girl is attractive, I wonder if I really want to go down that road again." Kristy stabbed a large broccoli floret, avoiding my gaze.

"But it's a part of who you are. You can't change that."

I wished I could be more helpful, but I didn't even know what it was to truly like someone. Every time I tried, it crashed and burned.

"My therapist says that too."

My eyes widened, unable to hide my surprise. "You see a therapist?" *I didn't know anyone our age that saw one.*

"My aunt made me go to one after everything that happened. It's actually not that bad."

"I wouldn't even know where to begin talking to one."

"It's actually easier than you would imagine. You talk about your life for fifty minutes and don't have to ask them how they're doing."

"Never thought of it that way. That does sound kinda nice."

Kristy stared at me for a second. "I know you have more questions."

"How could you tell?"

I hope she can't read my mind. The last thought I had was, would she talk to her therapist about meeting me, and if so, what would she say?

"Your leg is bouncing a mile a minute and your hands are clenched."

"You don't mind?" I unfurled my hand.

I didn't know what was okay to ask or if I even wanted to know more about her feelings being pansexual. My stomach kept getting more and more twisted, but I couldn't help but wanting to know more.

"Might as well keep them coming."

Here goes nothing. I took a deep breath. "What's it like being with a girl?"

"Soft and amazing." Kristy focused her gaze on a spot behind me. She cocked her head slightly to the right and a slight smile appeared as if she was recalling a favorite memory.

I gave her a quizzical look. "You lost me."

"Guys are mainly muscle, which sometimes can be hot. But girls are soft and sensual. And they smell really, really good."

I wrinkled my nose. "Unlike guys. Bryan sometimes smelled like a sweaty locker room."

"Ew," Kristy said. "No wonder you didn't want to kiss him."

"That and he's annoying. What else do you like about being with a girl?"

"Guys are less emotional during sex, and it doesn't take long with them. It's more about the actual act. But with girls, it's more about the exploration," Kristy said, glancing at me through her eyelashes.

I swear the look she gave me was almost seductive. But the glance was only there for a fleeting second and her emotionless face returned. My face grew warm thinking about sex and the look Kristy gave me. Hannah rarely talked about sex but maybe that's because I also dated her current sexual partner.

"I wouldn't know any of that because I've never had sex." It was my turn to start playing with my fork. The silence between us was deafening.

"Really? Never?" Kristy said, her emerald green eyes wide.

I stared off into the distance. "I've always said I'm saving myself until marriage."

Kristy raised her eyebrows. "Really? Why?"

"Church taught me to wait until I'm married, and I've stuck with that line. It was easy and it worked like a charm. If a guy had an issue with it oh well, on to the next one." I avoided her gaze.

"Sounds like an excuse to not sleep with them."

She doesn't beat around the bush, does she?

"I've never wanted to do it, so why not do what I'm taught?" *Maybe if the right person showed up but at this point, I doubted that would ever happen.*

"I didn't realize you were religious."

"My parents make me go to church on Sundays. Tyler, Hannah, and I go to the same Methodist church. Luckily Bryan is Catholic."

"My parents go too. Probably why they hate I'm queer. I'm surprised they didn't ship me off to some conversion therapy program."

"Oh my god, do those still exist? I've only seen those in movies or on TV."

"They do, mainly in the south, but they're still around. I bet I would've ended up there if my aunt didn't take me in." She pushed the rest of the food left onto her fork and took a bite.

"I'm so glad your aunt has been there for you."

"Yea, she's the best." Kristy wiped her mouth with her

napkin and set down her fork. "Enough about my parents. What about yours? You guys get along?"

"I'm lucky; they're pretty cool. My dad doesn't say much most of the time, but my mom makes up for it because she's always interested in my business."

"It's nice they care. Where are they right now?"

"My mom's a nurse at Dale Hospital and my dad owns the corner grocery store in town. They both work way too hard. My mom keeps taking extra shifts so they can help pay for my college. I keep offering to work more but they want me to keep up my good grades."

"Where're you going to school?"

"Temple University for communications in Philadelphia. It only takes about an hour on a good day to get there. I'm so freaking tired of living in Dale. There's nothing to do."

"You're telling me, this place blows. I have to drive to Philly to see any cool bands play. What made you pick communications?"

"I wanted to major in creative writing, but my parents were like, *we don't want you to be living at our house forever*. At least with communications I can still take some writing classes but find a job when I graduate. In the meantime, I'm working on some short stories. I'm hoping one of them sparks an idea for a book."

"Sounds like you have it all worked out." I saw a small smirk appear on her face.

My face hardened. *Did I hear a bit of sarcasm in her voice? Or was that jealousy? Either way, I was the last person to have anything figured out. I couldn't even find a boyfriend I liked.*

"I had no choice. My dad is big on planning for my future, so I had to pick something, even if it wasn't my dream major," I said in a defensive tone.

"At least you have a future. Now that my parents cut me out

of their life, I have no clue what to do. I was supposed to go where my dad went to college, Columbia for Business Administration, but now that they aren't paying for anything anymore, that can't happen. I'd be in debt, even after I died. Since my parents were so set on it, Columbia was the only place I applied to, so I'm not sure what to do anymore. I might have to find a job for a year and save up until I can apply to other places. I want to go somewhere in a big city though, like you. I'm so over this town."

My demeanor softened. *How awful. No wonder she was so bitter that I had parents that cared.* "You still have time to apply to other places. I could help you look."

Kristy stared at me. "Really? Why would you do that?"

I shrugged. "I'd like to help out if I can."

"That's really nice of you." She was quiet for a minute. "I didn't mean to get all worked up and come off like an ass. It's still hard for me to talk about all this. Only a few people know I'm pan and that my parents kicked me out. It's always scary not knowing how someone will react."

"You can always talk to me." Before I even realized what I was doing, I grabbed Kristy's hand and squeezed it. We looked in each other's eyes and she gave me a reassuring smile. Her green eyes had flecks of yellow. I could've stared at them all night and maybe I would've had the chance to if the door hadn't creaked open. I quickly pulled my hand away as if I touched a hot surface. I looked at my phone—seven p.m. My mom was right on time. We'd been talking for over an hour, but it only felt like a couple of minutes.

"Sam! Where are you? How was your ... oh you have a friend over, how exciting! Hi, I'm Mrs. Daniels." My mom outstretched her hand.

"Hey, I'm Kristy." Kristy stood and clasped my mom's extended hand.

I also got up. "Kristy's new to Dale. I'm showing her

around school, and we're partners for a couple projects. Hope it's okay she came over and had some dinner."

"Of course it's okay, honey! It's nice to see you're making a new friend. Hope Sam has been a good guide and hasn't already ruined your opinion on Dale. I'm sure you could tell she isn't a fan of her school. I keep telling her there are worse schools out there, but she doesn't believe me. Where did you go before Dale?"

"Archfield," Kristy said quietly.

My mom raised her eyebrows. "Then you probably also think Dale is a downgrade."

"It's all right. At least people say what they think at Dale instead of behind your back. Sam seems cool so it's not all bad."

"I'm glad you and Sam get along. I keep telling her she needs more girlfriends, instead of dating all those guys."

I almost choked. *I don't think her meaning of girlfriend was the same as Kristy's.*

I was in the middle of rinsing off our plates when my mom asked Kristy, "Do you have a boyfriend?"

Kristy's face froze. "Not right now."

A plate slipped out of my hand and the clunk of it falling in the sink reverberated throughout the house. I inspected the plate and luckily didn't see any cracks.

"Sam! Be careful with those. Money doesn't grow on trees you know." My mom folded her arms.

"Stop being so nosey," I said under my breath, gingerly putting the plates in the dishwasher.

My mom must have had super good hearing because she responded, "I'm trying to learn more about your new friend. It's nice you finally brought someone over here. I was starting to think you were embarrassed of us."

"That's because you ask a million questions, like you're

doing now. We're going to do some homework." I walked from the room not waiting for a response.

Kristy trailed behind me.

"Good luck with your assignments and don't stay up too late," my mom called after us.

I entered my room and sunk on my bed. I motioned for Kristy to close the door. After it was shut, I said, "Sorry, she's a lot to take in."

"She's fine, it's cute she cares."

Kristy surveyed my hot pink painted room. "Like pink much?" Kristy grinned.

I rolled my eyes. "It's always been my favorite color."

There wasn't anywhere else to sit except my bed. I moved my collection of stuffed bears onto the floor to make room for Kristy. She sat against the headboard, so close to me I could almost feel her leg against mine.

I picked off a piece of my pink, flaking fingernail polish. "Can you give me the iPad so I can start to download all the apps you need?"

Kristy pulled the iPad out of her messenger bag and handed it to me.

After a few moments of downloading the school apps and making sure all her settings were correct, I said, "It should be good to use now."

I handed it back to her and our hands touched.

Her green eyes were laser focused on me as our hands pulled apart. At this point her leg was touching mine.

I didn't want to seem homophobic if I moved my leg. Plus, I didn't mind that it was against me.

Suddenly a loud buzzing pierced the air. I jumped off the bed and grabbed my phone off the dresser and saw it was Zack.

For once I didn't mind hearing from him. It saved me from my ridiculous thoughts.

"Hey, what's up?" I asked.

"It's Hannah. Bryan's at her house and she's freaking out. I'm not sure what happened but she's apparently hiding in the bathroom."

"I'm going to kill him."

"He's still there. Hannah wants him gone."

"I'll go over and get him out of there." I gathered up my keys and slipped into a pair of flip flops.

"I can come too."

The last thing I needed was him and Bryan in the same room when tensions were already high.

"No, I've got this but thanks. I'll text you after." I hung up before he could say another word. I turned to Kristy. "I've got to go over to Hannah's. Bryan's being an asshole."

"I'll follow you there so you can have backup." Kristy gathered her bag and we sped to our cars after I hollered to my mom I'd be back in about a half hour.

How could I let this happen? I should've done a better job of convincing Hannah that having Bryan over was an awful idea. I hoped he didn't hurt her too bad.

CHAPTER TEN

I parked along the side of Hannah's parents' colonial house and rang the doorbell.

"Sam, I didn't know you were coming over." Hannah's mom said as she opened the front door a crack. She pursed her lips. "You do know it's a school night, don't you?"

I opened my mouth to reply when she also added, "Who's the friend you've got with you?"

Kristy stuck out her hand. "Hello ma'am. I'm Kristy and new at Dale. I already had biology at Archfield, so I offered to come over and help."

Hannah's mom fully opened the door and returned Kristy's handshake. Her face brightened. "Hannah's never been great at science and could use all the help she can get." Hannah's mom ushered us into the hallway.

"Happy to help. Our current project on earthworms is interesting. Did you know that earthworms don't need eyes because they have receptor cells in their skin?"

"No, I didn't. Hannah told me about their earthworm dissection but that's it. What other facts about them do you know?"

I was super impressed. Kristy provided the perfect diversion.

"They also move away from the light because heat from the sun will dry them out and kill them."

As she talked, I slipped past Hannah's mom to the basement steps. I ran down the steps, leaving the door open only crack. That was my secret for basement doors. Leave it open a smidge, so parents don't hear the closure of the door and think it's open.

Bryan was sprawled on the couch typing on his phone.

"Where's Hannah?"

Bryan's eyes widened and he jumped to his feet. "What the hell are you doing here?"

I hit him on the arm. "To make you leave Hannah alone!"

Bryan swatted at my hand. "I tried kissing her and she freaked out! That's it, I swear!"

"Of course she would. You know she has a boyfriend."

Bryan shrugged. "That didn't stop you from flirting with me last year."

Way to deflect it back to me. I was so done with his attitude. "What's gotten into you? You're being such an asshole. And for the record, we didn't kiss while I was with Paul! I would've freaked out too if you tried that."

Bryan's face began to resemble a ripe tomato. "I'm the asshole? What about you? Why didn't you want me? Am I not that hot? Is that why Cate cheated?" His voice continued to get louder with each question.

I put my finger to my mouth. "Shh ... be quiet. Hannah's mom is going to wonder what's going on."

Bryan lowered his voice a fraction. "Why did you keep leading me on?"

"I'm sorry. I did like you or at least I thought I did. But then I stopped, but it didn't have anything to do with you."

Bryan scoffed and rolled his eyes. "Whatever."

"You even said so yourself that you weren't the only one I did this to. I thought I could like you more than a friend, but it didn't work. You're hot, look at all the girls that like you. I don't know what I want."

His shoulders slumped. "Why did you have to drag me into it? You know I've been messed up ever since Cate cheated on me at prom."

"I'm really sorry. I thought we could work but I was wrong. I know you're pissed at me, but can you stop taking it out on Hannah?"

"I thought she wanted me to kiss her. Why else did she invite me over? It's not like we even have any homework yet."

I rubbed my temples. *Was I ever going to get through to him?*

"Bryan! How many times do I have to tell you, she has a boyfriend. Even if she didn't, this is literally the first time you guys hung out."

"You kissed me the first time we hung out alone."

I shuddered. *Don't remind me. It was about as gross as my first kiss with Zack. Wet and never-ending.* I ignored his dig. "How about you don't go after someone that's my best friend."

Bryan looked over my right shoulder.

I turned and saw that Kristy had her arm around Hannah. *When did Kristy escape from Hannah's mom?*

Hannah's eyes were red and puffy with black mascara running down her freckled cheeks. "You should go," Hannah said quietly.

"I was just leaving." Bryan picked up his blue backpack and trudged up the steps. He turned near the top and looked right at Hannah. "I'm sorry. I didn't mean to make you cry. Hope you don't hate me now."

Once he disappeared, I said, "Hannah, I am so sorry. I don't want us to fight."

Hannah's bottom lip quivered. She reached to hug me, and I embraced her. Hannah squeezed me so tight I could barely breathe. Her entire body shook as she sobbed into my dress.

I rubbed her back. "Are you okay?"

Her sobs subsided after a couple more seconds. Hannah pulled away. "I'm sorry too. I don't know what I was thinking. I should have told him he couldn't come over, especially after he was so mean to you." Hannah sniffled.

I pulled a tissue out of my purse and handed it to her.

Hannah gave me a grateful smile.

"It'd been a while since another guy paid attention to me and Bryan was being so nice. I should've listened to you, but it gets so boring here. I didn't know he would try and kiss me. As soon as he did, I freaked out because I don't want to cheat on Tyler."

"I didn't mean for you to think that you couldn't get a guy. Any guy would be lucky to have you, but something is really off with Bryan."

"He wasn't that bad to me. I didn't want to face him to tell him to leave, that's why I hid in the bathroom. I was embarrassed. That's when I texted Zack. Guess he misunderstood me. Sorry to make you guys run over here for nothing." She dabbed the tissue under her eye, causing her mascara to only become more smudged.

I rubbed her arm. "You were upset, that's not nothing." My phone vibrated in my purse, and I pulled it out. It was a text from Zack.

You guys okay?

I texted back a couple short sentences. After I hit Send, I

looked up and Hannah and Kristy were staring at me. "Zack was checking on you. I told him it was a misunderstanding. Figured you'd want to tell Tyler first about what happened."

Hannah released a shaky breath. "That'll be a fun conversation. My stomach already feels sick thinking about telling him. I wasn't trying to hook up with Bryan. I didn't want to be sitting here alone again."

Her eyes were close to spilling over with more tears.

I hated Hannah looking so sad. "Good luck with talking to him." I squeezed her hand encouragingly.

"Thanks, I hope he understands," Hannah said, her voice cracking.

If I knew anything about Tyler, he wasn't going to be happy.

"Sorry I texted Zack rather than you."

I gave her another big hug. "It's okay, but we're not allowed to fight ever again."

After a second, she pulled away. "I agree. It felt weird texting your boyfriend instead of you." She faced Kristy. "Thanks for coming over. You could beat Bryan up better than Zack."

I laughed. "After the fight we saw today, you're probably right."

"No worries. I think I convinced your mom that we're all studying biology."

I glanced down at my watch and saw it was past eight thirty. "I better get going before my parents start to worry about me. Are you going to be okay?" I gave Hannah a worried look.

She gave me a shaky smile. "I'll be fine. Thanks for your help."

"I'm always here for you, no matter what time of day."

"I know. I need to call Tyler and get this over with. Thanks for all your help."

"Let me know how it goes."

"I'm sure it'll be fine." Her lack of enthusiasm made it clear even she didn't believe a word she was saying.

CHAPTER ELEVEN

I woke up in a tangled mess of sweaty sheets. I flung them off me and still felt gross. My shirt was soaked, and my throat ached for water. It wasn't even that hot out.

I tried to recall the dream that woke me up so abruptly. I still felt excited and happy with whatever made me so hot.

I closed my eyes and attempted to remember what caused those feelings. I made out arms, legs, and ... breasts? I was pinned underneath a figure whose lacy black bra had been removed. My head reached up to kiss her when the figure's face came into view. Red hair tickled the side of my cheek right before her lips met my own.

I gasped as I jolted up in bed. The mystery person was Kristy.

It hadn't even been twenty-four hours since she came out to me, and I already had a sex dream about her?

In the bathroom I threw ice cold water on my face and looked at myself in the mirror. My panicked sheet white face stared back. *What was going on?*

Later that morning, as I picked at my honey bunches of oats, I couldn't escape my thoughts. I'd never had such a vivid sex dream, especially one where I woke up happy. I'm not going to lie, this wasn't my first dream about a girl, but they usually were about some cute girl from a TV show, not about someone I knew. I'd thought everyone had dreams about celebrities, no matter their gender.

Why was my subconscious cursing me like this? I had no time to dwell on that unsettling thought; school waited for no man, or woman.

Zack had set up camp, as I predicted, by my parking spot. *UGH!* He was the last person I wanted to see this morning after my confusing as heck dream. I guess his presence was going to be a daily occurrence.

I stepped out of my car and gave him a quick peck on the lips. "Morning. Thanks again for giving Kristy an iPad."

"No problem. Glad at least someone can use it." He sported his I-just-got-out-of-the-shower-look and a black Pearl Jam shirt. He reached down and took my hand as we headed to class.

Why couldn't things always be this simple? I could get behind this Zack, not the Zack that only wanted to make out whenever we were alone.

When Kristy appeared in homeroom I smiled and attempted to act like everything was normal, but I knew my face resembled a tomato. The blue low-cut shirt she wore wasn't helping me curb my thoughts about last night's dream.

"Hey, how's it going?" she asked, sinking into her chair.

"Not bad. Pretty uneventful." My eyes focused on every spot in the room, except her face. "You?"

"Eh, okay. I'm still trying to wake up." Kristy rubbed her eyes and yawned.

"Didn't sleep well?" *What were the odds she slept like crap too?*

"Not really. I could use another cup of coffee."

"Why couldn't you sleep?"

"Ever since everything happened with my parents, I've had trouble sleeping. I also randomly have dreams of Talia's jealousy. That's what happened last night." Kristy put her head down on the desk.

I'd take a hot sex dream over a dream filled with jealousy any day. "Have you seen her at all?"

Kristy raised her head and took a deep breath. "Not yet, but I've been avoiding places I could run into her, like this cool vegan café near Archfield we'd go to all the time."

"It really stinks you have to change where you go because of her."

Kristy shrugged. "Better than the alternative of seeing her."

"What would you do if you ran into her?"

"A million scenarios have gone through my mind but if it actually happens, I'd probably ignore her and go about my business."

"Let's hope you never have to worry." *I hated seeing Bryan, but at least I didn't mortally dread that I might run into him.*

"That's the plan."

I pointed to her device. "How's the iPad treating you?"

"It's awesome. I already started on the James Patterson/Bill Clinton book, and I have some ideas for our project."

"That's perfect because I don't feel creative at all. I need some inspiration to hit me," I said grimacing.

"Try reading the Stephen and Owen King *Sleeping Beauties* book we picked. That could help."

"Or it could give me nightmares."

On the other hand, maybe that's what I needed to stop my dreams of Kristy.

"We could use them as a starting point. Make sure you

write them down and we can decode them. Dreams always have symbols hidden in them."

My face froze.

"What's wrong?"

I made myself give a small breath, that came off shaky. "Oh, uh nothing,"

Did Kristy know about my dream? I dismissed the thought. That could never be possible. *Come on, Shorty. Pull it together! It was a dream. But Kristy did say dreams have symbols. Maybe my dream meant we were becoming better friends?*

"Sam! Where did you go? It was like you were in another reality for a second."

"Wait, maybe we can use that in our story."

Kristy tilted her head. "Are you sure you didn't start reading *Sleeping Beauties* because that sounds eerily like that plotline."

"Nope, not yet. I'll start it tonight after marching band practice, I promise."

The bell rang, and I picked up my stuff in a daze.

Kristy placed her hand on my shoulder. "Is what I told you last night bothering you? I know it's a lot to take in."

"No, it's not that. I woke up in the middle of a weird dream last night and feel like I'm in a fog."

"I hate when that happens. It throws off the entire day."

You're telling me. I kept having to avert my eyes from her because I couldn't stop thinking of that lacy black bra. *Did she have one on right now? She didn't seem like the lacy kind of girl.*

We sat in our normal seats for creative writing and class started with partner work on our outline and paper. *This won't help my neurotic thoughts.* I was thankful when Mr. T came over to us, giving my mind a short reprieve. "What ideas do you have for your paper?"

"We're still working on it, but I made a suggestion of an alternative reality."

"That sounds promising. How exactly are you thinking it would work?" Mr. T said, raising his eyebrows.

"Dreams are actually different realities, but you never know which one is real and which one is a dream."

"I'm intrigued to read more." He smiled and told us to continue to flush out the details to submit with our outline.

After he moved onto the next set of partners Kristy said, "Maybe we can think of different scenarios of how the dream worlds will work."

"And we could give each other pointers if we get stuck."

We smiled at each other at the exact same time, which caused me to stare at her slightly upturned lips.

What would it be like to kiss her? Would it be as exciting as my dream or like kissing the other guys I've been with?

Kristy studied my face intently. "You're doing it again. That must have been some dream."

I stared at the table. "I'm fine. Let's keep working."

I needed to focus on something way less sexy, like how Bryan was being super annoying.

By the end of class, we had a solid grasp on our idea and even outlined our respective sections.

When the bell rang, Kristy tucked the strand of red hair that fell in her face behind her ear. "Do you mind if I sit with you again at lunch? A table by myself isn't sounding great anymore."

Having Kristy around even more wasn't going to help curb my confusion, but I couldn't have her sit by herself. That'd be mean, and I liked her too much for that. As a friend, of course.

"Sure, why not. If Erin gets mad, she can leave." Inwardly my stomach was clenching about the impending disaster. *Erin couldn't be that awful, right?*

"If she starts to interrogate me again, I'm moving tables."

"Fair enough."

On my way out, Mr. T motioned for me to come over to his desk. I said bye to Kristy and walked over to him.

"Do you still want to contribute to the newspaper this year? We can always use more articles or essays and need help on the staff."

"I'd loved to," I gushed. *Another way to boost my resume and do what I love, write.*

"Great! First meeting is tomorrow after school."

"You're joking. That weirdo Kristy is sitting with us again?" Erin said, narrowing her eyes.

How did I ever think Erin would be okay with Kristy sitting with us at lunch?

"Yeah, what's the problem?" I asked, crossing my arms.

Erin pounded her fists on the table. "She must have a boyfriend to sit here. You know that!"

"Her boyfriend goes to Archfield."

When did lying become so easy?

"I doubt it, she has no fashion sense what-so-ever. Who does she think she is, a bank robber? Who'd want to go out with that?" Erin said in her shrieky voice that would even make dogs cringe.

Erin was wrong. Kristy didn't remind me of a bank robber. I felt more of a Russian spy theme going on, resembling Black Widow from the Marvel movies circa 2012, with her short, striking red hair and tight, dark clothes. *Who wouldn't have dreams about someone that looked like that?*

"She has nowhere else to sit and she seems cool," Zack tried to explain.

Props for him for helping me.

"We should accept her as a charity case?" Erin asked, glaring at him.

I put my hands on my hips. "Who put you in charge and made you the lunch table goddess?"

Erin faced me. "Shorty, this is *your* fault. Things were fine until you showed up."

"I want people to be included. Why does it matter so much to you?"

Erin ignored my question. "Zack, I miss Zoe. You guys were so much better together than with *this* one. She's caused nothing but trouble!" Erin's index finger pointed directly at me.

I shot her daggers. "At least people actually like me. Maybe you should be the one to leave the table. You're the only one that seems to care if Kristy is here or not."

Erin's mouth fell open like a ventriloquist dummy. "That's not true. Guys come on, back me up. Who else thinks this should remain an exclusive, couples only lunch table?"

Hannah, Tyler, Zack, and I all stared back at her, not uttering a response.

Dylan chewed on a loose hang nail and stared at the table.

My hands still rested on my hips, and my frown turned upward to become a smirk.

"Dylan!" Erin said, her voice raising to an even higher decibel.

"I don't think she's that bad," he replied as his face reddened, still not meeting Erin's gaze.

That's when I noticed Kristy standing off to the side, her arms crossed, near another lunch table but close enough to hear everything that had been said.

"Fine! If you think that, be her boyfriend for all I care. Don't come crawling back to me when you find out she's a serial killer." Erin stood.

I puffed out my chest. "Erin, the people have spoken."

"Whatever, you guys aren't as cool as I thought anyways." She grabbed her purse, flipped her highlighted blond hair, and rushed out of the lunchroom. *About time she's the one that leaves.*

I pulled out Erin's now empty chair and motioned for Kristy to join us. "Your throne awaits!" I said triumphantly.

"I've never had anyone do that for me before," Kristy said, her eyes wide. She lowered herself into the chair.

Dylan took a huge breath in and let it out slowly. "Shorty, you really helped me out. I've been trying to break up with her for a while now, but she'd never let me."

I gave him a curious look. "Really? I thought you really liked her."

Dylan shrugged. "She's hot, but all she talks about are clothes or who slept with who. I don't care about that. I'm much better off without her."

I reached over to give him a high-five. "Now that's the spirit!"

Dylan's hand connected with my own and he beamed. Dylan looked over at Kristy and gave her an apologetic look. "I'm sorry too for what Erin said to you. She can be downright evil when she wants to be."

Kristy gave him a small smile. "Thanks for sticking up for me, that takes guts."

Dylan beamed. I swore for a second I saw a hint of a flirty gaze pass between them, but maybe I was imagining things.

"Kristy, thanks for what you did for me yesterday. My mom loves you. Erin would never have done that for me. You're awesome," Hannah said.

Kristy nodded. "Anytime. Bryan's bad news."

"You can say that again," Zack said, his lips taut.

I noticed Hannah and Tyler hadn't said one word to each other or even given each other a hug or kiss. I pulled out my phone and sent Hannah a quick text.

What's going on with you and Tyler?

Hannah must have felt her purse vibrate because she reached in and began furiously typing.

Tyler's pissed. Needs time to think.

I frowned. Why did Bryan have to ruin everything?

Speaking of Bryan, I hadn't heard from him all day. I glanced around the lunchroom. He sat at his normal spot, but he wasn't talking to the rest of the guys at his table. Instead, his head was down, moving the cafeteria bought glue-like macaroni and cheese around on his tray. In all the time I had known Bryan, being silent wasn't part of his MO, but if it kept him from bothering me, I was all for it.

"Ready for practice tonight?" I asked everyone, trying to change the topic.

I heard four groans and a chuckle.

"If you guys hate marching band so much, why are you in it?" Kristy asked.

"If we play an instrument in the concert band, we're forced to do marching band no matter how much we beg or plead, unless we're a football player. But it's not all bad. It's how a lot of us became friends."

"Shorty and I wouldn't be together if it wasn't for marching band," Zack said, placing his hand on my leg.

I automatically flinched and hoped Zack didn't notice. *Yea, I'm so lucky that marching band helped us seal the deal.* If only I could go back to flirty Shorty and let her know dating Zack wasn't all she thought it would be.

"Do you have to go to all of the football games?" Kristy asked, taking a fork full of the salad she packed.

"Yep, even the away ones, which are the worst. They take up so much time," I replied, rolling my eyes.

"The bus rides can be fun," Hannah said. She tried to catch Tyler's eye, but he was laser focused assembling his cracker, bologna, and cheese lunchable.

Hannah looked away from him frowning.

"Are you going to enroll in any extracurriculars, Kristy?" I asked.

Kristy raised her eyebrows. "What's there to join?"

"There are lots of different ones but I'm guessing not as many as Archfield," I said.

"They had a bunch, but they were weird, like some math league group, model UN, chess tournaments, and other stuff that all sounded nerdy. What are you in?"

"Those sound awful, I hate math. Besides marching band, I'm student council president and in the spring, I'm in the musical and concert band. I also write for the newspaper. Mr. T asked me to come to a meeting tomorrow."

"Writing for the newspaper actually sounds cool."

"*Dale's Daily* isn't anything to write home about but at least we have a newspaper!" I said, smiling at my pun.

Tyler rolled his eyes. "Shorty, your jokes are the worst. Don't try any of those in the newspaper."

I glared at him. "Thanks a lot for the vote of confidence."

Will he and I ever not be mean to each other? I missed the Tyler who always had my back.

"You should come to the meeting with me tomorrow," I said to Kristy.

She thought for a second and nodded her head.

I took a bite out my peanut butter and jelly sandwich when I saw Bryan staring at me out of the corner of my eye. *Another ex with a grudge.* I stared back and raised my right eyebrow. Bryan pointed to his phone. While Zack was talking to Tyler and Dylan about some video game, I snuck a look at his text.

I messed up with Hannah. What do I do?

I tried to discreetly type back.

Apologize. Tyler is super pissed so I'm not sure how much she will want to talk to you.

Ok

After a couple more seconds more words appeared.

Btw I liked you a lot.

We weren't right together, and you know it.

But you and Zack r?

I thought so. And he has a lunch table with Hannah.

Crap. Did I send that?

I heard a snort. I looked up and saw Bryan shaking his head at me.

Do you even like Zack?

I fiddled with my phone. Did I want to tell Bryan the truth? But if I didn't, he might never stop harassing me.

I don't know.

This was a weird turn of events. Bryan and I were texting again like before we dated. Now I remembered why I thought we would work together; he was fun to chat with. Why did everything have to go to crap after kissing became involved? And why did he have to try and kiss Hannah?

I looked up and everyone at the table was staring at me.

"Did I miss something?" I said, placing my phone deep in my purse.

Hannah eyed me curiously. "Zack asked you if you wanted some of his chips."

"Oh, no thanks," I said, giving Zack a smile.

"Who were you texting?" Zack asked.

"My mom. She's on her lunch break asking what time I'll be home and what I want for dinner," I said blinking my eyes.

Hannah raised her right eyebrow at me. That's the problem about lying to your best friend, they always can tell.

The bell rang and we all gathered up our trash. As we walked out of the cafeteria together, I told Kristy I'd see her in bio.

She nodded.

"Wait, I'll walk with you since we're in class together," Dylan said.

Kristy shrugged. "Yeah, okay."

They walked off in the opposite direction as us.

Tyler broke off and walked by himself without saying a word to any of us.

I faced Hannah.

She bit her lip as she watched him walk away.

"It'll be okay," I said. "I'm sure he just needs some time."

"Yeah, he can't get over you that fast, you've been together for so long," Zack said, grabbing my hand.

We walked into Mr. Ricardo's class hand in hand. I wasn't going to lie, having someone so attentive wasn't always the worst thing. At least Zack made me feel special.

CHAPTER TWELVE

In bio, Kristy leaned over and whispered in my ear. "You'll have to thank Zack again for lending me this iPad. It's a game changer. Those books from the library looked super heavy and smelled like my grandma's basement."

I turned to her and smiled. "I'll tell him tonight at band practice."

Mr. Paul approached our table. "Miss Daniels and Miss Davis. I must commend you on your dissection's detailed analysis. It exceeded my expectations."

I smiled. "That's all thanks to Kristy. She was the brains behind the operation."

"Very nice, Miss Davis. I'm impressed," he said, rubbing his glasses on his shirt.

After he left our table, Kristy typed in the code he gave her to get the bio book. I tried to start reading our assignment but Kristy's right foot kept tapping the ground at a rapid speed, ruining any concentration I had mustered. After a couple minutes she said to me, "What are you doing this weekend? Do you have to perform at a football game?"

I shook my head. "There isn't a game because it's Labor Day weekend. I don't have any plans yet."

Kristy rubbed her chin. "Want to come to my family's beach house with me at Barclay Beach? We rotate who uses it and it's my aunt's turn to have it Labor Day weekend. We're leaving Friday after school."

She was already inviting me to the shore with her? I tried to hide my surprise but I never did have the best poker face, especially when I was taken off guard. Kristy's eyebrows scrunched to form a V, but before she could backpedal and uninvite me, I made my whole face erupt in a smile. "Really? I love Barclay Beach! That's where Bryan's and Zack's houses are too. Isn't Barclay the best?"

"I know. It's not trashy like some of the other Jersey shore towns and there's still enough to do but with charm."

If it wasn't for that stupid dream, I wouldn't have been second guessing every interaction with Kristy today.

I twirled a strand of blond hair. "Couldn't have explained it better myself. I really want to go with you, but I'll have to ask my parents. Can I let you know tomorrow?"

"Yea, no problem. It'd be nice to hang out with someone other than my aunt," Kristy said through her eyelashes.

Was she flirting with me? Come on, Shorty. Get it together. She's being a friend. I'd say the same thing to Hannah.

"Yeah! And I wouldn't have to be forced to *watch* a movie," I said with a smirk.

Kristy shook her head. "That poor boy. Speaking of relationships, what's going on with Bryan and Hannah?" Kristy nodded her head toward Hannah's desk.

I glanced over at Hannah, and she had a slight smile on her face as she gazed up to look at Bryan. *Wait, was she starting to like him? But what about Tyler?* Bryan put his hand on top of Hannah's. She let it sit there for a couple of seconds before she pulled away, turning red.

"What do you think they're talking about? It's like yesterday never happened," Kristy said, crossing her legs.

I let out a large burst of air. "He's charming her. I hope Hannah knows what she's in for if she dates him. Bryan loves football and everything else comes second after that."

Hannah looked down at her iPad and as soon as she did that, Bryan pulled out his phone, and under the lab table, his thumbs typed away.

My phone vibrated inside my purse. I stuck my right hand inside, and then looked down. "Now where is that stupid lip gloss?" As I pretended to root around for lip gloss, I skimmed Bryan's text.

I think she's into me. Can you ask her?

I gave another sigh and typed back with my right hand.

I'm expecting a full report from her about what's going on between you two.

And u'll let me know?

Maybe.

Come on Shorty. Throw me a bone!

If you're nice.

"You and Bryan are texting, right?" Kristy said, not looking up from her iPad.

My eyes widened. "What? How did you know?"

"I can clearly see him texting under the table like his life depends on it and it shouldn't take you that long to find lip gloss. Is that who you were texting at lunch too?"

I put up my hands. "Guilty as charged."

Kristy rolled her eyes. "You're terrible at being discreet. Why are you texting him? I thought you hated him."

I shrugged. "I don't hate him, he's annoying. He likes Hannah and is asking for advice."

Kristy wrinkled her nose. "Why would you want your best friend to date someone that's annoying? Wouldn't that be weird, your best friend dating your ex?"

"No weirder than her dating my other ex, Tyler."

"Touché. But Bryan's awful. Tyler at least seems nice, even if he's a little nerdy."

"Today Bryan's being a different person than the beginning of the week. And maybe if he dates Hannah, he'll leave me alone. Win, win!" As I said those words aloud, my stomach turned a little. *I'd only help Bryan if Hannah actually liked him,* I reassured myself.

Kristy twisted her mouth. "Except you forgot one thing. You can't control other people."

"It'll work out!" I gave a shaky smile. *But would it?* Kristy's statement reminded me of my texts at lunch with Bryan. *Why did I tell him I wasn't sure about Zack? What if he told Zack before I could?* Maybe I really did need the beach with Kristy, it would give me time to figure out what I wanted to do about Zack.

The bell rang and I turned to Kristy. "I'll talk to my parents and text you tonight if I can come this weekend. Does that work?"

Kristy smiled. "Sounds good. Have fun at marching band."

Hannah appeared next to us. "Can I call out sick? I don't want to see Tyler at practice."

"It won't be that bad," I said, placing my arm on Hannah's. "I'm sure we won't have time to talk to anyone. We haven't had practice in so long that Mr. Smith is going to run us ragged."

"I really hope I don't have to see him," Hannah replied, blowing a piece of hair out of her face.

We said goodbye to Kristy and trudged to dreaded marching band practice.

***

As predicted, practice was brutal. As soon as Hannah and I stepped foot on the field we had to stand at attention for over ten minutes. If we moved a muscle the drum major, Susan, with her brown large-rimmed glasses and perpetually messy hair, would scream in our faces. Once we began running through the show, Mr. Smith stopped and called out specific individuals for messing up the formation. I prayed that he wouldn't notice me, but God had other plans.

I was in the middle of trying to convince myself that going to the beach with Kristy would be fun and that I shouldn't worry about the steamy dream, when, at the same time as I moved forward, the jacked guy in front of me with a tuba backed up.

I yelped and catapulted myself out of his way before any damage occurred, narrowly missing a collision by a second. I wiped my brow and steadied myself. My gaze ping ponged around to see if anyone noticed, but the whole band was still in their formation, going through the motions. *Maybe I got away with it.* I sprinted to my spot, which was easy to find because it was a huge gaping hole and tried to get back into the groove.

A second later, the dreaded whistle pierced the air. Everyone halted in their place and returned to attention. Mr. Smith sprinted through the entire band and stood two inches from my face.

"What the heck was that Shorty? Get your mind out of

the freaking clouds and watch what's going on! No one has any time for lolly gagging on this field."

He was so close to me I could smell his coffee laced breath. I did everything I could to keep from coughing and bit my tongue. Talking back would do nothing to improve this situation.

"Because of Shorty's mistake, I'm keeping everyone for an extra ten minutes, standing at attention the entire time. Make sure you say thank you to Shorty after practice. Now let's start from the beginning," Mr. Smith said, jogging back up to the side of the field.

As soon as Mr. Smith was out of earshot, I groaned. I should have auditioned to become a drum major. All you had to do was wave your arms around and yell. Anything was better than being treated like a minion.

After a grueling practice with the extra ten minutes of standing at attention my whole body ached, especially my arm muscles from holding up the trumpet. I couldn't imagine how the tuba guy felt from lifting that instrument in place for ten minutes straight. This treatment was inhumane.

Zack found me after I put my trumpet away, rubbing my arm muscles. "Man, it sucks you were called out like that."

I sighed. "I feel bad everyone had to stay extra because of me. Hopefully they don't hate me."

"Mr. Smith was looking for an excuse to keep us late and he decided to take it out on you. He can be a jerk, and everyone knows it." Zack put his arm around me, bringing me in for a side hug.

My other bandmates came up to me and told me not to worry. The muscular tuba guy even clasped his hand on my shoulder and said, "I think I was the one that messed up that move. Thanks for taking the fall for me Shorty. I owe you!"

My face lit up. Everyone still liked me. It also probably helped that I had the most popular guy in the band in my back pocket. For some reason Zack could do no wrong in the eyes of the band crowd. Even Mr. Smith never critiqued Zack. Maybe Mr. Smith needed to know that Zack was my guy? We could be the band power couple and perhaps if we had enough people on our side, we could even be the next homecoming king and queen! *But was that what I really wanted? Wasn't I thinking of breaking up with him?*

Zack gave me a slight frown. "Shorty? Did you hear what I asked you?"

"Sorry! Can you repeat it?"

Zack sucked in a breath. "I asked, do you want to come to my parents' beach house this weekend at Barclay? It's the last time we could go before marching band takes over our life."

Oh no. I had to break it to him easy that I already made plans, without him.

I bit my lip. "I actually might be going to the shore with Kristy. We'd see you down there though. Her aunt's house is also in Barclay."

"Oh. I didn't realize," Zack said as he ran his hand through his hair. His charming smile was nowhere to be seen.

"She asked me today in biology and I couldn't say no. She's going through a hard time with her parents." I avoided looking him in the eyes.

Zack shrugged. "No problem."

I immediately felt guilty after seeing his downcast expression and before I could think, I said, "We can meet up if you want once I'm down there."

"That'd be great!" His face lit up.

"Perfect!" I looked down at my watch. "I better get home. See you tomorrow!" I gave him a quick kiss.

My hands trembled as I carried my trumpet case to my car, and it wasn't from the weight of the case. Telling Zack I was going to the shore with Kristy felt weird, it was as if I was doing something wrong. It didn't help that there was no part of me that wanted more *alone* time with Zack, especially at his beach house. I was ninety nine percent sure his parents wouldn't be accompanying him on this trip. I was about to pull out of my spot when my phone buzzed. It was a text from Hannah.

> Tyler broke up with me after practice. U still here?

> Yes! Where are you?

> My parking spot.

I jogged across the lot while dodging cars and found Hannah hunched over her steering wheel, her face buried in her hands. I opened her door and she collapsed onto me.

Her arms wrapped around my neck for dear life as she buried her tear-streaked face onto my shoulder. "It's really over. I completely messed everything up. And I loved him." Her voice broke.

"I can't believe he broke up with you like that. It's not like you actually kissed Bryan. You were being honest."

"Since I didn't tell him Bryan was coming over in the first place, he said he can't trust me anymore. We were together over two and a half years! Shouldn't that count for something?" Her sobs got louder.

I ran my hand over her long, curly dark hair and told her it would be okay.

"But will it? How can it? Everything is the worst right now. Now our lunch table is even more screwed." Hannah hiccupped and pulled away from me.

"Tyler doesn't have to sit there. And like you told me you can't worry about that. I always thought you were too good for him anyways."

"You're just saying that. I don't even know what to do now."

I looked her in the eye and her splotchy face stared back, tears still forming. "You'll be fine, I promise. You had a life before Tyler, and you can still have one without him. And you have me." I patted her shoulder.

"I know but that seems so long ago. It's hard to imagine being happy without him." The tears dripped down her face.

"It will hurt at first but over time it will get better. I promise!" I rubbed her shoulders.

"I sure hope so. Thanks, Shorty." Hannah gave me a shaky smile.

"Go home and try and relax. And text me if you need me!"

"I don't know what I would do without you." Hannah sniffled. After a second, she said, "Want to hang out this weekend? It will help keep my mind off Tyler."

Oh no. I didn't even think about what Hannah would say if I went to the shore with Kristy.

"I totally would but I promised Kristy I'd go to Barclay Beach with her. I also told Zack I'd hang out with him while I was down there," I said, avoiding looking at her.

"Really?" Hannah silently inspected me.

"Kristy invited me today and it was hard to say no. I know she's going through a rough time right now and you know how much I love the shore. This was all before I knew Tyler broke up with you. I'm really sorry!" I said, rushing my words, scared Hannah would be mad at me for ditching her.

"No, it's fine," Hannah said chewing her lip. Another tear slipped down her cheek.

"Hannah, I'm so sorry. You want me to cancel on her? I can tell her something came up."

I really hated seeing my best friend cry. I should bail on Kristy, but I really wanted to go.

"No, don't do that. I'll be fine," Hannah said, staring at the ground.

"Okay, but you don't seem sure."

"It's fine." Hannah glanced at her phone and gasped. "Oh no, it's really late. I better get home before my parents kill me!"

Hannah jumped in her car, shut the door, and sped off.

That didn't go well. I hoped she didn't think I was replacing her with Kristy.

Before I could even announce my arrival that I was home, my mom appeared in the doorway with a baby-blue dish towel wrapped around her arm and asked, "How was practice? Were you guys rusty from not having practice in a bit?"

Couldn't she at least let me put down my stuff before she came to bother me?

"It sucked. Mr. Smith totally called me out and told me to get my head out of the clouds, so that was fun." I rolled my eyes.

My dad made a grunting sound in his armchair.

"I'm really sorry honey. At least it's almost the weekend!" my mom said rubbing my back.

Maybe now would be the perfect time to ask about Kristy, when she's feeling bad about my day.

"Speaking of, can I go to Barclay Beach with Kristy and her aunt?" I asked, rubbing my hands on my dress.

"I don't see why not but your dad is pretty short-handed at the store. Can you come back in time to help him on Labor Day? I also would need to meet her aunt before you go with them."

"I thought you didn't need me during the school year. I signed up for the newspaper staff thinking I had some extra time."

"This just happened. My one part-time assistant up and left today without any notice," my dad said gruffly.

Her eyes pleaded with me. "It'd be great if you could help out here and there until he hires someone new."

An idea brewed in my head.

"Kristy might be interested in the position. She needs a job."

Not to mention, this way I could see more of Kristy.

"What experience does this Kristy have?" my dad asked while cleaning his glasses on his T-shirt.

"I'm not sure but I can text her."

I fumbled for my phone.

> I can go with you as long as we come back by Sunday night and my mom meets your aunt first. My dad's short-handed at the store on Monday and needs my help. He has a position available if you're interested.

> Let me talk to my aunt real quick.

My dad looked at me, cocking his head, and I explained she was talking to her aunt. He nodded and went back to sipping his beer and watching the Phillies lose.

My phone vibrated again.

> Coming back Sunday night works. She said to have your mom swing by Friday night before we leave so she can meet her. As for the open position, YES I'm interested.

> Awesome! What experience do you have?

A minute went by before the three typing dots appeared.

> Not much. I've shopped at a store. That count?

I had to hold back my chuckle.

That's okay, I had 0 experience when I started too.

But you're the store owner's daughter ...

I'll see what he says.

"She's interested, she hasn't had much experience but neither did I when I started at the store."

My dad grunted. "Have her come by Monday and we can test her out."

"Great, thanks Dad!" I ran over to his chair and enveloped him in a hug.

He patted my back as lightly as possible. "Sure."

I went to update my mom and found her in the kitchen pulling a pink flowery plate from the dishwasher and placing it in the cabinet. I grabbed the silverware container and began to arrange each piece in the drawer.

"Can you meet Kristy's aunt on Friday before we leave?"

She gave me a side glance. "Sure, that works. I'm surprised you didn't ask to go with your new boyfriend, Zack."

Why was she always so spot on? I needed to play it cool, or she'd see right through me.

"Kristy asked me first and it sounds like she needs a friend right now."

"That's really nice of you. Don't forget, if you want to go somewhere with Zack, we'll have to meet his parents too."

My face flushed. "Right. I'll let you know when."

I didn't want my parents meeting Zack's parents for many reasons, most importantly, he might get the wrong idea and think we're serious.

After I scarfed down my dinner, I shut myself in my room and relayed all the information to Kristy.

She replied:

Great, thanks for recommending me.

And thanks for inviting me to the shore! P.S. right after you invited me, Zack did too, but I let him know I already promised I'd go with you. Cool if I meet up with him at some point?

There was a couple minutes silence until Kristy texted back.

Sure. I'm heading to bed. Can't keep my eyes open. See you tomorrow.

I tucked myself into bed and couldn't shake the thought of Kristy also slipping herself into her bed sheets at the same time as me. It was as if we were almost in bed together. *Almost.*

CHAPTER THIRTEEN

And then there were five. Our lunch table numbers kept dwindling since Erin's departure. Tyler ignored us and plopped in a seat right next to Erin.

Hannah's face was dangerously close to crumbling when his butt hit the chair.

I reached over and rubbed her arm.

She gave a half smile, but her eyes were dull.

The next time I glanced at the other lunch table, Erin's hand was on Tyler's leg. I shook my head. I wasn't the only one to take notice.

Hannah's face was devoid of all its color. "How could he forget me so fast?" she whispered, her hands covering her face.

"He didn't. I'm sure he is trying to dull the pain."

Hannah uncovered her face and pools of tears formed in her eyes. "Or trying to hurt me, and if so, it's working," she said, wiping away a stray tear that dripped loose.

Erin caught my eye and smirked as she brought her hand further up Tyler's thigh.

I shook my head and said to Hannah, "Start flirting with Dylan. Two can play this game."

Hannah took a deep breath, jutted out her chin, and said to Dylan, "Didn't it suck we had to stay late at band practice last night?"

"It was the worst, and of course it was hot as balls out," Dylan responded, wrinkling his forehead.

Gross. Why did boys always have to refer to body parts?

After a couple more exchanges with Dylan, she let out her dainty laugh.

I kept my eye on Tyler and Erin and as I predicted, they couldn't ignore Hannah's distinct laugh. Tyler's head whipped around and once he saw what was happening, his face tightened.

Erin's mouth dropped and she grabbed Tyler's face and proceeded to stick her tongue down his throat. Luckily Hannah's face was turned when that occurred, but I was forced to watch the pathetic display of affection. As they pulled away, Erin wiped her face with the back of her hand with a look of disgust. A smirk appeared on my face. *Guess a towel was still a necessity when kissing Tyler.*

"This is all pretty messed up, Sam. Jealousy's awful," Kristy whispered in my ear.

"It seems like it." Jealousy was a bit of an unknown feeling for me. Seeing Hannah and Tyler together had been weird, but it was more like a third wheel kind of feeling, not because I cared they were making out.

My phone vibrated after Hannah's laughter reverberated in the cafeteria. *Crap.* That had to be Bryan and I'm sure he wasn't happy if he was watching Hannah's flirty display.

What the hell Shorty

She's only doing it to make Tyler jealous. He broke up with her last night.

Well if that's the case, c u soon!

I scratched my head. *What did he mean by that?*

"Hey Shorty, long time no talk," Bryan said as he slid into the empty chair next to Hannah.

Oh no. Zack was already shooting daggers at Bryan.

"What are you doing, man? No one wants you here," Zack said through a clenched jaw.

"Calm down percussion hero. I'm not here for your girl although it's interesting that she's been texting me for the past twenty-four hours. Betcha didn't know that," Bryan replied, leaning back in his chair.

I kicked Bryan under the table.

"Ow, Shorty! You're still fiery, aren't you?" Bryan said, rubbing his leg where my foot came into contact. He turned to Hannah and gave her a lopsided grin. "Do you want to work on our lab project together this weekend at my beach house?"

"Can I get back to you?" Hannah said, looking away from him, turning pink.

"Don't worry, I'll be the perfect gentleman!" Bryan said winking.

"Yeah, right," I said under my breath.

Bryan's eyes narrowed. "You never gave me a chance."

"Uh huh. I had to keep trying to fend you off me." *That and I wanted to curl up in a ball and take a nap every time he spoke.*

"That's because you didn't want to do anything!" Bryan said, throwing up his hands.

Zack's stare on Bryan kept getting chillier and chillier. "I think you should leave. No one wants you here."

"Hannah? You don't mind that I sit here, do you?"

"I guess not," Hannah responded, staring at her hands.

"Bryan, you've caused enough problems. I'm sure your

jock friends miss all of your boring banter," I said, motioning over to the table where all the occupants were blatantly watching us.

"I get the hint, I'll leave, but Hannah, if you want to come to Barclay with me this weekend, give me a holler," Bryan said knocking the table a couple of times as he left.

I rolled my eyes. "Sorry guys. I don't know what I ever saw in him."

"At least he provides entertainment, right?" Kristy said grinning.

"Maybe to you, but I want to smack him in the face," I replied, glaring at Bryan from across the lunchroom. All his jock friends were giving him high fives.

"Don't try it, it'll only land you in the principal's office," Zack said.

I gave a hollow laugh. "Good point."

"You and Bryan have been texting?" Zack asked quietly, pressing his lips together.

"Oh, just about Hannah. Nothing interesting," I replied. *Was Zack jealous too? He had nothing to worry about with Bryan, that's for sure.*

The rest of the lunch period wasn't much better. When Zack mentioned his beach party, Kristy gritted her teeth. I could tell a party with my boyfriend wasn't high on her agenda, but I already promised Zack. For the whole conversation about the party, Hannah looked down at the table and fiddled with her lunch. If it were up to me, I'd ask if she wanted to stay with me and Kristy, but I couldn't invite her to someone else's house. Maybe if I brought it up Kristy would invite her?

"Too bad you aren't able to come," I said to Hannah, giving Kristy a side glance.

"If I had a place to stay maybe I could convince them," Hannah said flatly.

"I already promised Tyler and Erin my guest room, otherwise you'd totally be invited," Zack stated.

My eyes widened. "What! Why?" I said, raising my voice.

"Tyler's my best friend, we go way back," Zack said, putting up his hands.

"I get that but when did this happen? He and Hannah broke up last night," I said.

That was the last thing Hannah needed to hear. She sat motionless in her chair.

"He asked me this morning. I guess he and Erin were talking after band last night," Zack stated, not looking me in the eye.

Hannah sucked in her breath as the bell rang. Her hands shook as she packed up her half-eaten turkey and cheese wrap. All of us walked down the hall in silence. As we approached Mr. Ricardo's classroom, Kristy said, "Well, once again, lunch was interesting. See you and Hannah in bio."

"Sam, are you ready for the first newspaper staff meeting tonight?" Mr. Ricardo asked as we sat in our seats. "I'm helping Mr. T with it this year."

Zack's eyes widened. "Wait, I didn't realize you actually joined the staff. I thought you wrote articles here and there. What else don't I know about you?" Zack slumped down into his seat.

That I had a sexual dream about the girl I'm going to spend the weekend with. Did that count?

"Get used to it man. That's Shorty to a tee. She'll never tell you everything," Bryan said scooting in the seat behind me, across from Hannah.

"Hey, that's my seat!" a girl with purple highlighted hair and bright blue-rimmed glasses said angrily to Bryan.

Bryan pointed over his shoulder to his empty chair. "Too bad. Take mine in the back."

"Bryan! Get out of her seat," I said, yanking on his arm.

I REALLY didn't want to be stuck in front of him during class or have him this close to Zack.

Bryan pulled his arm away from me and rolled his eyes. Looking directly at Zack he said, "If you're serious about Shorty, you have to get used to not knowing what's going on. I couldn't take it anymore."

This was downright dangerous. I liked it better when Bryan and Zack were enemies; at least then they didn't talk.

"You wanted *me* back."

"In a moment of weakness. Now I'm glad you didn't agree. Hannah is way better," Bryan said, leaning over to ruffle Hannah's curly hair.

Hannah turned bright red, but I saw a smile appear on her lips.

"I've been thinking. I want to go to the beach with you if the offer still stands," Hannah said, staring directly in Bryan's eyes.

Bryan pumped his fist in the air. "I knew you'd come around. You won't be disappointed."

My jaw dropped. "Hannah! What are you doing?"

"Are you sure you want to go anywhere alone with this jackass?" Zack asked.

"Yes. He was nice enough to invite me along, unlike anyone else. Plus, we have fun together, right?" Hannah asked

If that wasn't passive aggressive, I didn't know what was.

"We do. And I promise not to freak you out this time," Bryan said as he stuck out his hand.

"Deal," Hannah said, shaking his hand.

"How are you going to get your parents to agree?" I asked, pinching my eyebrows together.

"I'll tell them I'm going down with you and Kristy. You've used me for enough excuses I think I can finally start to do the same," Hannah replied with a smug look.

"Uhh ..." *Kristy was about to be implicated in a lie that I helped cause.*

"Hannah, you can come to my party while you're down there. I guess Bryan can come too, but no fights," Zack stated.

"You're one to talk. I'll bring beer and some of the guys. About time you did something cool," Bryan stated, giving Zack a high five.

I rolled my eyes. "Hannah, at least I won't be far away if you need me. And Bryan, if you hurt her, I won't go easy on you this time."

"Oh, I know. You were never easy to deal with," Bryan said chuckling at his own joke.

I was about to retort a response when Mr. Ricardo hovered over my desk. "Sam, are these two bothering you again?"

"Nope, we're all good." I flashed the fakest smile known to mankind, but he must have bought it, at least for the time being.

"Well, if not, make sure you let me know."

Mr. Ricardo looked at Bryan. "Bryan, get back to your normal seat. While he does that, everyone go to chapter three of your history book."

"Fine." Bryan got out of his chair and pushed the table-chair combo a couple inches towards Zack's direction. It made a loud screeching sound and I jumped.

Mr. Ricardo shook his head. "Bryan! Do you want to go visit Mr. Jergens again?" Mr. Ricardo asked.

"Chill out, Mr. Ricardo. I just tripped over my desk," he said, sinking into his assigned seat. When Mr. Ricardo turned his back, Bryan waved towards Hannah, and she gave a small wave back. *Was Hannah and Bryan getting together really happening?* It was weird when she and Tyler were together, but at least I could stand him. Bryan was a whole other level of awfulness. Would I ever want to hang around her again if they started dating?

I opened my iPad when Zack made a motion to his phone. I discreetly reached into my purse and saw a new text.

I'm not listening to Bryan. He's an ass and you're awesome.

"Sam, what's so interesting in your purse?" Mr. Ricardo asked.

"Looking for my lip gloss." Would the web of lies ever end? I could barely keep them straight anymore. I needed a flowchart to figure out what I've told everyone, including myself.

I looked over at Hannah and she was sitting with a small smile on her face. *I hoped she knew what she was doing.*

CHAPTER FOURTEEN

"Everyone, we have a few new faces with us today and a new co-advisor! Mr. Ricardo, why don't you introduce yourself and then we'll go around to all the new members," Mr. T said at the newspaper staff meeting.

Mr. Ricardo cleared his throat. "Hello, everyone. I recently graduated with a degree in secondary education from a small college in Ohio and moved to Pennsylvania for this job at Dale. I'm really excited to be helping with the newspaper this year because history and journalism are two of my favorite subjects."

Who moves to Dale for a job? There wasn't an education job at the million other cities in the U.S.?

"Great! Now let's start with someone most of you probably know. Sam?"

"Hi! I'm Sam, also known as Shorty. I've written a few articles over the years for the paper and Mr. T recruited me to help with the staff this year. I'm in some other activities in Dale and excited to see how I can help."

I felt a rush of excitement talking about how much I loved writing.

"And you're the Student Council President. Don't forget that. It'll be great to have you contributing more this year for the paper," Mr. T said.

"Thanks," I said, my face turning crimson.

I needed to set up a time to meet with Cashi about stupid student council stuff.

"Thanks, Sam. I believe you're Sam's friend?" Mr. Ricardo said looking at Kristy.

"Yep, I'm Kristy. If you didn't know already, I'm the *new* girl. I like writing and Sam suggested I join this group."

Mr. T made a motion for Kristy to expand more, but she shook her head.

"Short and sweet, I like it," Mr. Ricardo said, rescuing her.

A few other students that I had never seen before spoke about themselves. Maybe they were freshmen?

Mr. T ran through different article ideas for consideration and then asked if we had any other suggestions. When no one uttered a peep, Mr. Ricardo asked, "What about you, Sam? What do you want to write?"

An idea brewed in my head, and I spouted out, "What about an advice column? Something like *Ask Shorty*. I could ask for email submissions and have a box in the lunchroom for people to submit their questions."

"That's a great idea. Maybe you can start advertising around school tomorrow so you can have questions in time for our first issue?" Mr. T asked.

Kristy kicked me under the table. I raised my eyebrows and she whispered in my ear, "Maybe we can co-write the advice column?"

I nodded and asked, "Can Kristy help? It can be a joint effort."

Mr. Ricardo and Mr. T met each other's eyes for a second and Mr. T nodded and began assigning the other articles. Mr. Ricardo strolled over to us. "It's great both of you are on board. If either of you need any assistance with your column or someone to proofread, I'm happy to help."

"Thanks! Do you have any guidance on getting questions for our advice column?" I asked.

He scratched his chin. "Just that you might be surprised by the questions you're asked. Be prepared to receive some interesting submissions, especially since people could submit them anonymously."

"I figured that. Maybe there will be a gem among the dirt?" I replied, rubbing my chin.

"Let's hope so. If not, have a close friend or family member submit one so you have something to write about," Mr. Ricardo stated.

I turned to Kristy, and she threw up her hands. "I'm not having any questions I want answered for people to read."

I cocked my head. *What burning secret questions did she have?*

After all the articles were assigned, we were released. Once we reached my car, I didn't know if we should say bye, hug, or fist bump it out like the bros did, so I opted to give her a small wave.

She nodded her head. "See you tomorrow."

CHAPTER FIFTEEN

"Cheryl, it's very nice to meet you. Thank you for hosting Sam. I hope she isn't too much trouble," my mom said shaking Kristy's aunt's hand. Kristy's aunt's two-story Tudor house was super cute. It reminded me of something that belonged in Germany or somewhere else in Europe.

"Of course, happy to have Sam," Cheryl replied.

My mom passed her a piece of paper. "Here's my phone number if anything goes awry."

Cheryl looked like an older version of Kristy with her bright red hair and toned body but unlike Kristy, she wore more vibrant colors: an orange flowy tank, white jeans, and bright purple sandals.

My mom gave me a hug, said goodbye to Kristy and Hannah, and left. We entered through the large, brown door.

I looked around the entrance and announced, "We're free!"

"Thank God. It's been forever since my parents let me go away for a weekend. Thanks for covering Ms. Findley," Hannah said.

"Please call me Cheryl. Ms. Findley makes me feel way too old." Cheryl leaned against the front door. "My parents were super strict when I was your age. Kristy's mom and I couldn't do anything either. I always vowed if I had kids, I wouldn't be the same way. Guess the three of you are my kids for the weekend. Just don't get pregnant."

Hannah turned red. "Bryan and I aren't even dating yet. That wouldn't happen."

"You never know, especially with Bryan." *I had first-hand experience with how persistent he was.*

A car horn honked a couple times.

"Speak of the devil, I'd recognize that beep anywhere."

Kristy rolled her eyes. "He's too lazy to come up and get Hannah from the house?"

"I'm sure he doesn't want to meet your aunt," I replied. He always tried to avoid my parents, but I didn't blame him there. My mom would have a field day asking him a million questions. Football, his grades, his parents, and even his relationship with me would've all been fair game.

Cheryl opened the door. "Are you sure you'll be okay, Hannah?"

"I'm good." Hannah hugged me and said she would see me down at the shore.

"Text me if you need me and please go slow," I whispered to her before she left.

I peered out the window to see Bryan sprint to the passenger side of the car to open the door and take her luggage. *He really was pulling out all the stops.*

"You girls ready?" Cheryl asked.

"Yes! The sooner we get there the faster we can go in the hot tub," Kristy said.

That did sound relaxing.

Elton John blared through the speakers as we made our way to Barclay Beach in Cheryl's fire-engine-red Toyota

Camry. The interior was spotless, and I caught a whiff of *new car* smell.

Traffic was horrendous but I guess that was expected for a holiday weekend. As we crawled bumper to bumper up the Ben Franklin Bridge to cross into New Jersey, I asked Kristy, "If you could watch any movie right now, what would it be?"

"I love all horror movies, even the cliché ones like *Chucky*."

I wrinkled my nose. "Horror movies? How do you not get nightmares?"

"I already get nightmares about Talia; nightmares from horror movies wouldn't be worse than that. What do you like?"

I forgot about her Talia dreams when I mentioned nightmares, but at least talking about it didn't seem to bother her.

"I love all Marvel movies, thrillers, and epic movie sagas like *The Hunger Games*. But I also like classic movies like *Never Been Kissed* and *Clueless*."

"I can get behind that. Jennifer Lawrence and Scarlett Johansson look pretty sexy in tight black clothes."

I opened my mouth a little. "Uh, yea, I guess?"

It was odd hearing her talk so openly about her attractions, especially around her aunt.

Kristy shook her head. "Just so you know, I don't consider *Never Been Kissed* and *Clueless* classics. *The Sound of Music* is a classic."

"Don't knock them, they are staple nineties films. And *The Sound of Music* is like a million minutes long."

Kristy smiled. "But well worth the time spent. I guess we'll have to agree to disagree."

Another hour passed stuck in traffic. The sky was lit with reds, burnt oranges, and pinks from the setting sun. Piercing cries of seagulls could be heard through the closed windows, even over Elton John's *Crocodile Rock*.

The land became flatter and signs for Atlantic City and Wildwood passed by until one for Barclay appeared. We drove a couple more miles until finally, at the end of the island, after being in the car for two and a half hours, Cheryl put on her right turn signal and said, "We're here!"

I gasped. The house was three stories and didn't even resemble a beach house with pillars in the front and a two-car garage on the side. It was sad that their beach house was nicer than my normal house. When I went with Bryan to the shore, we'd take strolls around the neighborhood and I'd admire all the other elaborate houses, including this one. Bryan's was nice but it was nothing compared to *this* beach house.

Cheryl pulled into the garage and as soon as she put the car into park, Kristy opened her car door. "Come on, let's unpack!"

I grabbed my pink Vera Bradley duffel from the trunk and followed Kristy inside. The house had to be decorated by a professional. There were paintings of the ocean placed at exactly the right spot in each room, along with shells, starfish, and other beach accents hanging on the walls and laying on end tables.

At the end of the grand tour, Kristy showed me to my room and told me to put on my bathing suit for the hot tub. Once she left, I took time to admire the decor. Nothing looked like it came from IKEA—my mom's favorite furniture store. The bright white queen bed was adorned with a baby-blue and white comforter with modern shapes splashed all over. An expensive looking vase with fresh daisies was intricately placed on top of the white nightstand.

The flowers looked like they were just picked; how did that even happen?

Each beige wall in the room was decorated with ocean paintings that depicted the ocean in different times of the day. I stepped closer to the one nearest me to get a better look. In this piece, the ocean was tumultuous; towering waves with white crests looking for someone to suck under, as if during the beginning of a storm.

I opened my duffel and rooted around for my bathing suit and pulled out my itty-bitty-pink-polka-dotted-bikini. I slipped it on and inspected myself in the mirror. Just like I suspected, it barely covered the essentials. At the time when I begged my mom for it, I thought about how fun it would be to wear with Bryan, thinking maybe on that trip I'd want to lose my virginity. *But no such luck.* He sure liked the bikini but every time he went to undo the strings on my top I hyperventilated and stopped him. I couldn't go further; my body and my brain wouldn't let me.

Now I wished I had thought more wisely before I bought this scandalous suit. At least I remembered to bring my pink Victoria's Secret coverup that I pulled on over top.

A knocked rattled the door. "Come in!"

The knob turned and Kristy appeared wearing a midnight black bikini showcasing her amazing abs. The bikini top was strapless, and her large breasts were threatening to spill over. She didn't seem the least bit embarrassed. My voice wouldn't work for a second but before I could try to utter anything Kristy stated, "Come on, hot tub is right down here."

She grabbed my hand and pulled me with her. Her hand was so soft and warm. *It was strangely natural to be holding hands with her, like we had always done this.*

Kristy let go once we made it to the hot tub outside and my hand felt tingly, as if her hand were still clasped to mine. I slowly removed my coverup and averted my eyes from Kristy's lingering stare.

"You sure like the color pink but I can't argue, it's your color."

"And black is yours," I replied bringing my gaze to meet hers.

"Money is tight, so I had to wear my suit from a couple years ago. I think I've grown a bit since then."

You're telling me. I was afraid when she bent over, I would see more than I bargained for.

"I hear you there. This is the only suit I have too and as you can see, it's kinda skimpy," I said, picking a string off my bikini bottom.

Kristy sat on a lounge chair beside the hot tub and looked at me. "It's cute. I like it."

I sat on the lounge chair beside her. "Is your aunt joining us?"

"She's making us margaritas but then she'll probably go watch TV. I thought we could drink some of the margaritas and then go in the hot tub?"

Margaritas???

Right on cue, Cheryl appeared with two slushy green drinks in extra-large margarita glasses complete with little blue umbrellas and salt around the rim.

"Wow, thanks so much Ms. Findley, I mean Cheryl. Are these non-alcoholic?" I blurted out.

"Oh, wait. How old are you?" Cheryl asked.

"Seventeen," I replied. *How did she not know our ages?*

"Huh. I thought both of you were eighteen for some reason. I was drinking way earlier than that. Plus, there isn't much alcohol in there, I promise!"

"You don't care that we drink?" I asked incredulously.

"I'd rather you do it here, then I know you'll be safe. You only live once, right? Enjoy!" Cheryl said, walking off.

After we were alone, Kristy raised her glass. "To new friends."

"To new friends!" I replied and clinked my glass against hers.

I took a sip. "Your aunt is super chill. I can't believe she brought out margaritas." I licked the salt off my lips. *Wow, her aunt had to put more alcohol in here than she realized.*

"She offers me wine at dinner most nights, but I've never said anything. It's like she thinks it's okay to drink if you're eighteen."

"That is the legal age in Europe."

I sipped on the drink again and grimaced. Either Kristy's aunt was lying about the low alcohol content, or I wasn't used to margaritas because it seemed like it was drenched in tequila. It made it hard for me not to stare at Kristy's half naked body. My eyes tried to settle on her face, but they kept getting distracted.

"Have you been to Europe?"

"Not yet, it's on my bucket list. I really want to go. Have you?"

"Yeah, a couple times with my parents. It's gorgeous but would've been more fun with someone I actually liked," Kristy said, giving me the side eye.

Was she talking about me?

"Where was your favorite place?"

Kristy picked up her margarita and took a large sip. "I fell in love with the Czech Republic. I'm part Czech and have some relatives that still live there. We visited their town, Třeboň, and I never wanted to leave. I finally felt like I belonged somewhere."

My margarita was already half gone. *How did that happen?* "What was it like?"

"The town was quaint, and everybody knew everyone. There were cobblestone streets with a brewery from like the 1300s that served the best beer I've ever had. Not like I've had much beer to compare it with, but it was so good."

I grinned. "Holy crap that's old. I want to go!"

Kristy stood and held out her hand.

"Maybe after senior year is over, I can convince my aunt to take the three of us to Třeboň. We wouldn't have to pay for anything other than the flight." She helped me lower into the hot tub. My legs felt a little wobbly. I shouldn't have drank that margarita so fast. And was I hearing her correctly? Kristy invited me to a foreign country with her? I had only dreamed of traveling to Europe and going with her would be so fun. *Hannah would be so jealous.*

"That sounds *amazing*!" I gave her a hug in the hot tub.

Kristy laughed and hugged me back.

I realized this was our first hug.

Her body was pressed up against mine, and I could feel her lack of clothing against me. *I'd better be careful and not accidentally unlatch her swimsuit top.* My face burned red thinking what could happen, and I quickly pulled away. *These were thoughts people had about their friends, right?*

We settled next to each other on the hot tub ledge, with Kristy's leg touching mine. I was aware of how close we were, even though the hot tub was large enough to fit at least four more people.

After a moment of silence, Kristy spoke. "Thanks for being there for me this week. If it wasn't for you, my week would have sucked. Meeting you was by far the highlight."

"Hanging out with you is fun. You're really cool and easy to talk to, even if you're a bit intimidating and a badass."

Kristy smiled. "Me a badass? I don't know about that, but I'll take that as a compliment."

I should have eaten more for dinner, but I was in such a hurry to get to Kristy's I only ate a small veggie burger. I could tell the margarita was already going to my head. I didn't drink often, mainly at the shore when adults weren't around. This also was the first time I ever had an adult serve me alcohol. Imagine if my parents saw me now. Scantily clad sipping alcohol next to the girl from the only sexual dream I've ever remembered.

That dream was so hot, but would it be like that in real life?

"Thanks for not freaking out on me when I told you I'm pansexual. Not everyone I've told is so chill."

"Of course! You are who you are." Kristy's arms were very muscular, which led me to reminisce how we were intertwined in each other's arms in my dream. And then the part where her bra came off and ...

"You seem distracted."

"Oh, it's this margarita. I think it's stronger than I'm used to. I rarely drink."

Kristy scrunched her eyebrows. "You should slow down. I don't want you to get sick."

"How did you know you were into women?" I blurted out.

Man, I really shouldn't drink; I have no filter right now and I can't stop thinking about that unsettling dream.

Kristy was quiet for a moment. "When I realized I had a crush on my best friend at school. When we were hanging out, I wanted to do more than talk. I wanted to run my hands through her hair, remove every single piece of her clothing, and kiss her all over."

"Uh that would do it." I picked a fleck off my pink nail polish. Kristy's hair did look really nice, and that bikini was so distracting. *What would happen if a hot tub jet would propel it to float off?*

"When I confessed to her about my crush, she never spoke to me again."

"What? Are you kidding me? That's awful!" *I don't know what I'd do if Hannah ignored me for the rest of my life.*

"I was devastated. That's when I went on a downward spiral and started dating any girl from the internet, which is how I ended up with Talia."

"How do you know you are pansexual and not a lesbian?"

"I find all people attractive. To me it's more about the

attraction than their biological sex, gender, or gender identity."

"That must be so confusing!" I met Kristy's eyes and I could see them grow weary.

"You have no idea. When people find out about me, and they say, *Oh you have the best of both worlds*, I want to scream. To be honest, somedays I don't understand it. One moment I'm checking out a guy's butt and then someone's cleavage and still feeling hot at both."

"That has to be so hard. I can't even imagine. Especially since I've never been attracted to any guy I've been with ever." As soon as I uttered this admission, I covered my mouth with my hands.

Why did I say that aloud?

Kristy stared at me for a second. "Never?"

I bit my lip and shook my head.

"No. That's why I always get bored and look for the next prospect when they can't keep their hands off me. It becomes so annoying that I break it off."

Kristy's eyes went wide. "You've never fantasized about Bryan or Zack naked?"

I blinked back tears as I whispered, "No."

Kristy sucked in a deep breath. "That's okay you know."

"Are you sure? But then why does it feel like something is wrong with me? Most of the guys I dated have been hot. Why wouldn't I like them?" I asked, not sure if I was ready for Kristy's answer.

Kristy's eyes bored into mine. "This is going to be an awkward question, but I have to ask. Have you thought about girls?"

"I don't know." My mouth felt so dry. *Why did I drink that margarita so fast?* My heart pulsed in my head.

Kristy moved closer to me; her leg pressed up against mine.

"You don't have to be scared to tell the truth. I'm someone that can understand," she said softly.

"Um," I said, staring at her full lips. "I had a dream about you," I whispered.

Kristy's right eyebrow shot up and she gave a small half smile and placed her hand on my bare leg. I began to tingle where my leg met her hand. My face began to flush, and I felt a sense of warmth over the entirety of my body. *That was from the hot tub, right?* I tried to take a deep breath and it became ragged.

"I'm not going to lie either. I've thought about you, too, but I wasn't sure if you felt the same way."

"It's all pretty confusing. We've just met. And I have a boyfriend."

"But sometimes that's how it works."

She looked so hot, with her auburn hair falling in her face, which complemented her black bathing suit perfectly.

"It feels like I've known you so much longer." I inched my body closer to hers. If we got any nearer, I'd end up in her lap.

Her hand continued to rub my leg, causing the tingling to become more pronounced. My brain cried out in confusion but something deep inside me took over and I shut off my mind. I turned to Kristy and before I could doubt myself, I tucked a loose strand of hair behind her ear.

Kristy made a deep sound and placed her other hand on the side of my face, leaned in, and our lips met. At first the kiss was hesitant but then it became more insistent, with tongue slipping in and out. Kristy's hand found itself in my long hair, pulling me closer, pressing ourselves against each other. After a few more minutes Kristy let go and pulled away. "Still okay?"

I nodded and realized for the first time ever I was disappointed that a kiss had ended.

"Just making sure. I didn't want you to regret this after

you woke up in the morning without any margaritas clouding your judgement."

"I don't think this is the margaritas. It helped bring out what I couldn't say."

"Okay good. If that's the case then ..." Kristy leaned her head toward me, and we picked up where we left off. Her fingers trailed around my stomach and a small moan escaped from my mouth. *So this was what I'd been missing out on? I couldn't think straight, and this time it wasn't from the margarita.*

After a bit, Kristy pulled away. "Let's go somewhere more comfortable."

We agreed to meet in her room. As I was getting ready, I tried to sort out the thoughts in my head. *Was I a lesbian? What did this mean? My parents would kill me if they found out. Holy crap I cheated on Zack. What was I doing?*

I rummaged through the clothes I packed and noticed I'd brought sexy pajamas. Very tiny plaid pink and black shorts and a pink string tank top. *Did I subconsciously pack them on purpose?* I took a deep breath and left my room into the unknown.

I knocked on Kristy's door.

"It's open."

I turned the door and saw Kristy propped up on her bed wearing a black ribbed tank top and gray shorts. She patted the spot next to her. I shut the door and I laid by her side.

"No regrets yet?" Kristy pulled me close.

"None," I said firmly. When I was with her all my confused thoughts left as fast as they had arrived.

"Good." She kissed me gently and I hesitantly kissed her

back. Then, as more time went by, the kissing became more frantic and hotter. I wanted more.

After a bit, Kristy pulled away. "Maybe we should stop before this goes any further. We're both a little tipsy and I don't want you to regret anything in the morning."

I was still on a high from Kristy's kisses and missed her lips on mine, but I nodded. "All right, but I have to say, I've never enjoyed making out like that before."

Kristy smiled and pulled me closer.

I placed my head on her chest and closed my eyes.

Her heart was still racing.

"Does this make me a lesbian?"

"You know I'm not a fan of labels. I say you are whatever you want to be."

"I guess I knew I found women hot, but I didn't realize that it was more than just friends."

"It's not something that you can bring up to your friends either without sounding creepy."

"Exactly! I couldn't bounce off Hannah, *Hey, I had a sexy dream about some girl, what do you think that means*? I'd also worry that she would think I would hit on her."

"You never know how people will react, like my ex best friend. Plus, you might not have even let yourself realize it was true." She combed her hands through my hair, and it relaxed me.

"You're probably right about that."

I heard a low vibration of my phone that I threw somewhere.

"Do you need to get that?"

"Probably. No one usually calls me."

I reluctantly left Kristy's side and found my phone. I had two missed calls: one from Hannah and one from Zack. There was no question in my mind who I'd call back first.

"Hey! Zack was worried about you because he said you

didn't answer his texts or phone call. You good?" Hannah asked.

Why did he have to care about me so much?

"Yea, I'm fine. Just chilling at Kristy's place. How are you enjoying Bryan's? It's pretty sweet right?"

"It really is, and Bryan is being quite the gentleman. Probably trying to make up for the other night. It's like he's afraid to touch me."

I chuckled to myself. *It sounded like he was more afraid I would come after him.*

"If you need me, let me know. I'll text Zack I made it."

"See you tomorrow."

"Oh right, yep."

I hung up and turned to Kristy.

"Zack was freaked out because he didn't hear from me."

"Oh, man. That boy has it bad for you."

"What am I going to do?" I whined.

"Let him down gently. That's all you can do."

I turned my attention back to my phone and texted a few lines to him explaining I'd been in the hot tub, away from my phone. All I got back was a *k*.

I could tell by Zack's one letter response he was pissed but that was the least of my worries. A barely dressed hot woman was waiting eagerly for me to return to bed.

"Everything okay?"

I set my phone down and laid next to her. "Zack's being a pain and wondering what I've been up to."

"What if you told him the truth?"

I laughed but Kristy's face didn't change. "Wait, are you serious?"

"It would give you an out and a reason to break up with him."

"I can't do that! No one knows that I like women, except you, and I still don't even know what this is between us. It's all too new and I want it to be special between you and I before the rest of the world gets involved."

Kristy propped herself on her elbows, distracting me because I could see right down her shirt. I wanted to see more.

Kristy saw where my eyes lingered. "Well, I know what you want, but I'll respect that you want to keep this between us for a bit."

"Thank you," I said and scooted closer. "Can we make out some more?" I whispered in her ear.

"Are you sure? You're going to have to stop me though, because it's hard to not go further with you."

"I'll do my best."

CHAPTER SIXTEEN

The next morning, I opened my eyes to see light spilling through the windows in Kristy's room. We were so caught up in each other we forgot to close the blinds when we passed out. I looked down at myself and all my clothes were still intact.

Phew. I managed to stop us before I ventured into uncharted territories.

Maybe I wasn't ready yet like Kristy had predicted or perhaps I felt like what we were doing was wrong, and not only because I had a boyfriend. My Christian upbringing was emerging. Was I going to hell like all the *gays* that my pastor warned us about? And how would I even go about *coming out* to people. What would I tell them?

Even thinking about *coming out* felt weird. It was obvious I liked females, but was I completely gay? My whole life I assumed I was straight for the most part. I mean occasionally I questioned my sexuality, but who didn't? I did sometimes stare too long at an attractive female like Erin or couldn't get a cute girl on a TV show out of my head, but I never admitted to myself that I liked women until Kristy arrived in my life. Now my whole perspective of myself had changed.

Also how was it fair that I would now have to *come out* to people? No straight person ever had to do that. Why couldn't we live in a world that let us love whomever we wanted to? A world where we didn't have to justify our attraction? A universe where it would be normal to date anyone, no matter their gender or identity. Wouldn't that be the dream world?

I took a deep breath and closed my eyes. I was going down a rabbit hole. *Maybe my phone would take my mind off things?* I got up off the bed and rummaged in my purse and found more text messages from Zack.

> I thought we would see each other more once I asked you out.

> Are you still up?

> Fine. Night.

And then one from Hannah.

> Zack is bugging me again. u need to deal with him …

I sighed and put down my phone and shook my head. What a mess I made, and I didn't know how to clean it up.

Kristy stirred from the bed. She propped herself on her elbows and gazed at me. "Good morning. Still no regrets?"

I sat on the side of the bed. "No regrets but I'm feeling more confused than ever about myself this morning, like you said."

"That's normal, I had the same thing happen too." She reached over to squeeze my hand.

A tear slipped down my cheek. "It feels like I did something wrong and unnatural."

"I know. Come here." Kristy reached toward me.

I moved closer to her, and she wrapped her arms around me. I buried my face into her neck as she ran her hands through my hair.

What was I doing? I was fairly popular at school, had a good-looking boyfriend, amazing best friend, and supportive parents. Why would I want to throw it all away to be with this girl that I had just met? What would people say if they found out? I wanted to stay in this room forever and not face the real world.

Kristy pulled me back and gazed into my eyes. "It'll be okay, I promise. I get that this is scary. How could it not be? Everything you thought about yourself has changed. But I'm here to help you figure things out and we can take this slow."

I took a deep breath. "Okay. Thanks. I think I'm having a minor freak out, but I'll be better soon I'm sure."

Kristy smoothed out my hair. "I've been wanting to ask you. Should I call you Shorty or Sam? I felt weird when we first met calling you by your nickname, but now I feel like we might be more in nickname territory."

"Honestly, I answer by both names, so whatever you feel like calling me. After last night though, you for sure have the right to call me Shorty."

Kristy nodded. "What about going to breakfast? Maybe that will take your mind off everything."

I gave a small smile and nodded.

After we got ready, Kristy and I walked down the block to the famous pancake house. As soon as we got to the counter, I heard a high voice call, "Shorty!"

I turned to the sound of the voice, and it was Hannah and Bryan in a nearby booth. I should've known to not go to this pancake house. It was the Dale hangover haven.

I sighed. Guess reality was about to hit me before I had any say in the matter. I plastered on my best fake smile. "Hey!"

Bryan stood and said to the counter attendant, "These two can sit with us." He grabbed our menus and strolled back to their booth.

I looked at Kristy and she rolled her eyes. Probably not the romantic breakfast she had planned. *Why did we even leave the house?* Bryan sat next to Hannah, and Kristy and I slid in the other side.

"How are you guys? Did you answer Zack yet?" Hannah asked.

"I'm good but I'll be better after breakfast."

"And lots of coffee," Kristy chimed in.

That was the exact time the waitress came over and asked for our drink orders. I can barely stand the taste of coffee so I ordered an iced latte with whipped cream. I had to hold back my surprise when Kristy ordered a black coffee. Who was this girl?

After the waitress left, I turned to Hannah. "What about you two, how was your romantic evening?"

Hannah's face reddened. "Good."

Bryan slung his arm around Hannah's shoulders. "More than good. Better than uh ..."

"Were you about to say better than all our times together? Or better than me?" I asked. *At least he was starting to realize we were awful together. Maybe him and Hannah together wouldn't be the worst thing in the world.*

"You said it, not me," Bryan said with a smirk.

"The two of us didn't work. That's why I didn't want to get back with you. We're different people. I'm glad you and Hannah had fun together."

"What about Zack? It doesn't seem like you guys are that great either," Bryan said.

"I don't want to talk about it."

Bryan pointed toward the entrance. "You might have to, he just walked through the door."

"Shit!" I said and covered my hand with my mouth. I whipped my head around to where Bryan pointed. There Zack stood in the flesh. His hair was freshly washed, and he wore a Rolling Stones navy-blue tee and khaki shorts.

Kristy gritted her teeth.

Guess Zack wasn't the only one showing signs of jealousy. Zack strode over to our booth. "I didn't realize you were going out for breakfast. I would've met you here."

"It was a last-minute decision. I didn't think you'd be up." *It wasn't even nine a.m., and I was already getting grilled.*

Zack's eyes bored into mine. "I haven't seen much of you lately."

"If you haven't noticed, Shorty's always busy doing something. You should get used to it. I never saw her much either," Bryan said leaning back in the booth with his hands behind his head. His shirt lifted up showing off a small portion of his abs, and I noticed Hannah take a peek. She saw me catch her and quickly looked away. *She really did find him attractive. He wasn't bad looking, I guess.*

"She also didn't like you that much," Zack retorted.

Bryan opened his mouth, saw me giving him daggers, and then proceeded to shut it.

"I haven't seen her either, so you're not the only one," Hannah said under her breath.

It was going to be harder than I expected keeping whatever was between Kristy and I a secret. I somehow needed to reassure Hannah that she wasn't being replaced.

"You didn't ask Bryan and Hannah to meet you here?" Zack asked looking between us.

"No. Kristy and I woke up hungry and this is where we ended up. End of story. But you're here now so why don't you pull up a chair?" I said, trying to keep my frustration out of my tone.

I didn't really want him here, but I didn't know what else to do.

Kristy gave me an annoyed look and I shrugged. Not much else I could do while I still had a boyfriend.

"I was meeting Erin and Tyler, but I'll let them know I'm with you now," Zack said.

After pulling over a chair from a vacant table, Zack grabbed his phone out of his cargo shorts and began furiously texting. "They decided to stay in anyways."

Hannah avoided my penetrating gaze. At least we wouldn't have any other unwanted visitors at this already super fun breakfast.

After all of us ordered—a veggie omelet with breakfast potatoes cooked with onions for me—we stared uncomfortably at each other. I heard laughs from other tables and the sound of the cash register, but no one at our table uttered a word. I had to say something before it got even weirder. The waitress dropped off our drink orders which bought me more time to think of something to ask. After she left, I asked Zack, "How many people are coming to your party?"

"Not sure but I mentioned it to a lot of people. My parents' house can hold a ton, so it really doesn't matter, as long as they bring drinks. Tyler's helping me pick up a keg today, too. His brother is hooking us up."

Every time Zack mentioned Tyler, Hannah cringed. I knew she couldn't have gotten over him that fast.

"Will you be okay seeing Tyler with Erin?" I asked Hannah.

"I guess I'll have to be. Besides, I have Bryan now," Hannah said smiling over at him.

"You guys all seem to date the same people," Kristy said.

"There aren't many different options here," I said. "Plus, we're all in the same classes so it's bound to happen."

"Kristy, we'll have to find you a boyfriend. I'm not sure who's single right now but maybe you can find someone at Zack's party," Hannah said.

I had taken a large sip of my iced latte and was so surprised by Hannah's statement, it went down the wrong way and I started coughing.

"I doubt it. I'm picky," Kristy said. "You okay, Shorty?" She rubbed my back, which freaked me out at first and then I realized no one would think it was out of the ordinary except me.

"My friends are coming with beer. And some of them are single too," Bryan said winking at Kristy.

"Thanks, but I think I'll pass. I'm not exactly a jock magnet," Kristy said, removing her hand from my back even though I wished she hadn't.

"A lot of my friends don't care; as long as you're a warm body with good boobs."

"Bryan! That's disgusting! Yet another reason for me to not like your friends." I reached across the table and hit him in the arm.

"It's okay, Shorty. Unlike Bryan's friends, I need more than a warm body and a large penis," Kristy said.

I was waiting for her to divulge she was into girls but luckily so far she didn't reveal that information. I wasn't ready for people to start questioning her even more. It could lead to them figuring out why I was hanging out with her more than usual.

When I woke up today I didn't think that my current boyfriend, my ex-boyfriend, my female lover, and my best friend would share a meal together discussing sexual preferences. But if I had learned anything, my life was slowly becoming less and less predictable. Perhaps if I closed my eyes I could reappear in Kristy's bed again and have a *Groundhog Day* moment where we never left her place.

Nope, no such luck. When I opened my eyes, everyone stared at me.

"What'd I miss?" I asked.

"Kristy told me to ask you what she likes," Bryan asked raising his eyebrows.

"Someone that acts older than anyone we know," I said giving Kristy a side glance. *I hope that stopped them from asking any more questions.*

"Is that what you two were talking about in the hot tub last night?" Zack asked.

"Yep, you know, girl talk." I couldn't stop myself from blushing as I looked down at my hands. *I needed to learn how to lie better, without giving myself away.*

By saying that I knew that Hannah would feel left out but I didn't know what else to do. There was no way I was going to utter the truth, that what we were doing in the hot tub last night was way more than talking and it had nothing to do with men.

I gave a grateful sigh when our food arrived. We ate in silence. All I heard was the sound of chewing and slurping of coffee. Normally I was all about filling long pauses but today I didn't know what to say and I also didn't want to accidentally blurt out my newest secret. Inwardly I was screaming: *OMG. What is going on? I want to tell the world that I finally found someone that made me happy, but I can't because it feels like I did something wrong, and people are going to judge the crap out of me. What is happening and why can't my life be drama free?*

After I scarfed down my food, I looked in my wallet and found two twenties my mom gave me for the trip. That should be more than enough. I needed to get out of there before I had a major freak out. I threw the money on the table and stood. "Sorry to eat and run but we promised Kristy's aunt we wouldn't be gone too long. She wants to hit the beach early before it gets crowded. I'll see you guys later at the party. Ready to go?" I asked Kristy.

"Sure, thanks for covering my bill. See you guys."

Zack stood as we slid out of the booth. He placed his arm around my waist and brought me close to his body.

"See you tonight. Looking forward to making up for lost time," he said whispering in my ear.

He placed his lips on my own and I quickly pulled away before his tongue could make an appearance.

"See you then." I turned around and was met by Kristy's piercing glare. *How was I going to make this work?* We were silent for a couple of steps as we walked out of the restaurant when Kristy said, "I know we just got together but seeing you kiss him was awful. I almost threw up my scrambled eggs."

"I'm sorry. I don't know what to do about Zack. You have to admit he's a good cover. I'll have to keep avoiding contact with him. I'll try harder."

"How long will that last? He's going to realize you aren't into him like Bryan did."

I didn't know how to respond which gave Kristy the chance to add, "Why do you even need a cover? I get you not wanting to tell people about us yet, but how's breaking up with him connected?"

"I don't want to let him down yet, plus I could always tell my parents I'm seeing him when you and I hang out. That way they don't wonder why we are together so much."

"Okay," Kristy said tightly.

"Just give me time, that's all I'm asking. I was trying not to have a panic attack at breakfast because of everything running through my brain. I need to comprehend everything happening."

"I'll try and be patient." Kristy looked over at me. "Good call by the way on your excuse to leave breakfast."

I smiled. "Why thank you, I was proud of that moment."

At Kristy's place, her aunt was eating a bagel at the kitchen table and reading something on her iPad. She looked up at us. "Hey girls! I was going to let you know I had brought some breakfast items along, but you were already gone by the time I got up."

I inwardly groaned. *We really should've stayed in for breakfast.* I'd take a stale day-old bagel any day over awkward moments between frenemies.

"We'll eat here tomorrow. Want to get ready for the beach?" Kristy asked me.

"I thought you'd never ask!"

In my room, my bathing suit was still wet from the hot tub last night, but I didn't care. I wanted to see the ocean and relax. I grabbed my beach bag, complete with a fluffy murder mystery, and knocked on Kristy's door.

"Come in!"

I pushed the door open and sucked in my breath. Kristy stood there in her skimpy bathing suit where her breasts were once again threatening to break free. I had never moved so fast to be next to someone.

Kristy gently cupped my face, and we slowly kissed each other. "I've wanted to do that to you all breakfast to make sure this was actually real," Kristy said whispering in my ear.

"I was wishing we never left your bed," I said softly.

"That too. We could stay in if you want."

"As much as I'd like that, I want to go to the beach while it's sunny. Plus, your aunt is wide awake downstairs."

"Okay, but we should come back early before the party starts," Kristy said rubbing my shoulders.

We kissed a couple more times and finally made ourselves pull apart and headed for an afternoon of relaxation.

CHAPTER SEVENTEEN

"What's your favorite part of the beach?" I asked Kristy. I was sprawled out on my back on top of my pink Vera Bradley towel.

"That I can do nothing but lay here and listen to the sound of the waves."

I snuck a glance at Kristy. She was laying on a plain navy-blue towel close to me, so much so that if I reached out my hand, I could grasp hers. Kristy's skin glowed from the suntan lotion that I helped her apply. My hands had lingered a little too long on each part of her body as I tried to rub in any remaining splotches, but I didn't hear her complaining.

She also helped apply my lotion and it gave me the shivers, even though the temperature was in the high eighties. I hadn't wanted her to stop but I couldn't have anyone from school seeing anything out of the ordinary happening so I'd faintly told her that maybe we should save some lotion for later.

Kristy sat up on her elbows and her midnight black sunglasses slid down her nose. "The sun is hotter than I thought, I need to cool down. Want to come in the ocean with me?"

"I was thinking the same thing!" I slipped my sunglasses into my beach bag and jumped to my feet. I weaved to avoid people laying on the sand.

"These shells are hard to walk on. Come on, we need to go in deeper in the water to smoother sand." Kristy extended her hand.

Who from school might see me holding her hand? Maybe it wouldn't look too odd since friends would sometimes hold hands?

I caught her hand and we waded into the water. The waves weren't too over-powering, but I braced myself each time one smacked us on our way out to deeper waters. Finally, we were out where we could bob up on a wave before the wave's breaking point.

"This is also one of my favorite things about the ocean. Just being in the water, floating around aimlessly," Kristy said, letting go of my hand. She floated on her back; the tips of her black bathing suit top barely could be seen above the murky water.

"I don't usually come out this far. My mom was scared I'd get swept away and Bryan would boogie board the entire time, leaving me on the sand by myself."

"Try floating, it's so relaxing."

I laid on my back, barely needing to move to keep myself afloat. I squinted against the sun to gaze at the powder blue sky and puffy white clouds. Seagulls came in and out of my viewpoint, squawking, waiting for the next unsuspecting person that left their sandwich unattended. The sound of the waves breaking mixed with the chatter of excited people either jumping to get out of their way or the thrill seekers, trying to overcome each wave. After a few moments I noticed Kristy standing right next to me, eyes focused on my face. My feet found the sandy ground and I turned toward her.

"Sorry, I didn't mean to interrupt your moment, but you looked so beautiful I couldn't help staring," Kristy said putting her arms around my waist and bringing me closer to her. My first thought was, *Oh my god who could see us* but as I looked out at the shore, everyone was indistinct and unrecognizable which had to mean they couldn't recognize a single soul out where we were, especially two girls with their bodies almost completely submerged.

"That's okay, it's even better now that you're here." My face was so close to hers. I could see specks of sand dotting her cheek and a lone streak of suntan lotion on the top of her right ear. I reached to rub off the spot but as my hand was closing in on her ear, she leaned her face in and grazed my lips with her own. *No one could see us, right?* I tried to quiet my insecurities and I kissed her back.

The heat from the sun warmed my back as we kissed, and a peace filled my body. We bobbed up and down, not caring when we floated overtop an impending wave. That was what I'd always wished for when I was at the beach with Bryan. Someone I had fun with that I also enjoyed kissing.

Back on the beach, after drying off, I spread out on my towel and cracked open the fluffy murder mystery.

"How'd you know you liked me?"

I stuck in my bookmark and rolled over to face Kristy. "From the beginning I've always thought you were sexy. And then even more so after we started talking but my dream made me wonder that it might be more than friends. That's when I was like oh, so that's what I'm feeling. What about you? How'd you know you liked me?"

"I noticed right away you're super-hot, but I thought you were the typical straight girl that only cared about her boyfriend. The more we hung out though, the more I realized you were different than that, especially when you stuck up for me and helped me out. That only made me like you even more. You also had your boyfriend give me an old iPad. How could I not like you?" Kristy smiled.

I returned her smile. "Is this what you were hoping would happen when you invited me to Barclay?"

Kristy removed her dark sunglasses. "It turned out better than I expected. I wasn't sure how you felt about me but either way I wanted to chill with you. It's nice having a friend around, since all mine either hate me or I can't see any more. The other stuff with you is an extra bonus."

"I feel the same way. Of course Hannah's my best friend but I don't have many other close friends. Everyone else I see at class or band. They're nice but it's hard to open up to other people because I don't have much to say."

"That might also be because you're hiding who you are from people, and I don't mean just liking girls."

I shrugged. "Maybe. I'm pretty boring."

Kristy moved to get her book out of her beach bag. "No, you're not. I don't hang out with boring people. And maybe if you're really yourself, people will like you even more."

"I doubt it, but you never know," I said, re-opening my book.

CHAPTER EIGHTEEN

Sun, sand, and relaxation were exactly what the doctored ordered. My head felt clearer after reading my mindless mystery. I even forced myself to contemplate what was so quickly happening with Kristy. I realized I needed to tell Hannah about this newest development. She was my best friend and I had never kept secrets from her before and didn't want to start that nasty habit. I really wanted to tell someone how excited Kristy made me feel.

Maybe I could try to tell her at Zack's party?

After I showered in the guest bathroom, I threw on a tank and jean shorts. There was still some time before the party, so I figured I'd be comfortable until it was time to go. I stood outside Kristy's door and was about to knock when she called, "I hear you outside my door. Come in."

I opened the door and noticed immediately how hot Kristy looked propped on her bed. She wore a low-cut tank and skintight black shorts. I jumped into bed next to her and she moved her head close and placed her lips onto mine.

After a bit of time passed, we laid back in bed next to each other. My body was still warm from Kristy's embrace, but I couldn't get enough of her. I cuddled up to her and laid my head on her chest.

"What caused you to freak out inside your head this morning before breakfast?"

I traced the bottom of her chin with my index finger. "Liking women feels wrong. I know that sounds stupid and so old school, but that's what's going on right now for me."

Kristy ran her fingers through my hair. "No, that's not stupid at all. I thought something similar too, especially since my parents are so conservative."

It was the perfect opportunity to divulge my plan of sharing about myself to Hannah.

"Hannah should be cool about it but expect her to be a little freaked at first. It's a big bombshell you are about to drop."

"True. How about I go in expecting the worst and if it goes well, I can be pleasantly surprised?"

"I like that! Maybe once you tell Hannah, it will make you feel less like you are doing something wrong because at least one person will know, and it won't feel like some big secret?"

"I hope. I want to be really excited about this because for the first time I'm attracted to someone, although I have no idea what I'm doing," I said, blushing.

"What're you talking about, you've got skills!"

I blushed even more. "I just go with my gut. It's nice I'm not bored when we're making out with my mind thinking about other things."

Kristy chuckled. "Is that what usually happens? How did you survive?"

"I could have composed a whole book during all of the times I wasn't thinking about kissing them."

"If you ever get bored with me, please tell me, unless the book you're writing in your head is a Pulitzer winner. If that's the case, give me a cut of the profits."

I laughed. "I promise!"

My phone vibrated and I groaned. It was from Zack.

See you soon, right?

It was like he knew I was having too much fun without him.

"It's Zack checking to see if we're still going to his party."

"Guess it's about time for it," Kristy said looking at the clock on her nightstand.

"Do you want me to bail for us? I'm sure going to a party with my boyfriend is the last thing you want to do."

Kristy shook her head. "No, it's fine. If it's important to you, I'll go."

"If you're sure ..."

"As long as you promise me hot tub time tonight." Kristy rubbed my leg.

I began to tingle. *Maybe we could stay at the party for a little. The hot tub did sound inviting.*

"I think I can do that," I said moving closer to her.

"Topless?" Kristy asked slyly.

I sucked in my breath. *Was I ready for clothing to get removed? Was I ready to face the hard truth that a naked woman would most likely turn me on? Verdict unclear.*

"Open for discussion," I said, my face warming.

"Sorry, I didn't mean to make you feel weird. I was kidding around," Kristy said with a concerned look on her face.

I nodded and mumbled I was going to get ready.

But was she really kidding? God knew she was way more experienced than me and I'm sure she wouldn't want to go slow forever.

I went into my room to look at what I packed in my overnight bag. A skintight, short red dress and my black

Michael Kors sandals. I squeezed into the dress and when I was finished, I opened the door to Kristy's room. She was wearing her typical clothes, black pants and a tight red tee.

"Hey, we kind of match!" I said.

"Oh no, it's already starting!"

"Now we need a joint name. Kriory? Sisty?"

Kristy rolled her eyes. "Those names are awful! You look super-hot by the way. I'm going to have to watch Zack to make sure he doesn't defile you."

"Don't worry about that. I've avoided having sex with guys for seventeen years that I have it down to a science."

"You just needed someone that didn't have a penis."

"Or that."

We stared at each other for another second. "Guess we should get going before Zack sends out a search party."

Kristy took a deep breath. "If it sucks, can we please peace out early so we can get some hot tub time in? And I promise, we can be fully clothed."

"Deal."

CHAPTER NINETEEN

No sooner than two minutes after Kristy and I had arrived at Zack's beach house, he sought me out and wouldn't let go. *Staying away from him might be harder than I thought.*

"Shorty, you look amazing. I want to take you to my room right this second," Zack said at a higher decibel than I would have liked.

Woah. How much did he already drink? I wasn't used to these direct comments from him. In a way it was kind of sweet that he found me that attractive. *Why couldn't I feel the same way about him?*

"You don't want to neglect your guests. I can wait. Is Hannah here yet?"

Zack turned his head to survey the room. "I saw her and Bryan wandering around. Tyler and Erin are here too somewhere. I'm really hoping I don't have to break up a fight."

"Hi Zack," Kristy said loudly, getting closer to me.

"Oh. Hi, Kristy."

"I think I saw someone else come in, maybe you should greet them?" Kristy nodded toward the open front door.

"Oh, uh okay. Shorty, don't go too far."

"I'll try!" I said brightly. I smiled until Zack couldn't see me anymore.

"Oh, geez. He's already plastered. Please don't go anywhere alone with him. I don't think I could stand it," Kristy pleaded.

"I won't, I promise. I should have worn sweats or something." I squirmed to get comfortable in my skintight dress.

"Don't you remember? That wouldn't have mattered for Bryan's friends and the same rule probably applies to Zack. He wants to sleep with you."

"That can't be all he wants. We were friends first. That couldn't have disappeared once he asked me out, right?" I saw out of the corner of my eye a flash of dark curly hair.

"Oh, there's Hannah! I'm going to try and tell her about us. Maybe you can keep Bryan company and out of trouble?"

"That sounds grand, small talk with your awful ex-boyfriend to distract him from your other ex-boyfriend, Tyler. Is there anyone here you haven't been with?"

"Uh, that guy!" I pointed to a jock who threw a shot into a beer.

"You missed out there, he looks like a real winner."

I rolled my eyes. "All of Bryan's friends are. Hey, Hannah, over here!" I waved at her.

"Shorty! You made it," Hannah said. She was wearing her usual—skinny jeans and a lavender V-neck tee.

Her arm was wrapped around Bryan's waist.

He gave me a smug smile. "Long time no see, Shorty. Kristy, I brought lots of my friends for you to choose from."

"I can't wait to see my fantastic choices," Kristy deadpanned.

"You won't be disappointed!" Bryan said, elbowing her.

"That's one of them over there, right?" Kristy said as she pointed to the guy that finished chugging the car bomb. He let out a large belch.

"Him and many others. He can show you a good time," Bryan said wagging his eyebrows.

"Before or after he vomits all over Zack's parents' carpet? I think I'll pass."

"You guys are getting along great. I'll leave you two to talk all about Kristy's options. Hannah, I need to tell you something. We'll be right back!"

I pulled Hannah away before anyone could protest.

"Where are we going? What's so important that it couldn't wait?"

"You'll see in a minute."

I drug Hannah up the steps and opened doors to rooms until I found the one I assumed was Zack's; the one with *Star Wars* and *Zelda* posters and a navy-blue bedspread. I plopped down on his bed and Hannah sat next to me.

"We need to make this fast before Zack finds us and thinks I'm here waiting for him."

Her brown eyes stared at me full of questions. "Okay, well what is it?"

My stomach clenched and I had to hold back the urge to throw up all over Zack's bedspread. My whole body felt cold. I had to tell her and get it over with, no matter what happened. I couldn't stand this awful feeling any longer. *I hoped she wouldn't hate me.* "Kristy and I kissed. Like more than once. And I think I want to have sex with her."

Hannah's mouth opened. "Wait. What? When did this all happen? You just met her on Monday!"

"We got closer last night in the hot tub. It first started off as talking and the next thing either of us knew we were on top of each other. And then in her bedroom later that night and this morning and then this afternoon."

Hannah's eyebrows shot up. "I was going to ask if this was a one-time thing but clearly not."

"Yea, I don't think so. I like her a lot, and now I finally understand why people want to have sex."

Hannah was silent.

"You don't hate me, do you?"

"No, of course, not! You're still Shorty to me, but I'm not going to lie. It's different to think about since I've known you forever, but I'll get used to it. Thank you for telling me, I know that was probably hard."

"It really was. My hands are still shaking. You're the first person I've told."

Hannah grabbed my hands. "Shorty, it's me! How could I possibly hate you for this? You're my best friend, and I'm always here for you!"

Tears welled up in my eyes. "Thank you so much; thank God we have each other!" I gave her a huge hug.

"So what are you going to do? Break up with Zack?"

"That's what I don't know and need your help figuring out. I'm not ready to come out to the world yet. I thought I could use Zack as a cover for a little bit until I figure out what to do."

Hannah scrunched her nose. "I don't think that's a good idea. Zack adores you. If you don't feel the same way, you need to let him go. Forget what others think. You don't have to come out and say you're dating Kristy, be *single* for a bit."

"What about my parents?"

"Do you really think they will care?"

"My mom kept trying to pull the whole guilt card that I was going to miss church and youth group by being at the shore on a Sunday. My mom lives and breathes church so I'm pretty sure they won't approve since our church teaches that what I'm doing is a major sin. That's why I thought it might be important to have a cover."

"But then you'll be hurting Zack. Say you're hanging out with me or even Kristy. They would never know it wasn't as friends."

I was about to say more when Erin and Tyler appeared in the doorway in the middle of a heavy make out session.

Crap. How did I forget to shut the door?

I gave a loud cough and they quickly pulled apart.

"Seems like this room is taken by both of your exes," Erin said giving us the death stare.

"Oh, hey Erin. I heard you and Tyler were here. You do realize this is Zack's room right?" I was greeted by silence. I rolled my eyes, grabbed Hannah's hand, and quickly exited the space before she could witness the scene unfold any further. I slammed the door behind Hannah. Her lip quivered, and she covered her face with her hands.

"Hannah, you're too good for him, especially if he's interested in someone like Erin," I said, pulling her close to me.

Hannah sobbed. "I can't believe how fast he moved on. And into a bedroom with her!"

I rubbed her back while she cried. "But you moved on quickly with Bryan."

"I didn't want to be alone. He's nice and all but not Tyler. I was hoping it would make Tyler jealous and want me back. Plus, it gave me a place to crash at the shore this weekend so I wouldn't feel left out."

"Well, that's great. I'm glad that I'm once again being used by a girl. I'm so done with the two of you!" Bryan leapt up off the floor beside us.

I yelped and jumped back.

"What the hell? Were you sitting outside the door this entire time?"

"For most of it, and I've sure heard some juicy information about *you*. No wonder you never wanted me. You wanted—"

Before Bryan could complete his sentence, I held my hand to his mouth. "Shut up! You don't know what you heard."

"Oh, Shorty, I really do. Now I know why Kristy keeps trailing behind you like a lovesick puppy and isn't interested in any of my friends. You're both lesbos together!" Bryan said, his voice rising and slurring at the same time.

Great, he must have also drunk too much from the keg.

I grabbed his arm. "Bryan, stop it. You're so drunk you must have misheard!"

"I can handle my booze, unlike your pussy boyfriend. I saw him running to the bathroom on my way up here."

"He's not a pussy!"

"No, but you wish he had one!" Bryan said with a hollow laugh.

"Bryan, what is wrong with you? Stop being such a douchebag!" *This was getting out of hand. There was no talking to him.*

"I'm the douchebag? You're the one that didn't want to be with me! What you did to me was worse than Cate. At least she liked me at some point before she cheated. You never liked me. Screw you Shorty. Everyone's going to know who you really want and it's going to gross them the eff out," Bryan screamed, pulling his arm out of my grasp and running in the opposite direction.

I heard his footsteps descend down the steps. I stared at Hannah for a split second, said a word that would've made my mom cringe, and then sprinted after Bryan. I went so fast that I tripped down the last three steps and sprawled out on the floor. My dress wasn't as skintight as I thought because it hiked up past part of my butt exposing my bright pink thong. I specifically picked out that underwear because I had high hopes of maybe going a little further with Kristy tonight, not showing my bare bottom to the entire senior class of Dale High.

Everyone nearby stopped talking and laughed as I attempted to pull down my dress. I saw a few flashes of light that could only be from people taking pictures of my naked ass. *Great. This would be recorded in infamy.* I tried to stand but my ankle gave way and I landed down on my backside.

Bryan shot me a look of disgust and was about to open his mouth when I pleaded, "Bryan, please help me up. I'm sorry. I'll do anything if you help me up right now and not say anything about what you heard."

Bryan thought for a second and said loudly, "Anything for a lady in need." He reached down and roughly pulled me up. "I own you now," he whispered in my ear.

Before I could react, I readjusted my stance and one of the sharpest pains I've ever felt shot down my left ankle. Flashes of light blinded my vision for a couple seconds. I groaned and leaned into Bryan.

"Looks like you hurt yourself, Shorty. Might need your lesbian lover to help you," Bryan hissed in my ear. He put his arm around my waist and held me close to his body.

Everyone still stared at me. I knew I had to say something. "Thank you everyone for watching the rise and fall of the great Shorty! Now for my next act, I'll disappear in disgrace. Thank you and good night!"

A few kids chuckled and one guy said, "Yo Shorty, you have a tight ass. Don't make that disappear!"

I smiled sweetly at him. "Thank you. I'm sure Zack, my boyfriend, would love to hear you say that louder!" *Phew, smart thinking Shorty, throwing in that Zack was my boyfriend, in case Bryan leaked my news.*

The guy shut his mouth and quickly looked around and sure enough Zack was heading in his direction. While Zack was distracted, I said to Bryan, "Thanks for not saying anything. I'm not ready to tell the world yet."

Bryan looked down at me with his relentless dark eyes. "I meant what I said, I own you now. If you do anything wrong, I'll let everyone know you like the ladies. First off, you need to stay with Zack."

"Wait what? Why?"

"So you can play him like you played me. He shouldn't be let off so easy; you need to break his heart too. Juggling him and Kristy will make your life complicated, which will please me greatly."

I shook my head. "No way. I was going to break up with him."

Bryan gave a throaty chuckle. "Not anymore. You need to hang out with him even more now. Give him blue balls until he breaks and can't stand it."

My mouth dropped. "I don't want to do that! Why do you care so much about hurting him?"

"That's what you did to me every single time we hung out." His face was so close to mine we were almost kissing.

I could smell the stench of alcohol laced on his breath. "I didn't mean to." *Did I really cause Bryan that much pain?*

"Well, you did. And now Zack thinks he's better than me because you're with him. He needs to stop trying to show me up and making me look stupid."

"Sorry, Bryan, but you do that on your own." *I needed to get away from Bryan stat and get off this ankle.*

"Shut up. No I don't. Zack thinks he's so cool, trying to punch me in front of everyone. Well, joke's on him; he didn't hit me or get the girl. You're going to help me ruin him."

I tried not to gag from his foul breath. "You're crazy! I don't want to do your dirty work because you don't like Zack."

Bryan squeezed my waist harder and moved his mouth to

my ear. "If you don't do what I tell you, the entire world, including your Bible hugging parents, will know your gross secret. I don't think they'd like finding out you're having sex with a goth lesbian."

Before I could respond and explain that Kristy was actually pansexual, not at all goth, and that we haven't had sex yet, Zack appeared by my side. "Hey, what happened? I heard you fell down the steps. Are you okay?" He glared at Bryan. "I got her now."

Bryan released me as Zack reached around my waist.

I let out the breath I held and placed my left arm around Zack's shoulders. *Thank God I could get away from Bryan's grasp and manipulative words.*

"You finally done spewing your brains out, nerd?" Bryan asked.

Zack's eyes widened. "Who told you I threw up?"

"I know everything. Have fun with Shorty here. We had a chat and she's going to make sure she spends more time with you. You can thank me later."

Zack turned his head to me. "What? Why would you talk about us with him?"

"Don't get your girly panties in a bunch, I'm the one that started it. Oh, and this party is lame as eff. My guys and I are going to blow this joint and find something better to do." Bryan took a few steps, then turned. "Shorty, Hannah's no longer welcome at my house, so she better get her shit and peace out."

Bryan turned back around and made a beeline to his jock friends. He made a few hand gestures pointing to the exit and all, but Bryan exited Zack's front door a few seconds later.

"What's going on? It's too early for people to leave." Zack looked down at me. "Why can't Hannah stay at Bryan's place anymore?"

"He heard Hannah say that she was using him to make

Tyler jealous. Oh, I forgot to mention, Tyler is probably having sex with Erin in your bed right now."

"Not again! For some reason Erin is insistent on doing it in my bed. I found her trying to sneak in with Tyler earlier today."

I had heard of strange fetishes, and I'm sure I'll find out I had some of my own now that my sexual beast had been awakened, but why would someone fantasize about having sex in their boyfriend's best friend's bed?

"Gross and TMI. Good luck with that." I shifted my weight to be more on Zack. "Just so you know, Bryan's pretty pissed about Hannah and wants to now make both my life and hers a living nightmare. Since you're my boyfriend, I'm sure you're also included on his list of enemies. That's probably why he told his minions to leave your party."

"But why did he stay?" Zack asked, motioning to Bryan downing a red solo cup near the kitchen.

"Probably to keep harassing us." I did a quick scan around the room. "Where's Hannah? I hope she's not still upstairs outside of your room."

"You stay down here; I'll go up and deal with that situation. Kristy, can you help Shorty to the couch? She hurt herself."

Kristy miraculously appeared beside me and gently placed her arm around my waist and moved me to the couch. I noticed in my peripheral vision Bryan taking pictures.

"Get a room!" He hollered at us snickering.

Kristy set me on the couch, placed her hands on her hips, and asked, "What the hell happened? I left you alone for fifteen minutes and now I find you with a hurt ankle, Bryan screaming for us to get a room, and Zack disappearing to deal with a *situation* involving Hannah outside his bedroom? Do I even want to know?"

"No. You really freaking don't. I can't even explain how

things have gone bad to awful in the span of fifteen minutes. Once again you were right, we never should've come here. What I really want is to get out of here and sink in the hot tub with you and forget about the rest of the world."

"Are you kidding? I was going to try and keep an eye on Bryan but was sidetracked when Dylan caught me to talk about a band we both like coming to Philly soon."

Since when was she friendly with Dylan?

"What's the status of everything now?" Kristy asked.

I brought my hand to my face and rubbed my temple. "Hannah needs somewhere to stay now, and it can't be here since Tyler and Erin are also crashing. Oh, and Hannah might or might not be standing outside of Zack's room crying while Erin and Tyler are having sex on Zack's bed."

I paused to catch a breath. Kristy looked at me expectantly and I continued. "I'm really sorry to ask this but is it okay if Hannah crashes at your aunt's?"

Kristy's face showed no expression. "She could stay in your room, and you can either share the bed with her or me."

"I'll share it with you if you don't think your aunt would care."

"She won't even notice."

I took a few deep breaths trying to figure out how to tell her about Bryan's blackmail when he strolled over to us.

"Oh, look Shorty, there's your boyfriend now and Hannah. Don't forget what I told you."

Hannah approached Bryan warily. "Bryan, I'm sorry. I do like you. But I also know I'm not over Tyler yet."

"You should have told me that to my face. Instead, I had to revert to my own devices to figure it out. We're finished. Time to find someone new."

Bryan turned his head. "Oh, I've heard stories about that one." Erin was sneaking down the steps alone in only a bright orange tank top and a short white skirt with material so thin you could see clear as day her orange thong. Her tank must also have been flimsy because you could clearly see she wasn't wearing a bra. Did she purposely leave her bra in Zack's room or maybe she didn't wear one tonight?

"Shorty, don't forget our little chat. Hannah, you need to get your crap from my house because no way in hell you're staying over," Bryan said moving toward Erin.

"But where will I go?" Hannah asked but Bryan had walked away without answering.

"You can stay with us," Kristy said.

I could tell she was being nice and didn't actually want her to stay. Hannah probably also heard it in her voice and said timidly, "I don't want to impose."

Hannah turned to look up at Zack with pleading eyes.

"You can stay here but fair warning, Tyler and Erin are also crashing," Zack responded.

"I'm not so sure about Erin. Looks like Bryan is already charming her. That must be record time for him," I said pointing across the room.

All of us turned our attention to the other side of the room where Bryan had slung his arm around Erin's bare shoulders.

She giggled like a hyena.

I rolled my eyes and told Zack to go get Tyler.

He nodded and darted up the steps. A couple minutes later, he and Tyler appeared.

Erin's back was to the steps, so she didn't even notice she had an audience.

Tyler's face turned from confused to pissed in a millisecond.

Zack physically grabbed his shoulders to hold him back.

Bryan whispered in Erin's ear and led her into another room.

Tyler looked wildly around until his gaze landed on Hannah, who shyly stared at him.

Zack let go of Tyler's shoulders and Tyler walked over to us.

"Hey, looks like your new girl and my ex might be in the process of hooking up," I stated.

"Thanks for pointing out the obvious. What does anyone see in that guy?" Tyler asked.

"I've been wondering that since I moved here. He's the worst," Kristy said shaking her head.

"He knows the right thing to say and makes you feel important but then after he has you, he's another boring jock, and you start to notice his not so nice qualities. And he is excessively handsy. Isn't that right Hannah?" I said.

"Yea, he's not that great. I don't know what I was thinking. Last night all he wanted to talk about was football. Like *all* night. It seems like he doesn't have any other thoughts, besides sex."

"Sounds about right."

Bryan and Erin reappeared.

"New plan guys. Erin's staying with me tonight. Sorry, Tyler. Seems like women are dying to get away from you. Erin, go get your stuff."

Erin quickly darted up the steps.

A flash of anger appeared on Tyler's face and Zack stood in front of Tyler before he could move.

"No man, it isn't worth it. Trust me, I tried. Hannah why don't I drive you to Bryan's place to get your stuff and you can crash with us tonight?"

"Are you sure?" Hannah asked.

"Yeah. Shorty, can you stay here with Tyler and make sure he doesn't do anything stupid?"

"Zack, you've had too much to drink. I'll take Hannah and Shorty can come along," Kristy said.

I saw Bryan out of the corner of my eye, and he yelled, "Shorty should stay here and keep the boys in line. She's been away from Zack all night."

Tears formed in my eyes. I felt so confused. I didn't want to piss off Kristy, but I also didn't want my parents finding out about my desire for girls from Bryan. A shot of pain coursed through my entire body, originating in my ankle.

"Ow!" I winced. "Kristy, my ankle is killing me. I'll stay here until you get back." I took a deep breath to subdue the pain. "What about Bryan though? He's probably too drunk to drive."

"One of Bryan's friends drove us here. He probably forgot," Hannah said faintly.

Kristy gave me a long look. "Fine. I'll drive Bryan and Erin too."

Bryan overheard Kristy and said, "You're not as bad as I thought. I'll invite you to my upcoming bonfire extravaganza. Come on Erin, let's go make our own party."

Kristy rolled her eyes at me as she shut the door. I inwardly cringed. I owed her bigtime.

CHAPTER TWENTY

I inspected the room from my spot on the couch. Cashi, Dylan, and a few other band members mingled around the keg but other than that, the party cleared out after Bryan and his friends left.

Zack also looked around the room and sighed. "Not exactly the party I thought I'd have. I'm going to tell everyone it's over so we can chill."

After Zack left, Cashi came up to me. "Are you ok? That fall looked like it hurt."

I shrugged. "As good as I could be. My ego is more bruised than anything else."

Cashi laughed. "You always did know how to put on a good show."

"Or do you mean I always have been a klutz?"

Cashi leaned on the arm of the couch closest to me. "That too. I'll never forget the time you fell on a potted plant playing tag in my yard as a little kid. You totally smashed that plant like no one's business!"

"Oh my god. Your mom wouldn't stop yelling in Hindi!"

"That's because I think she likes her plants more than people."

Zack showed up as we were laughing about Cashi's mom's obsession with plants, and he gave a pointed look at Cashi.

Cashi straightened. "Looks like everyone's leaving so I'll head out too. Thanks for the invite, Zack. Shorty, hope you feel better!"

"Thanks. I'll see you around."

I guess Cashi couldn't be too mad at me that I won president. I'd have to hang out with him soon to talk about our first student council meeting.

Zack handed me a bag of ice, a towel, and a large glass of a reddish-brown liquid in a wine glass.

I accepted his offerings. "Is this wine?" I tried not to appear shocked that he was thoughtful enough to bring me ice and a drink. Bryan would've made me fend for myself.

"A special drink I made just for you. Try it."

I took a sip and held back the automatic urge to gag. The liquid tasted like rubbing alcohol with a hint of grape.

Zack sat next to me. "It's my specialty cocktail. Vodka, grape juice, and a splash of whatever soda is open. Do you like it?"

My stomach turned as I listened to the contents. Guess I wouldn't be drinking any of that. I really didn't need to get drunk anyways after the margaritas from yesterday.

"It's interesting but should help numb the pain. Thanks."

Zack frowned. "I knew I shouldn't have added the Pepsi. Next time I'll try adding Sprite."

I was situated in the middle of the couch, so Zack and Tyler sat on either end. After I propped my ankle up with the ice and took the smallest sip possible of the drink mixed with grossness, Zack pulled me close.

"Thanks for helping me out," I said. It did feel comforting

to be in his arms. His aftershave smelled so good. This felt almost right.

Maybe I wouldn't have to pretend I liked him? Who knows, maybe what I felt for Kristy was only lust. Or maybe I was like Kristy and pansexual?

"I'm sorry you guys. I know I'm the one that started all this with Bryan. If I knew he would be such a psychopath I would've never even dated him."

"How would you know? I'm glad both you and Hannah are done with him. Hopefully he doesn't hurt Erin," Zack replied.

"I'm sure Erin can take care of herself. Tyler, did you even like her?" I asked.

Tyler stared straight ahead. "She was good at helping me forget Hannah. Other than that, no."

I shifted my ankle and tried to get comfortable in Zack's arms. "You know Hannah still loves you, right? She got caught in Bryan's tangled web and was stuck getting out."

"She does? Erin was fun but she wasn't Hannah. All she did was talk bad about other people." Tyler motioned to my ankle. "What happened to you?"

"Oh, you know me, I had to get some extra attention falling down the stairs after you guys took over Zack's room. I gave the entire room a show of my ass."

Tyler laughed. "Wow. Too bad I missed that."

"It was almost one of those movie worthy moments where the girl hits rock bottom. But I'm resilient!"

"You should probably get your ankle checked out," Zack said looking worriedly down at my leg.

"I know. I'll make my mom look at it when I get home. My dad's making me work at the store on Monday so that should be fun."

We talked for a couple more minutes. When Tyler turned

on the TV, Zack whispered in my ear, "Do you feel up to hanging out in my room? If not, that's okay."

I sucked in a breath. What if Kristy returned to find me behind closed doors with her arch nemesis? But Bryan's words continued to haunt me. Did I really want to continue this fling with her if Bryan might tell my parents? Being with Zack would make life a lot easier; I wouldn't have to come out to the world, and I could keep plugging along like nothing happened with Kristy. Zack and I were good friends before we got together. Maybe we could make it work so no one would ever have to find out I was attracted to women.

If I remembered correctly, Bryan's house wasn't that close. Maybe I should give it one last try to make sure I wasn't making a big mistake. Zack was my boyfriend, so I wasn't technically doing anything wrong.

"Okay, I need help getting up the steps."

"Sorry man, we're going upstairs but you understand, right? Just don't go after Bryan," Zack told Tyler.

Tyler kept his gaze on an old Godzilla movie. "I won't. I'd rather wait for Hannah to return."

"Can you shout a warning when Kristy pulls up so we can come down? I don't want to make her wait."

"Yea, no problem," Tyler said.

Zack helped me limp up the steps. He opened the door to his room and assisted me in sitting on his bed. He shut the door behind him and all in one motion, he descended on the bed while pulling me down to lay beside him.

"Are you sure you're okay?" he asked.

"Yeah, I'm fine." I lied. *What was I doing? Why did I agree to this?*

He stroked my cheek. "This is what I've been waiting for all week."

He moved his mouth close and as soon as his lips touched mine, guilt overcame me. If Kristy saw us now she'd be devastated but on the other hand, Zack was my actual boyfriend. What really was she? My side toy? And there I went again, thinking of other topics while making out with a guy.

We kissed for a while, and I had to keep myself from yawning. *When was this going to be over? The sheer desire I felt for Kristy wasn't here at all. Now that I finally knew what attraction felt like, not having it with Zack only made this even more intolerable.*

While my mind was distracted, his hand inched down the neckline of my dress, attempting to go underneath my bra. *Really?* I was hoping I wouldn't have to fight him off again so soon. I tried to clear my mind and enjoy what was happening but after a few seconds, I gave up.

It wasn't the same as kissing Kristy. With her I lost myself; I never wanted her to stop touching me, and I wanted to rip off her clothes. But with Zack, I honestly had more fun working at my dad's store. At least there I knew I had an exact time where I could go home. Here, every single second was a chore, and I was praying it would end. Next thing I knew, Zack's shirt was off, and he was inching my dress up. I grabbed his hand and pulled it away. "No, not yet. I'm not ready to go further and my ankle is still killing me. Kristy also should be here any minute and I don't want to make her wait for me. But you know what I realized. I have no pics of us."

I pulled out my cellphone from my dress. Don't let anyone kid you, dresses with pockets really were the best. I teased my hair a little bit, adjusted the angle I was sitting against Zack, and snapped a selfie of us before Zack could protest. I quickly texted it to Bryan.

Hello from Zack's love nest.

The picture was perfect. From the way I took the picture, all you could see was Zack's naked torso. My hair was so messed up that if it didn't scream sex hair, I didn't know what did. *That should keep Bryan off my back for a little.*

"I'm going to head down to wait for Kristy. I can use the banister to help me. I promise I won't fall again," I said limping to the door.

"Uh, okay. I'll be down in a bit," Zack said, placing a pillow over his lap.

I closed the door and let out the sigh I had been holding in. *How much longer could I come up with excuses to not go further with him?*

I took each step carefully and Tyler glanced up from the TV. When he saw me alone, holding onto the banister for dear life with both hands, he quickly rose and helped me to the bottom of the steps. I scanned the room and breathed a sigh of relief. No Kristy.

Tyler led me to the couch and helped me prop up my leg. He found the ice and towel I had left and handed it to me.

"You guys done already?"

"We were worried Hannah and Kristy would be back soon."

"You mean you were worried," Tyler said giving me a side glance.

I forgot that Tyler was so blunt.

"I didn't want to hold Kristy up."

Tyler studied me carefully. "Can I ask you something?"

I nodded as I reached for my *cocktail* that was still chilled and took a big gulp. *Screw the foul taste, I needed something strong after being with Zack.*

"Have you and Zack even done anything else besides kissing?"

My mouth was still filled with the vile liquid, and I was so taken aback, I started coughing. Driblets of the mixture escaped from the corners of my mouth running down my dress. At least the dark spots were a similar color to my outfit.

I was not expecting that question. I forced myself to swallow the awful drink. "No. Did Zack say something?"

"No. I was curious. What about with Bryan or Paul?"

"Just making out."

"So, you still never had sex? I mean I know we never did it, but I thought you had by now."

I crossed my arms. "Well, I haven't. Is that a problem?"

"No. I guess I assumed you did, especially with dating Paul and Bryan, who are known to sleep with all the girls at Dale."

"I'm waiting." I knew it was one of the lamest responses ever uttered.

"Why?"

"I dunno. My church and my mom have always told me I should wait. I guess I'm also scared that it won't live up to the hype. But maybe in the future." I automatically thought about Kristy.

"You should, I bet it's more fun than you think." Tyler was silent for a moment and then glanced over at me.

"I'm afraid I'm part of the reason Hannah liked Bryan's attention. Her parents won't let her do anything and it's hard. At first I'd be creative how we could see each other but that got old. I stopped FaceTiming and texting her as much or trying to find other ways to see her because my grand plans would never work."

"I was wondering. Hannah mentioned you weren't talking to her as much."

"Maybe that's why she went for Bryan. He was her lab partner and easy to see. And who knows what he was saying to her." Tyler looked over at me. "Just so you know, I didn't go the whole way with Erin; I couldn't do it. I was too busy thinking of Hannah. I guess I should've tried harder with Hannah, but I thought she'd always be there."

"Try talking to Hannah about all of this. I'd mention for sure you didn't sleep with Erin."

Tyler focused on the floor. "Yeah, I should do that. I'm nervous though."

"Why?"

"We never really talk about our feelings much. It's scary to be that open with someone."

"But you're doing it with me right now!"

Tyler shrugged. "Yeah, but you're you. I've always been able to talk to you about anything, until after we broke up. That's how we've worked and probably why I've missed talking to you."

How much did he have to drink? Probably a lot if he was actually being nice to me and opening up.

"I've missed talking to you, too. Now all we do is fight."

Tyler looked over at me. "Yeah, I'm sorry for that. I was embarrassed you broke up with me. I guess fighting made it easier to swallow."

I frowned. "I figured as much, but you know we weren't right together. We've always been good as friends, boyfriend and girlfriend, not so much."

Tyler nodded. "No, you're right. You and I sat around and watched all the new movies. So that's what I thought it would be like when I started dating Hannah. But our relationship is, or I guess I should say was, completely different. If we ever found time together, we needed to make up for whenever we couldn't see each other."

"You and I worked well together because we enjoyed hanging out. I dreaded breaking up with you because I knew things would change. You were my best guy friend and not being able to talk to you anymore was rough. And seeing you having fun with my best friend sucked. I tried not to think about it since Hannah was so happy, but I kinda wish we never dated so we could've stayed good friends."

"That had to be weird to see us together."

I shrugged. "I got used to it. Honestly, it was weirder seeing you with Erin just a few minutes ago."

Tyler stared at me straight in the eyes. "I should say thanks for breaking up with me. I would've never been able to do it. I know I was hurt, especially since you were my first girlfriend, but you're right. We didn't belong together."

I returned his look. "It's nice to hear that. I didn't want to hurt you because I cared, and still do, about you. You're awesome but we should only ever be friends. Can we stop fighting so we can actually talk like real friends?"

Tyler nods. "I'll stop being such an asshole."

"Now you and Hannah, you two do work, even if it is weird for me. She made a mistake with Bryan, and she's so sorry."

"Yeah, I know."

"What if we had a movie night if you and Hannah get back together? You, me, Hannah, and Zack? We can watch the newest Marvel movie!"

"Zack's movie room is a pretty sweet setup, right? He told me he showed you his place. And if it works out, maybe it can be a weekly thing?"

Tyler and I gave each other a high five.

At that moment Zack strolled down the steps with his hair still rumbled. "Kristy and Hannah are here. I saw them pull up."

I glanced back at Tyler. "Talk to her. It will help, I promise."

Tyler nodded. "Thanks Shorty."

He looked like he was about to say more but at that moment the front door opened, and Kristy appeared.

Hannah trailed behind, mascara stains trailing down her cheeks.

"How did that go?"

"We could hear Erin's moans echoing throughout the

house while Hannah packed up her stuff, so you tell me. How about here? Anything exciting happen?" Kristy asked.

I willed myself to not turn red and stay cool. "Nope, watched TV with the guys."

Kristy walked over and looked down at my ankle. "How are you feeling?"

"Not terrible. It still throbs but the ice and the drink Zack mixed me helps."

"A mixed drink? I didn't think it was that kind of party." She picked up my drink and sniffed. "What the hell is in that? Zack, are you trying to kill her?"

"No! It's grape juice, vodka, and Pepsi, nothing too crazy!"

Kristy rolled her eyes. "That's your idea of a mixed drink? Don't quit your day job. Are you ready to go, Shorty? We can have some real drinks at my place, my aunt won't notice some missing."

I tried to avoid Zack's gaze. "Yep, I'm good." *He couldn't tell I was imagining her in her tight black bikini, could he?*

Kristy helped me up.

"Hannah, you okay staying here?"

"As long as I'm welcome," she said giving Zack the most pitiful look.

"For sure," Zack replied.

"I think Tyler wants to talk to you too," I said.

"You do?" Hannah asked, moving closer to where Tyler sat.

He stood and put his hands in his pockets. "Want to go upstairs?"

Hannah nodded and followed him up the stairway.

Zack came over and gave me a quick kiss. "If you get out of working at the store Monday, let me know and we can hang out after I get home."

That settled it, I was going to work at my dad's store, even if I sat and was like a Walmart greeter. "I'm sure my dad will find something for me, but I'll let you know. See you!"

Kristy snuck her arm around my waist, and I continued using her like a crutch. She helped me into her car. She reversed and pulled onto the road. "It's always a pleasure hanging out with your friends."

I sighed. "I'm sorry. You used to think it was funny."

"That was before we started hooking up. There's so much drama."

We were quiet the rest of the way back. When we arrived at the beach house, Kristy's aunt asked how the party was and if her car was in one piece. After that, she told us to help ourselves to anything in the fridge.

Kristy helped me limp to my room. "Do you need help with your clothes?"

"You just want to help me undress!"

Kristy's eyes glittered. "Or maybe I don't want you to hurt yourself again."

"How very thoughtful of you," I said smiling. "I can get changed myself but if you could help me get to the hot tub that'd be great."

Kristy nodded and shut the door.

I inched out of my skintight dress, threw off my thong and bra, and slipped on my slightly damp bathing suit. *Another reason why I always needed two bathing suits.* I sat on the bed while I waited for Kristy.

After a couple of minutes, Kristy knocked on the door and I told her to come in. She grabbed my towel from me, held out her arm, and I latched on. We hobbled down to the hot tub at a glacial pace. She helped me in, and I sank down.

I turned around and Kristy had disappeared. After a few moments, she appeared out of the screen door with two glasses of white wine.

"My aunt said to help ourselves to anything in the fridge. Wine counts, right?"

My eyes went wide. "She won't care?" *If it were my parents, I would've been scared they'd see me drinking and ground me for the rest of my life.*

"You saw her yesterday; she wouldn't think twice if she saw us with this."

"It's amazing how different she is than my parents." I took a sip and placed it behind me.

"And mine." Kristy slid in the hot tub and wrapped her arm around my shoulders.

"This water feels amazing on my ankle. I'm not going to want to leave."

"We can stay in as long as you want."

Being alone with Kristy helped me to forget about my ankle but instead, feelings of guilt began to arise. I reached for my glass and took another gulp of wine. I tried not to hear the voice of my grandma or my parents' voice condemning me to hell. I was also feeling awful about making out with Zack and not telling Kristy.

Nothing much really happened with him, but I blatantly lied to her right after I promised I wouldn't go anywhere alone with him.

Kristy tapped my head. "What's going on up here?"

"I'm trying to process everything that happened at the party," I said, sadness weighing me down.

"Maybe this will help." Kristy pulled me close and brought her lips to mine. They felt so soft compared to Zack's. And she was so gentle and caring. We kissed for a bit, her nipping my neck while circling her fingers around my exposed stomach. I gasped.

"Mmm, is this helping?"

"Uh, for sure. I almost can't remember my name." I still felt awful about what I did, but what Kristy didn't know wouldn't hurt right? It wasn't like much happened with him anyways and he was my actual boyfriend.

In mid kiss, I inched myself onto Kristy's lap. We pressed against each other and continued onward. There was no question if I was attracted to her. I had to take everything that was bothering me and put it in a large box under a lock and key and enjoy the one thing that currently made me happy. I'd figure out everything else later.

CHAPTER TWENTY-ONE

"Sam, why are you limping? What did you do?" my mother asked, her forehead creasing.

"I fell down some steps. I might need you to look at it," I said as I attempted to walk from Kristy's aunt's car to meet my mom.

My mom rushed to my side and let me lean on her.

"Don't worry, we took care of her last night and made her ice it," Cheryl said from the car.

Cheryl was an accomplished liar; she didn't even notice my limp until this morning.

I was also pretty sure she thought it was a sexual activity injury because she winked when she asked if we had too much fun last night.

Kristy came behind me with my duffel bag.

"What are you going to do about marching band? The first football game is this Friday," my mom asked.

Crap. I didn't think about that.

"There is no way I can march. Can I also sit at the cash register tomorrow at the store?"

My mom sighed. "I'll let you be the one to break it to your dad."

"Kristy's still available to work and not broken like me," I said glancing back at her. Her hair was slicked back from her shower in the morning. I tried to not turn red thinking about our evening in the hot tub together. I ultimately decided I still wasn't ready to go the whole way, especially with my ankle pain, but we found other ways to have fun that would make my mom throw Kristy out of the house if she ever found out.

"That's really nice of you Kristy. Can you be at the store at seven tomorrow morning? That's a half hour before we open so it will give my husband some time to give you the rundown."

"No problem. Happy to help out."

My mom patted Kristy on her shoulders and thanked her again. "You're welcome anytime at our house. Do you and your aunt want to stay for dinner?"

I was dying inside. It was stressful enough seeing my mom and Kristy speaking. I wanted to go inside and hide and pretend that everything was normal. That I didn't have this dirty little secret that was already starting to haunt me. I was praying to the gods, whichever ones existed, that Kristy would decline my mom's generous offer. I couldn't even imagine her and Cheryl eating with us. And what if one of us slipped up and the truth came out?

"Kristy and I need to get home to clean the house and do laundry but thanks for the invitation," Cheryl called from the car.

Saved by the cool, smooth aunt! I was sure she didn't feel like spending her free night sharing a meal with a family that had no clue that her niece was having heated relations with their daughter.

Kristy gave me a small wave. "See you tomorrow, Shorty."

I really wanted to hug her goodbye but not in front of my mom.

I returned her wave. "Bye! Thank you guys for taking me to the beach. I had a great time."

She climbed into the car, and they drove off.

"They're both very nice people. Besides hurting your ankle, did you have a good time?" my mom asked.

"It was a lot of fun! I even managed to not get sunburnt."

"Good, now let's go take care of your ankle."

After my mom's inspection, she declared that it was probably sprained and rushed me to urgent care to get treated. I was told I shouldn't put any pressure on it, so I had to use crutches for the next two to three weeks. They also gave me an attractive boot to wear. Luckily it wasn't my right foot, so I'd still be able to drive. But that meant marching band was out for the month, oh darn! Hannah would be so jealous. It also meant I didn't have to stock shelves at my dad's store tomorrow. I did feel bad I couldn't work like I'd promised but at least I had recruited Kristy to help although, that'd be more time she had to be around my father. Maybe I didn't think this plan through.

A little before seven a.m. the next morning, Kristy sauntered into my father's store sipping coffee from a travel thermos, wearing black dress pants, a maroon blouse, a leather jacket, and looking sexier than ever. She hadn't noticed I was sitting in the corner so I could have free reign to check her out longer than necessary. Little did she know, my dad was going to make her change and put on a lovely bright lime green polo that displayed the text *Phil's Market* across the chest. I had tried for years to get him to change the horrendous color, but he still hadn't embraced my fashion sense.

Kristy finally noticed me. "Hey! How'd you sleep?"

"I slept okay." I motioned for her to come closer. "I would've slept better with you next to me," I whispered.

"Same. I woke up in the middle of the night wondering where you were." She was about to put her hand on my leg when I heard a noise and saw my dad approaching. Kristy quickly pulled her hand away and I straightened up on my chair.

"Dad, this is Kristy Davis."

Kristy moved toward my dad and stuck out her hand.

He shook it. "Very firm handshake. I'm always telling Sam a firm shake is important for first impressions. It can immediately show someone's character."

"Thank you, sir."

This was going well so far. My dad sized Kristy up, walked away for a second, and then returned with the dreaded polo. "Here, try this on and see if it fits. The bathroom's around the corner. You're going to be assisting in a variety of tasks today since Sam got herself hurt and can only do the cash register."

I rolled my eyes. Like I purposely fell down the steps and embarrassed myself to the world to get out of stocking shelves.

Kristy nodded her head and walked toward the bathroom.

"While I'm training Kristy, you can open up the cash register and unlock the doors at seven-thirty. Got it?" my dad said to me.

"Sure, easy peasy. Sorry I can't help more."

My dad grunted. "At least you found a friend to help and she's taller than you."

That was my dad's way of saying everything was fine. I grabbed my crutches and hobbled over to the cash register.

Once I opened the doors, the day crawled by. Everyone must have still been at the shore because we only had a few customers until around eleven a.m. In the meantime, I had the best view of watching Kristy stock shelves. My dad must've given her the smallest polo size because it was tight on her, especially around the lettering *Phil's Market*. Even though the color was hideous, she still managed to rock it, unlike me.

I had nothing to flaunt, and the polo fit me like a sleep shirt. Even when I tucked it in, there was so much extra material it looked like I was hiding something in my black jean pants, which were way too short. My mom had to hem them for me, but she misjudged, and they sat above my ankles. It looked like I was waiting for a flood to occur. To complete this fashion nightmare, I sported my shiny new crutches and the large cast boot. Good thing Kristy already liked me because today I wouldn't earn any points toward looking cute.

My dad released me for a lunch break at noon and took over the register. I went to find Kristy where she was stocking fruit.

"Nice melons," I said loud enough so only she could hear.

Kristy stopped moving with a watermelon still in her hands. She gave me a bewildered look. "Shorty, you're as bad as a dude. How'd you ever think you were straight?"

"Shhhhh! Don't make comments like that so loud!" I hissed. I whipped my head around to see who might have heard. The coast was clear, but it was too close of a call for my tastes.

"Sorry, it's going to be hard to restrain myself when you provoke me like that."

Kristy gingerly placed the watermelon in a bin with the others.

"I'm on lunch now. Did my dad say when you could go on break?"

"When you come back."

"That's what I figured. He usually lets me eat something off the salad bar. When I get back, I'll ask him what you should do."

"I don't want him to do anything special. He could take anything I buy from my paycheck. I think that's usually what happens at places."

"I can ask. I'll eat fast so you can have your break."

I wanted to kiss her goodbye but knew I couldn't. *What a cruel trick.*

In the past I had my pick of guys to kiss, and I couldn't have been bothered with them. Now I had someone that I wanted to kiss nonstop, and I couldn't for fear of who would see us.

I hobbled over to the salad bar and came to the awful realization I had no idea how I was going to make my salad on crutches. Maybe a bag of crackers would have to work. I turned away in frustration when Kristy appeared beside me.

"Need help?" She picked up a to-go salad box.

"Are you sure? I feel bad having you make my salad."

"I wouldn't offer if I didn't want to help." She opened the box and reached for the romaine lettuce.

Looks like she won't take no for an answer. "Thank you," I said softly. I hated not being able to do basic tasks myself. It had always been hard for me to ask for help and now, when I needed it the most, it was still difficult.

Kristy's salad making skills were superb. She added the right number of veggies and didn't overdo it on the Italian dressing. I loathed soggy salads. She followed me to the break room with my salad. I picked a chair closest to the door and collapsed. "This sucks! I had no idea crutches would take so much work. I want to be me again."

Kristy brought over a chair and helped me prop up my left leg. "I'm sure you'll get the hang of them in a couple of days. And Zack will be more than happy to help you at school tomorrow," Kristy said flatly.

My gaze connected with Kristy's. Her look was unreadable but if that wasn't a passive aggressive comment, I didn't know what was. "I wish I didn't have to go to school tomorrow." *Could we return to the beach house where everything was a perfect bubble?*

"If it gets too bad, think about the hot tub," Kristy said, bending over and giving me a lingering kiss on the lips.

"What're you doing?" I yanked myself as far away from Kristy as possible.

Kristy stepped back and crossed her arms. "Geez, Shorty. Relax, no one's around. You're acting like I'm repulsive."

"I don't want my dad to see us," I said defensively.

"Fine. Have a nice break." Kristy turned her back on me to return to her shift.

"Thanks for your help!" I called after her but received no response. I sighed and stabbed a piece of romaine lettuce. How was I ever going to make this work?

CHAPTER TWENTY-TWO

I pulled into my spot at school and my gaze darted to the rearview mirror. Zack was jogging up next to my car.

Kristy was right; he was more than ready to help. At least he wasn't pissed at me like her. After we finished working at the store, she only said a quick goodbye and I didn't hear from her for the rest of the night. Why couldn't she understand I wasn't ready to tell the world about me? Not everyone could be as confident and cool as her.

Zack waited for me to open my door. "How's it going?"

"Living the dream." I swung my left leg, complete with my big cast boot, out of the door. Using the open door as a crutch, I attempted to get out of the car.

Zack held me steady as I opened my back car door. I reached for my crutches and almost fell over in the process.

"Here, let me." Zack effortlessly extended his arm to grab my crutches and handed them to me. "I guess you sprained your ankle?"

I adjusted the crutches under my arm. "I did, hence the cast boot." His face was so close to mine, and he moved in for a kiss. After a couple of seconds, I pulled away. *It was way too early to make out.*

Zack's face crinkled. "I didn't hear from you yesterday."

"Sorry, I was working at my dad's store. He put me on register duty and when I'm up there I can't even check my phone."

Zack reached into my car and grabbed my lunch and iPad. "Tyler and Hannah made out in my backseat most of the way back from the shore yesterday, so that was real fun."

I laughed. "Thanks for putting up with them. Hannah texted me yesterday pretty happy. Things are back to how they should be." *Except that I was falling for someone that wasn't Zack.*

I knew I needed to keep Zack around a little longer, at least until Bryan found someone else to blackmail, which hopefully was sooner rather than later. I also had to figure out how to be with Kristy without having to shout to the world *I like women!* And speak of the devil, out of the corner of my eye, I saw Bryan walking toward me. Might as well take advantage of this situation.

I began kissing Zack again, but with more feeling. It was easier to stomach once I closed my eyes and imagined that it was Kristy's lips locking mine. I discreetly opened one eye to see if Bryan was watching. He was but so were about ten other people, including Kristy. My daydream shattered.

Her arms were crossed, and her mouth pursed in a thin line.

I pulled away. "We should probably go in. I don't want to be late."

"At least you have a good reason, you can blame it on the crutches."

By the time we were ready to go in, Kristy had disappeared. I hobbled to the entrance, and we made our slow trek to my homeroom. He followed me into the classroom and put all my stuff on my desk, helped me into my seat, and leaned my crutches against my desk.

"Thanks Zack for your help. I really owe you."

He leaned in for a kiss. "No worries, that's what I'm here for. See you at lunch."

I waited until Zack left before I turned around.

Kristy's face was buried in her iPad.

I whispered, "I'm sorry. I didn't mean for you to see that in the parking lot and just now."

Kristy raised her head to meet my gaze. "It sucks seeing you with him. I wanted to punch him in the face but then I realized, I'm the one doing something wrong."

"What do you mean?"

Kristy looked around and lowered her voice. "You're cheating on him with me. I can't legitimately ask you not to make out with him, he's your boyfriend. That also means I have to watch scenes like that unfold every single day. You need to figure out what you're doing about him ASAP because I can't handle much more of that."

My stomach flipped. "I told you I'm trying to figure out what to do. It's not so easy breaking up with someone, especially when you consider them a friend."

"If you aren't one hundred percent sure you don't want to be with him, then we shouldn't be messing around. It's not fair to Zack or me."

I sighed loudly. The thought of telling her about Bryan's blackmail crossed my mind, but I didn't know the consequences if Bryan found out I told her. I bit my tongue. "I'm super confused right now."

Kristy's eyes softened. "That makes sense. I'm sorry. I keep forgetting this is all new for you."

"I'm not ready yet to make any decisions when my mind's so fuzzy."

"That's fair, but please don't shut me out. I can help you work through this. I've been there too."

I nodded and thanked her.

Mrs. Jacobs cleared her throat. "Sam, are you finished talking so I can give a few updates?"

"Oh, sorry." I faced the front of the classroom.

I knew I should do the right thing and break up with Zack, but what if Bryan told my parents about Kristy? Zack made more sense for the time being and gave me time to figure out my next step. I hoped Kristy actually understood.

In creative writing class, as we took our seats, I heard a small clink. I turned around just in time to see Kristy bending over to pick up her phone. I could see directly down her shirt. I bit my lip to avoid any noise escaping my mouth. I squirmed in my seat.

Every time I wondered if maybe being with a guy would be easier, my body came back to remind me it had other plans. I was insanely attracted to this girl, no matter how complicated our *relationship* was.

Kristy straightened and caught me gaping. She sat and gave me a small smirk. "Want to come over after school?"

"Yes!" I quickly replied. *That'll give me a chance to convince Kristy that I'll break up with Zack when I'm ready.*

At lunch, I was the first to arrive at our table. Kristy was second to arrive and claimed a spot next to me. As soon as we sat, Tyler slipped beside Hannah and draped his arm on her shoulders.

"Is it okay if I sit with you?" Tyler asked while gazing at Hannah.

"Of course," she replied beaming.

Zack plopped on the open chair next to me. "Want to come over after school? My parents won't be home until late." *I didn't think through having to make excuses to my own boyfriend when I spent time with Kristy.*

"I'm going over to Kristy's tonight, sorry." I avoided his stare by pulling out my PB&J sandwich. I took a large bite.

"Uh, okay. Hope you guys have fun," he said, giving me a half smile.

"We're working on our creative writing project," I said quickly. *That wasn't a complete lie, right? I'm sure we would at least mention it tonight.*

I turned to Kristy and she was giving me a cold stare. I quickly looked down.

These interactions with Zack in front of her were the worst.

"What about tomorrow after marching band?" he asked while placing his hand on my leg.

It felt like lead sitting on top of my skin. I snuck a glance over at Kristy again.

She made a discreet shrug.

"Sure, okay," I said half-heartily. I was about to take another bite into my sandwich when I felt my iPhone vibrate in my purse. It was a text from Bryan.

> I see who you really want. The rest of the world will know too if you don't keep leading Zack on.

I whipped my head around and found Bryan sitting at his usual table with his left hand stuck in the back of Erin's jeans. *Ew.* He winked at me and went back to talking with his jock friends.

What the hell? Why did he even care, especially since he had a new distraction.

As I tried to unravel Bryan's evil plan, everyone, minus Kristy, discussed tomorrow's dreaded marching band rehearsal. I tried to pay attention, but my thoughts kept drifting.

When the bell rang, Zack grabbed my hand. "I'll walk with you to class."

Kristy gave me another chilly glare and marched off without saying a word.

Kristy opened the door to her aunt's house. "You're here."

"Of course! Why wouldn't I?"

Her eyes challenged me. "I was afraid you'd blow me off for Zack."

"No way. I've been daydreaming about you since creative writing," I said, giving her a lop-sided grin.

"Why, pray tell?"

"Because of that peep show you gave me! I think you dropped your phone on purpose."

Kristy smirked. "I would do no such thing."

I followed her into the house as fast as I could with my crutches. Kristy led me to a door. "Can you make it down steps?"

I nodded and handed her my crutches. I clung on the railing as if it was my only lifeline. I finally reached the bottom and took a sigh of relief.

Her aunt's basement looked like something straight out of a seventies movie, complete with a blue lava lamp on a bookshelf in the corner. Kristy helped me to the retro multi-colored couch. She sunk next to me and put her arm over my shoulders.

"Sorry I walked off at lunch, but it was better that way. I would've said something I'd regret and make things worse."

I leaned my head on her shoulder. "I know it's hard to see me with Zack. He's so handsy."

"That's because he likes you; how could he not be?"

"I guess."

Kristy tipped my head up to meet hers and grazed her lips against mine. My body instinctually melded into her lap.

We began to kiss slowly, with long, deep kisses. I wrapped my arms around her shoulders to close the gap between us. After a bit, her right hand began to trace my spine, and she slowly worked her fingers to trace the outline of my bra. I sucked in my breath.

"You like that?"

"You're killing me. When does your aunt get home?" I asked Kristy between kisses.

"Don't worry, I told her you were coming over and she texted back she would make herself scarce," Kristy responded, rubbing her hand over my leg.

What was happening to me? I always dreaded *alone time* with Paul and Bryan but today was different. The entire drive over, my speedometer read forty-five in a thirty-five zone and I was a second away from blowing through a stop sign.

We kissed some more. Her hand reached behind me and hovered over the zipper of my dress.

"More?" she asked between kisses.

Is this what I wanted? Kristy instead of Zack? And poor Zack. He didn't deserve this.

"Uh," I said stammering, pulling away. "I don't know. Maybe not while I'm still with Zack."

Kristy stood and put her hand on her hips. "That's what I've been saying all along. Now you're getting all moral on me? What the hell, Shorty?"

"I guess going further makes it even more real," I said, twisting my mouth.

Kristy's eyes pleaded. "Why can't you break up with him? I don't get it. Help me understand."

"I told you, I'm not ready for the world to know about me." It was becoming harder and harder to not tell her about Bryan's blackmail but what if he found out I told her and released my secret.

"If you break up with Zack it doesn't mean the world is

suddenly going to start pointing a finger at you screaming, *You're queer*! How would they know? Can't you be single, and we can wait to tell everyone about us until you're ready?"

Kristy's reasoning made perfect sense if Bryan didn't have a vendetta against me and my current boyfriend.

"I can't do that, I'm sorry." I wiped a tear from my eye.

"Fine. You should probably go then." Kristy motioned to the steps.

My stomach throbbed. Being with Kristy was beyond anything I had ever dreamed of but lying to her sucked. "Right. Well, see you tomorrow." I was unsure of how to say goodbye. I grabbed my crutches and hobbled toward the staircase. I latched onto the railing and heaved myself up the steps.

"I don't like to share," Kristy admitted from behind me.

I sniffled. "I know. This sucks. I'm doing my best."

I heard her take a deep breath. "I'll try and be more patient."

"Thank you," I whispered, another tear silently falling down my face.

CHAPTER TWENTY-THREE

Kristy was already engrossed in her iPad when I collapsed the next day in my chair. Zack, the ever-obedient boyfriend, had been waiting by my car to help me to class. He sat my iPad down on the desk for me and gave me a quick kiss. "Hi, Kristy."

"Hey," she mumbled back.

He shrugged and said he'd see us at lunch.

Once he left, I turned around and asked, "Whatcha reading?"

Kristy rolled her eyes. "*The President's Daughter*. It's long and terrible. Why did you have to pick this?"

"I didn't realize it was like over 500 pages. *Sleeping Beauties* isn't much better. It makes no sense!"

"It's not supposed to. It's fantasy horror. What part of that would make sense?"

We glared at each other, which gave me time to meticulously assess her attire. She was wearing her typical ensemble that I was growing to love, a low-cut navy-blue T-shirt, and black skinny jeans. She even wore a black corded bracelet with the colors of the pansexual flag: pink, yellow, and blue. How had I not noticed that before?

"You look nice," I said breaking the silence.

"You do too. That dress looks good on you. Pink really is your color," she said speaking softly.

I smiled. My efforts paid off. This soft pink cap sleeved dress was the third one I tried on this morning.

"Can I toss your phone on the floor so I can get a repeat of the show you gave me yesterday?"

"Not my phone, that's too expensive. How about the iPad your boyfriend gave me? The case seems pretty indestructible."

She had to bring up Zack. It crashed me back to reality and stopped my brain from having steamy daydreams about removing Kristy's shirt. As I grappled with a response, Mrs. Jacobs took attendance, made a few announcements, and the bell rang.

I was the first to arrive at our lunch table. Kristy trailed in a few moments later. We spent creative writing class arguing over our collaborative writing paper, making no progress what-so-ever. *How did James Patterson and Bill Clinton make it work?*

"How was math?" she asked, sitting next to me.

"Horrible as always. Why do I have to take it? I'm going to be a writer."

"Why do we need most of what we learn in high school? Are we going to go out and dissect a worm in real life?"

I shuddered. "We better not."

Out of the corner of my eye I saw Zack striding toward us.

Zack kissed the top of my head. "Hey guys." He pulled

out the empty chair next to me and sat. I avoided looking at Kristy; I didn't want to be on the receiving end of her judgmental glare.

Dylan, Hannah, and Tyler soon arrived after. I chewed a piece of my sandwich when I felt a finger lightly circling my left knee cap. I gave a small yelp and jumped forward. There was no way that finger was Zack's, he was sitting on my right and both of his hands were accounted for. That meant only one thing.

"You okay?" Zack asked.

"Oh yea, thought I felt a bug on me. Must've been a loose hair!"

He went back to talking about the newest Zelda game for Nintendo Switch with Dylan and Tyler as I snuck a glance at Kristy. A smug grin was plastered on her face and her hand still rested on my knee. *No one could see it, right?*

I tried to take more bites of my sandwich but was incredibly distracted. Kristy motioned with her head to the door, and I nodded.

"I'll be back, gotta pee!" I said.

Kristy stood. "Wait, I'll come with you. Just in case you need help opening the doors."

Hannah's right eyebrow raised as we left. Hannah was usually my bathroom buddy. I'm sure she was judging me that I hadn't broken up with Zack but I honestly couldn't yet, not with Bryan breathing down my neck.

We barreled down the hallway as fast as I could on crutches. Suddenly Kristy veered towards a pair of double doors. I followed her without question in a dark nook under a set of stairs. Without a word, Kristy's lips grazed my own.

"Wait, someone could see us," I said softly, still an inch from her face.

"Has anyone told you that you worry too much?" Kristy asked, her right hand stroking my cheek.

"Once or twice." I leaned up against the wall for support and one of my crutches clattered to the floor.

"I've got you," Kristy whispered, wrapping her arm around me.

I happily leaned my body toward her, tipping my head up to meet her lips. Kissing Kristy made any questioning thoughts vacate my brain. Her lavender scent enveloped me, taking me to a sunny field full of purple flowers, a place where anything was possible.

A creaking sound abruptly brought me out of my daydream.

I whipped my head to the location of the sound and yelped. A crippling cold feeling enveloped my body. The worst person I could possibly fathom to see me in this position was standing before us. One of Bryan's arms was extended, his phone pointed in our direction.

"What the hell are you doing here?" I said, my voice raising.

Kristy unwrapped herself from me and reached her arm out to grab Bryan's phone but missed by a few inches.

"Too slow!" Bryan said as he sprinted out the double doors.

"I'll be right back!" Kristy said to me. She flung the door open and disappeared. I sunk to the floor, my other crutch clattering beside me and my foot with the boot extended.

My life was ruined.

Every single person would soon know I was a fraud and that I liked women. As I inched on the ground to grab one of my crutches, Kristy reappeared in the doorway, lips pursed with her hands on her hips. Her red angular hair fell into her face. "You lied to me."

My mouth dropped. "What're you talking about?"

"Bryan showed me the picture you texted him Saturday night from Zack's room. You said nothing happened!"

Bryan really was the worst.

"Nothing happened! Well, nothing really. I went up to Zack's room to make sure I didn't have any feelings for him, and I didn't."

"He had no shirt on," Kristy said flatly.

"But I was fully dressed! I wouldn't let him go any further."

"It didn't look like that in the picture. But who cares, you still lied. What else are you lying about?"

"Nothing, I swear!"

Kristy shook her head. "I wish I could believe you, but I don't." She opened the double door and turned back around. "By the way, Bryan still has a video of us. Just thought you should know, since you're so scared to have anyone find out."

I gasped. "You're only telling me this now? He could've already posted it on YouTube or TikTok!" *It was official. My life was over.*

"I don't care about the video. I want you and don't care who knows it," Kristy replied.

My face flushed. "You can't tell me that a video doesn't worry you."

She was wasting precious time. I needed to get that video back.

"You only care because Zack will find out. You're probably scared he's going to break up with you. I'm so done with this. Have fun with Zack." Kristy walked out the door.

"Wait!"

Kristy spun around and stared at me.

"I need help up." I gave her a desperate look. I was still sprawled out on the floor, legs splayed in different directions nowhere near my crutches.

"That's your response to we're done? Screw you." Kristy pushed the door open with both hands and disappeared from sight.

That did not go well. I should've responded that I wanted her, and I wouldn't care if Zack broke up with me, but you know what, I didn't want to. She was right about one thing; I wasn't ready for Zack not to be my boyfriend.

I liked the thought of Zack; he made me feel like I could have a normal senior year. He was safe; Kristy was not. I became reckless around her; Zack kept me grounded. Maybe this turn of events was for the best. I could focus more on school and graduating with great grades, not lurking around the halls making out with Kristy.

I needed to find Bryan ASAP to delete the video before it went viral but first things first, I had to somehow get off the floor. I crawled over to the left crutch and once it was safely in my hands, begun using that to bring the other crutch over to me. I wasn't having much luck. They were much heavier than I remembered, and my stupid leg with the boot kept me from crawling. I sighed and reached into my pocket for my phone. Dresses with pockets really were the best fashion invention, especially in dire times like this. I sent Hannah an SOS text and a few moments later the doors quickly opened.

Hannah gasped when she saw my disheveled state.

I was in the process of trying to hook the left crutch with my non-boot leg to bring it toward me.

"Are you okay?" she asked, rushing down to me.

"I'll be fine. I'm having some trouble getting up. But more importantly, Bryan filmed Kristy and I in a compromising position and I need to delete that video like now."

"Where did Kristy go?"

"Long story short, Bryan told her some stuff about me and now she's pissed."

Hannah held my gaze. "Is what he told her true?"

I looked down. "Yea, which is why she left me here."

Hannah reached for my left crutch and held out her right hand.

I grabbed hold, with my right crutch in my other hand. Once I was upright, Hannah helped position the crutches under my armpits. "Thanks so much. I owe you."

"That's what I'm here for." Hannah opened the door so I could hobble out. "Zack was wondering where you were. I said you weren't feeling well and that I had to check on you. To be honest, I really hate lying for you."

"That's not a lie, I'm not feeling good."

"Because of something you brought upon yourself. You made the choice to come in here with Kristy, even though you had a boyfriend waiting for you in the cafeteria," Hannah said, her voice sharp.

That stung.

"You should talk. What about you and Bryan?"

"You should've learned from my stupid mistake. And I didn't actually cheat on Tyler." Hannah put her hands on her hips.

My shoulders deflated. "I know. I'm sorry. I'm on edge. I didn't mean it."

Hannah squeezed my arm. "It's okay, you've got a lot going on right now. Let's go find Bryan."

As soon as I stepped foot into the cafeteria, the bell rang. I moved to the side to avoid the barrage of students headed my way. I frantically attempted to look at each person passing me by, but spotting Bryan was hopeless. It might have been too late anyways.

"Are you okay? You were gone so long," Zack stated coming alongside me.

If Zack was still talking to me, that meant Bryan didn't share the video yet. I still had time to stop him.

I leaned over and kissed Zack. "I'm feeling much better now."

He gave me a large smile. "Oh, good. I was worried. I

brought your stuff from the table." He motioned to my iPad and my bubble gum pink lunchbox in his hands.

Getting a glimpse of my lunchbox reminded me of Kristy. Eating my PB&J sandwich with Kristy's finger teasing me seemed like a lifetime ago. A wave of regret hit me like a truck.

What did I do? Yes, Kristy made me act irrationally but that was only because I wanted to spend every single second of my day with her. *Was that so wrong?* And maybe if we didn't have to be some big dirty secret, I wouldn't have behaved so recklessly.

If I hadn't felt so guilty about being with a girl, I wouldn't have tried to see if I had an attraction to Zack. But instead, I made the wrong decision by going to his room and lied to the one person I wanted to be with. *And now she hated me.*

I gave a half-hearted smile up at Zack. I had trouble meeting his eye.

Zack was the comfortable choice. I thought I had a crush on him because he made me smile. But my steamy daydreams were certainly not about him. If Kristy had never come along, I would have settled for Zack, but now that I knew what real attraction felt like it was hard to settle for less.

I tried to discreetly catch Bryan's attention in history, but he completely ignored me. And at the end of the lesson Bryan slipped out before I had a chance to even get out of my chair. *These crutches were going to be the death of me.*

In bio, Kristy sat as far as humanly possible away from me while still at our lab table. If she moved her chair an inch more, she'd be in the aisle.

I turned to her. "I'm really sorry. I made a mistake."

Kristy placed her thumb on the iPad to unlock it and kept her head down.

"I know you hear me. Can we at least talk this through?"

Still nothing. She was now scrolling through her unread emails, not stopping to read any.

It was as if she was deaf or mute or both.

At the end of class, Kristy quickly gathered up all her stuff and shot out of her seat. On her way out the door she said over her shoulder, "Have fun with Zack tonight, although he deserves someone better than you."

Bryan overheard her comment and laughed uncontrollably. "Lover's spat?" he asked, coming over to me to my chair.

"Thanks to you, my entire life is now over. Can you *please* delete the video?"

"Hell no! That's the best piece of evidence I have on you." An evil grin appeared on his face. "Now I officially own you. I didn't think you would make things so easy."

A shiver ran down my back. *What did he mean?*

"Why did you have to show Kristy the pic of me and Zack?"

"Didn't you hear? I want to ruin your life. I could tell you were still going to see her even if you had a boyfriend. You shouldn't be so happy when I'm miserable. Now things are even more complicated for you." Bryan bared his teeth; his creepy grin couldn't get any wider if he tried.

Hannah appeared by my side.

"Oh look, it's your lacky Hannah. You better watch your back too. We'll see how long Tyler stays with you once I tell him what you and I did," Bryan said as he marched out the door.

Hannah's face paled. She turned to me. "He wouldn't, right?"

We walked down the hallway for a couple seconds at an extremely slow pace thanks to my crutches when I blurted out, "What happened between you and Bryan?"

Hannah chewed on her lip. "We went a little further than making out before the party on Saturday."

I gaped at her.

"Like sex?" I asked. When I was with Bryan, I had to do everything in my power to push him away. I couldn't believe Hannah willingly chose to be with him.

"Not completely, no. But more than I should have."

I rubbed my chin. "I take it you haven't told Tyler."

"Not yet. I will, I promise. But I was waiting until he trusted me again."

"If you don't say anything and he finds out from Bryan, he's going to trust you even less. You need to tell him. You were broken up at that point so it's not cheating but if you don't tell him, it's lying."

A tear trickled down Hannah's face. "I know. I've already done so much to mess up our relationship. I'm so scared he's going to break up with me again."

I grabbed Hannah's hand. "I have a plan. Why don't we have Zack invite him over to his house tonight after marching band so you two can talk and I won't be that far away. You can tell your mom you have homework for Mr. Ricardo's class with Zack and me."

"I don't know if my mom will buy that, but I'd kill to see Zack's house!" Hannah replied.

I texted Zack part of our idea. Didn't want him to spill our full plan to Tyler. Only a couple seconds went by before he responded that Tyler could come over.

"Now you have to convince your parents. How can I help?"

"Maybe if you follow me to my house after practice and drive me? That way my mom knows you're going to be there. I can't believe I'm finally going to see Zack's house!" Hannah said, excitement in her voice.

"Go team!" I gave her a high five. I was secretly happy my

idea made Hannah smile again. She didn't need to know she was also helping me out because now I'd have her and Tyler around as an excuse in case Zack wanted to go further.

CHAPTER TWENTY-FOUR

The only positive outcome that came out of spraining my ankle was getting out of marching at band practice. I still had to sit in the stands and *watch* the rest of the band make formations, but when Mr. Smith wasn't looking, I completed my homework assignments. For once, I didn't feel super behind in all my schoolwork by being at practice.

In between chapters, I gazed onto the field at my trumpet section. Cashi was doing an impressive job at filling in my missing spot, so much so it was like I wasn't supposed to be there. *Crap.* That reminded me, I still needed to find a time to meet with him about his ideas for the school year.

I scanned the rest of the field. Erin was in front of the band with the rest of the guard girls, throwing her baton in the air. She flawlessly caught it and gave a dazzling smile. Since she deemed herself head of the guard, she was the only one that had a shockingly short blue and white skirt and tight top exposing her midriff. All the other girls wore blue and white dresses with the hem coming to the knee. The outfits had to be from like the nineties because the white really wasn't that white anymore.

Erin always got away with everything. Maybe I'd get lucky, and she'd do a flip to keep me entertained. Even though Erin made me want to tear my hair out, I couldn't deny she was hot, and it wasn't like I was going to see any other action any time soon.

After practice was over, I spotted Cashi walking to his car. I called his name a couple of times. After the third time, he made a head nod and headed my way with his trumpet in tow. His dark black hair was gelled, and he was dressed nicer than most of the guys at band, a plain navy-blue polo and khaki shorts.

"Hey, Shorty. How's your ankle?" he said, pushing up his glasses.

I motioned to my crutches and boot. "I'm not in as much pain but I can't wait until I lose these."

He placed his trumpet case on the ground. "I bet. The section misses you."

"You guys look great."

"We'd be better if you were able to march." He raised his eyebrows. "So, what's up?"

I clenched and unclenched my hands. "Want to find a time to talk about student council stuff?"

"Sure! I have some great ideas I think you'll really like. Are you free tomorrow night?" he asked, his face lighting up.

"I can come over after I'm finished at the newspaper."

"Great! I can have my mom make us dinner and then we can talk about my ideas."

"Yes, please. I remember your mom's food being the best. Oh, and I'm kinda vegetarian now."

"Really? Guess it's been a while since we hung out," Cashi said twisting his mouth to the side.

Cashi lived across the street and my parents were friendly

with the Patels. Cashi and I had been the best of friends in elementary and middle school. We hung out together all the time, especially on snow days. We'd roll up large balls for the snowman we started to make but never actually finished. By the time we were working on the snowman's midsection, one of us would throw a snowball at each other, and the snowman was suddenly forgotten. The day would end with Mrs. Patel serving us large cups of steaming hot cocoa with large, fluffy marshmallows that I would slowly sip to savor each drop.

Our families always joked we were going to end up together, but then high school happened. Even though we were in the trumpet section together, we drifted apart. I started dating Tyler and instead of going to Cashi's every night after school, my nights became filled with seeing Tyler and schoolwork. Then last year when we both ran for Student Council President we stopped talking, but it seemed like Cashi got over the fact I won. Maybe we really could be friends again.

"Vegetarian is no problem for my mom."

"Can't wait!" I said giving him a huge smile.

Cashi saw Zack and Tyler headed our way. He picked up his trumpet case. "See you tomorrow!"

As soon as Tyler and Zack reached me, Tyler glanced toward Cashi hurrying away. "Woah, you and Cashi are talking? I thought you guys hated each other?"

"That was so last year. He doesn't really seem that upset I won president. He came up with some ideas he wants to talk over Thursday."

Zack's face looked conflicted. "Oh, cool."

Hannah appeared. "What'd I miss?"

"Cashi and I might be friends again?" I said, clapping my hands together.

"That's great news! Cashi's so nice." Hannah took a deep breath. "We should go convince my mom to let me hang out with you guys. Tyler, I really need to talk to you tonight," Hannah said with furrowed eyebrows.

"Oh," Tyler said, his face turning grim.

"Hannah let's go work our magic. See you soon guys!" I said hobbling away with Hannah in tow.

CHAPTER TWENTY-FIVE

It wasn't as hard as we thought sweet talking Hannah's mother to let her come over and *study* with me. Not going to lie, most parents loved me. I really didn't seem all that threatening and usually was a good influence, until I started secretly sneaking around with a hot girl.

I pulled into Zack's long driveway, where Tyler's blue Honda Civic was already parked.

"So that's what his house looks like," Hannah said in awe, gazing out the window at Zack's massive house.

"Wait till you see the inside. Who knew houses like this existed in Dale City?" I said shaking my head.

We stepped out of the car. "I can't do this. Tyler's going to kill me when he finds out what I did," Hannah said, rubbing the palm of her hands on her dark blue skinny jeans.

"Yes, you can. And I'll be here for you," I said, looking her square in the face. "And he was seeing Erin too, so it's not like he's all innocent."

"I know. I guess I should suck it up and get it over with," Hannah replied.

We walked up the brick pathway leading to his door. I had

to be careful not to get my crutches stuck in the cracks. I rang the doorbell and after a minute the door opened to reveal both Zack and Tyler. Tyler had a blank look on his face, probably dreading the worst. No guy wanted to hear that their girl wanted to talk.

"Thanks for coming over," Zack said giving me a quick hug.

Hannah and Tyler also hugged, and he gave her a quick kiss on the lips.

I looked away. "Zack, where can Hannah and Tyler go to be more alone?"

"They can take the basement and we can go into my room."

Of course we would take the bedroom. Maybe if we talked the whole time it wouldn't have to lead to anything else?

Tyler nodded, reached for Hannah's hand, and led her away.

She turned back to give me one last look and I gave her a thumbs up.

We climbed the stairs to Zack's room. Each time I took a step forward, it felt like I was one minute closer to my life sentence. *Is this what I wanted?* I could tell him the truth and then plead for Kristy to take me back. Then I thought about my parents' disapproving faces if they saw the video of me and Kristy. I couldn't have them kick me out and not pay for college when I was so close to graduating. I sighed when we reached the top and entered his room. *My fate was sealed. I had to accept that and get on with the lie.*

Zack led me to his bed, but I pulled him back toward his couch.

"We have plenty of time for that. I feel like we haven't talked much lately," I stated.

"Oh, okay. What do you want to talk about?"

I took a deep breath and realized I had absolutely nothing

to say to him. With Kristy, I could find a million topics to talk about like what books we wanted to read or movies to watch, but with Zack, I'd rather actually watch a movie and have the least amount of interaction possible. He made me feel safe because he didn't challenge me. When we were *friends* we'd make fun of each other. Now that we had each other, there was nothing to say. This moment would have been the perfect time to break up with him, but that video and my insecurities were still hanging around in my head.

"I've been meaning to ask you, what's the deal with Kristy? You hang out with her more than Hannah these days. Is she your new best friend?" Zack asked.

He was even providing me the perfect opening, but I couldn't take it. "She's actually not talking to me. I guess I offended her or something."

"Weird. She seemed cool. Maybe you'll make up like you and Hannah did?"

"I don't know." *I already missed her sarcastic comments.*

"I'm happy we're alone," Zack said, moving closer to me and pinning me against the side of the couch's armrest. He pressed his body against me, and his lips met mine. After a couple of minutes, it was obvious how very happy he was to see me. *Why couldn't I feel the same way?*

As we kissed, my thoughts turned to Hannah and Tyler. *Was everything going okay?* I didn't hear any screaming or crying, but then again, they *were* in the basement.

I pulled away. "Should we check on Hannah and Tyler? Hannah had to talk to him about something serious and I'm worried."

"Mmmm they'll be fine," Zack mumbled as he began sucking on my neck. He'd better not leave a mark for Kristy to see, or my parents.

"I'm going to check my phone real quick."

Zack continued to kiss my neck as I reached down into my

purse. I prayed for any new messages that could pull me away from Zack. Praise be to God, there was one! I read it to Zack.

> We're going to need some more time. Still working things out. 😖

I inwardly sighed. *Guess Tyler was not taking it too well. He really did have trouble with change.*

"Maybe I should go see if Hannah needs to talk? Or I could try talking to Tyler?"

"That might make whatever is going on between them worse. Let's take advantage of our alone time. They'll text us if they need us," Zack said as he pushed back the hair from my neck and began kissing it again. *What was with the neck thing? A hickey was the last thing I needed.*

I moved him away from my neck and brought my lips to meet his. I tried imagining Kristy as the person I was kissing but it didn't work very well. Their kissing styles were completely different, as were their smells. I enjoyed getting a whiff of Zack's aftershave, but it couldn't compete with Kristy's distinct lavender scent. Zack groaned and kept attempting to move my hand to the front of his pants. I would lay my hand there for a couple minutes and then move it to wrap around his back.

After what felt like an hour, but only was fifteen minutes since the last time I snuck a peek at my watch, Zack's fingers fumbled with the back of my dress and started to slowly unzip. My gut reacted and I jumped off the couch.

"What's wrong?" Zack asked alarmed.

It was time to play my final card. "I'm saving myself."

Zack's eyes grew wide. "What? Really? But you've had so many boyfriends!"

"That doesn't mean anything."

Zack's face turned serious. "I didn't realize."

"If that's a problem, you've got to let me know."

Zack shook his head. "I'm not that shallow, I had no clue. Not even with Bryan?"

"Especially not with Bryan. It's why he got pissed and broke up with me. I have Christian values to uphold," I said, lying through my teeth.

"You should've told me sooner; I wouldn't have tried anything."

I stared at my hands. "I was embarrassed."

I was hoping this time I'd want to break *my values. Funny thing was I finally wanted to, but not with him.*

Zack and I discussed my boundaries some more when my phone thankfully vibrated, and Hannah said they were finally done talking. We found them all smiles with their clothes disheveled. *Huh, that was surprising given Hannah's earlier text.*

I insisted we watch the newest *She-Hulk* episode on Disney+. During the show Zack held my hand but didn't try anything further. Maybe this whole saving myself schtick would work for a couple weeks until I figured out what I wanted to do.

On my way to drop Hannah off, I inquired how her conversation with Tyler went.

"At first he was upset but I brought up the point he also had been with Erin at the time, so it wasn't like I was doing anything wrong. I was just trying to be honest, which made him start to open up to me more. He told me more about how he was only with Erin to help forget about me, which is exactly why I was with Bryan. That helped him understand where I was coming from."

I smiled. I'm glad they were able to work through it without too much of a mess.

"We both promised to tell each other the truth from now on and actually talk when issues come up."

I nodded. "Smart plan." *If only I had done that with Kristy before I lost her.*

I made it home again before my mom arrived, but only by a few minutes. I barely had time to warm up and gobble down the veggie pizza and salad my mom left in the fridge for me when I heard her pull into the driveway. I ran into my room to pretend I was working on the newspaper advice column due tomorrow. Since I hadn't heard from Kristy all night, I assumed I would be writing it on my own. I ran my eyes over the last sentence I'd written earlier, *the riskiest things are sometimes the best,* when I heard my mom call, "Sam?"

"In my room!"

My mom appeared in my doorway. "How was school and marching band practice honey?"

"Oh, you know, fine. I got a lot of homework done watching them rehearse."

My mom's face erupted in a smile. "Good! How's Kristy?"

"She's good, I think. I didn't see her much since she's not in marching band." *Did she have to bring up the one person I didn't want to think about?*

"Your dad wants you to tell her she's welcome to work at his store anytime. He was very impressed with her work ethic."

And now I had to contact her?

I sighed. "I'll text her and let her know."

"Can you also see if she wants to work soon?"

"Can't Dad ask her? I'm not her assistant," I said, my tone sharper than I intended.

Her forehead creased. "He can do that, I just thought it would be easier since you were her friend."

"It's better if he talks to her. I'll let her know to expect a call from Dad." *The last thing I wanted to do right now was text Kristy asking her to work at my parents' store, who were the reason I was afraid to be with her in the first place.*

"How's your new boyfriend Zack? When are we going to meet his parents?" *She really was testing my patience.*

I gritted my teeth. "He's fine. I haven't thought that far ahead yet."

"Well, invite him over here sometime so we can at least meet him!"

"Okay, someday," I replied, my eyes glued to my iPad.

Not if I could help it.

CHAPTER TWENTY-SIX

I woke up the next day hoping everything was one bad nightmare and more importantly, that Kristy would talk to me again. Homeroom proved that would not be the case. She didn't even raise her eyes to meet mine when I said hi. I'd texted her last night to expect a call from my dad and all I got back was *k*.

In creative writing I tried again. "You can't not talk to me. We have a paper to write together." *I didn't want to get a terrible grade because of this fight.*

"Try me. I'm sick of being hurt," Kristy said, still not looking up.

"I'm sorry and want to make up for it. I'm not like Talia."

"You hurt me when you lied to me."

I already felt bad enough, why did she have to keep bringing up the lying?

"I know I should have told you. I'm sorry. Can we start over? I won't lie again, I promise," I pleaded.

"Are you still with Zack?" She finally lifted her gaze to meet mine and it was stone cold.

"Yes." *Even though I desperately wished I wasn't.*

"Then no. Until you break up with him, I won't even consider seeing you. I'm not some dirty secret."

"What about this paper? I can't flunk. I'm going to be a communications major."

"I don't want to fail either. We can put it in a Google doc and edit that way."

"What? And have no plan?"

"Should've thought about that before you screwed me over," Kristy replied, eyes still down.

I turned around, livid. How dare she attempt to mess up my grade. How was this paper going to work?

At lunch I said hi to Hannah, who was the first to arrive at our table. I sat in my normal seat, waiting to see if Kristy would sit next to me. When she appeared in the cafeteria doorway, she avoided eye contact with everyone and sat at a table that held a couple of band guys.

Dylan slid into the chair next to her, a smile on his face. The rest of the guys gave them a shocked look, probably identical to the look on my face. *What was going on?*

Zack sat at his usual seat next to me. "Why are Kristy and Dylan over there?"

"I have no clue. Kristy still isn't talking to me, which is going to be horrible for my creative writing grade."

"Did you ask her what her problem is?"

I pondered what to say back to him when Hannah saved me. "Thanks for having me over last night Zack."

"Oh yea, it's no problem. Glad you and Tyler are finally good again."

"Me too, we need more double dates together," I said. *It would make hanging out with Zack a heck of a lot easier.*

"I agree," Tyler said as he descended into his seat and slung his arm around Hannah's. He gave her a kiss on the cheek and her face lit up. Even an extra spark shone in her eyes as soon as Tyler had appeared.

"Hey there," she said turning her face toward Tyler's and kissing him directly on the lips.

I looked away and held back a sigh. I wanted that. To be that excited to see the person I was dating. Not dreading setting up a date or devising plans to get out of seeing them. And even if I was with a girl that made me happy, would I even let them kiss me in public? Would I ever be able to enjoy these simple pleasures and feel comfortable being myself?

I peered around the cafeteria until I found my target, who already had his eyes locked on me. Bryan took his index finger and middle finger, pointed them to his eyes and then pointed them in my direction. As if I didn't already know he was always watching. I was waiting for the day I would wake up and find him in my bed watching me sleep. Couldn't he find a new obsession?

I turned my attention back to the lunch conversation. Zack and Tyler were comparing notes on their progress in the Zelda game they were obsessed with, and Hannah stared worriedly at me. "Are you doing okay?" Hannah whispered across the table.

I shrugged my shoulders. "I mean, I kinda have to be. I don't know what else to do."

"Maybe we can steal Bryan's phone?"

"Trust me, I've thought about it, but I don't know his password."

"Have you heard from Kristy?" Hannah continued to whisper.

I shifted to look at Zack. He was making tons of hand motions and I kept hearing the word Link. *Reminder to myself, if I ever wanted him distracted, ask a Zelda question.*

I leaned toward Hannah and said under my breath, "No. I need to forget about her. That chapter of my life is over."

Hannah frowned. "I don't think that's how it works."

"It's the only way right now for me to get through senior year."

Thinking about hacking into Bryan's phone reminded me of the texts Kristy and I had sent each other. There were quite a few I needed to delete in case my parents or Zack accidently looked at my phone. My heart dropped thinking of those texts from Kristy.

Would I ever receive ones from her again that said *Hot tub time?* or *Miss your face* ?

CHAPTER TWENTY-SEVEN

That night after the newspaper staff meeting was over, I found myself knocking on Cashi's door almost in tears. I couldn't stop thinking about how I messed things up. I still had a thread of hope that Kristy would rush into the newspaper staff meeting at the last minute and offer to help with the advice column, but my life wasn't a Hallmark movie, so of course, she was a no show.

When Mr. T and Mr. Ricardo asked where she was all I could do was shrug. They even liked the answer I created for my fake question, since no one submitted one yet. The advice column was here to stay, and I was the sole author.

What I really needed was the answer to all my problems, not spending my time helping everyone else with theirs.

"Hey! Come in," Cashi said as he opened the door.

I walked in and automatically slipped off my one sandal, which proved to be difficult clutching crutches.

"You remembered my mom's anal habit," Cashi said, smiling.

"Guess there are some things you don't forget."

"True, especially since she'll run after you if you take one step off the mat with any type of shoe on."

I laughed. "It's nice to know some things don't change. Unfortunately, she'd have to pry this stupid boot off me."

Cashi frowned. "It sucks you still have that on."

I shrugged. "I'm getting used to it by now."

I attempted to follow Cashi back to the kitchen. Each time I took a step, my crutches hit the linoleum floor causing echoes to fill the hallway. I cringed. Anyone would be able to hear me coming a mile away.

"Sam! When Cashi told me you were coming over I couldn't believe it," Mrs. Patel stated. Her straight black hair was up in a bun, and she wore a stylish navy-blue suit. Whenever I'd asked Cashi what Mrs. Patel did for a living, he'd shrug and say, *business stuff*. It had to be something important though because she was always dressed to impress.

"Yeah, it's been a bit."

"Cashi said you're vegetarian now?"

"Kind of. I don't eat much meat if I can help it."

"I made a vegetable korma curry that hopefully isn't too spicy for you. Please, have a seat. Dinner's ready." Mrs. Patel motioned to an open chair at their dining room table. She passed me a basket filled with steaming naan that glistened with oil and garlic.

Mr. Patel was already sitting at the head of the table wearing a button-down brown shirt and khaki pants. A few gray hairs were mixed in with his slightly thinning, slicked back black hair. He nodded toward me. He didn't talk much, similar to my father.

I used my fork to take a large portion of the curry and as soon as the sauce reached my tongue, I let out a small sound of approval. It was the best curry I had ever tasted, even better than our local Indian place. I could taste so many different flavors all at once, even with the spice.

Mrs. Patel quizzed me on my life the whole-time during dinner. She wanted to know the classes I was taking, what teachers I had, and my favorite subject. I needed to come over here more and not just for the curry. I couldn't remember the last time I had a family meal where the three of us would sit together at the table and talk about our day.

After dinner, Cashi had me follow him into his room. His mom didn't even make us leave the door open. He gestured for me to sit at his desk, and he plopped down on a plaid bedspread. The room hadn't changed much since our middle school days—still wall to wall books, with one corner dedicated for his music stand and trumpet.

Cashi stared at me. "Are you okay? You looked like you were about to cry when I answered the door."

I cringed. "Was it that noticeable?"

Cashi's eyebrows scrunched together. "You're usually so happy but you looked like someone died. What's going on?"

"I don't want to bore you with the stupid details of my messed-up life."

"Try me."

Was I ready to talk about my problems, especially with Cashi of all people?

"Maybe later. Can we work on school stuff first?"

Cashi gave me a long look with his dark brown eyes and then nodded. He gave a really detailed summary of all the ideas he had for the school year starting with homecoming.

I sat there and shook my head in agreement. I offered some input, but he had everything so well thought out. We looked at dates for our first student council meeting and devised a plan of attack. It was great having his help. Cashi made everything seem less daunting.

Maybe it would be okay to talk to him about what's been going on. He didn't seem to hold a grudge against me.

I took a deep breath. "The reason I was so upset when I

first got here is I got into a big fight with the new girl Kristy. And I think I totally messed up whatever was between us."

"What do you mean whatever was between you?"

Here went nothing.

"I was starting to like her more than friends and we made out a couple times, but she's super pissed at me because I haven't broken up with Zack. I was scared to tell her the real reason I haven't left Zack; Bryan keeps threatening me he's going to tell my parents I'm gay if I don't stay with Zack." I spewed out all of this information as fast as I could, so I didn't have to prolong my embarrassment.

"Woah, Shorty, that's so messed up. Not that you have feelings for Kristy, but what Bryan is doing."

"Yea," I said looking down at my feet. "I'm so confused about myself and stuck in this boring relationship with Zack."

"For what it's worth, not sure if you knew, but I'm gay."

My head shot up. "Wait what? I had no idea!" *Cashi was gay? Since when? I never even heard any rumors about it.*

"I'm not officially out at school but I bit the bullet last year and told my parents."

"Oh my god, really? How did that go?"

"The whole time I felt like I was going to throw up but I'm still alive to talk about it, so it didn't go that bad."

"I'm so impressed that you told them! What did they say?"

Cashi rolled his eyes. "My mom is still convinced it's a *phase* I'll grow out of, and my dad never mentions it. My mom still tries to suggest girls for me to date. Your name comes up a lot."

"That has to be so frustrating."

"It is but to be honest, it's been better since I told them. I don't feel like I'm constantly hiding something from them."

"That I get." My voice broke. *I wanted to talk about how it felt like I was hiding myself from everyone in my life, but I didn't think I could keep talking about myself without crying.*

Instead I diverted the attention. "I seriously had no idea you were gay."

"It's not like there has been anyone for me to date anyways at Dale, so I keep it on the down-low and make myself busy, like running for Student Council President," Cashi said, his voice trailing off. *And there was the elephant in the room.*

"I'm so sorry," I said, going over to where he was sitting. I plopped down next to him and took his hand into mine.

"What? Why?" Cashi asked, continuing to hold my hand.

"That I became president over you. I had no idea you wanted it that much." I pulled my hand away and put them over my face.

"Hey, it's okay. I'm not mad. You involving me in the planning today has been great. We can keep working on it together," Cashi said.

I placed my head on his shoulder. "Thank you. I've missed you. No wonder we've gotten along so well, there was no chance of either of us liking each other more than friends."

"I've missed you too. But you shouldn't have to hide yourself to everyone. Have you thought about telling your parents?"

"I can't do that!" I said straightening.

"Why not? What's the worst that could happen?"

"They could cut me off and I can't go to college. Or even worse, kick me out and I could be homeless."

"Shorty, have you met your parents? They wouldn't do that."

"I don't know. They might. How do you keep it a secret at school?"

"I'm not keeping it a secret on purpose, I just haven't been interested in anyone."

"Then how did you know you were gay?"

He raised his eyebrow. "I get excited when I see a guy

shirtless. I get obsessed with cute guys I meet, and I've never once wanted to kiss a girl."

That sounded almost like me but with girls.

"I guess that would do it. I hadn't officially realized I was gay or whatever I am until I met Kristy. Why didn't I know sooner?"

"Everyone figures it out differently. I was a freshman when I got a crush on Tyler and that's how I knew."

My eyes widened. "Really? Tyler?"

"Yep. He's cute and nerdy, my type. That's why I stopped hanging out with you once you started dating him. I knew I'd never actually be with him, and it hurt too much to see you guys together."

"I had no idea. I thought it was something I did."

"Nope. You were even nice and invited me along with you guys, but it was too weird."

"I wish I knew that was the reason you stopped hanging out with me. We could have done stuff without Tyler."

"I should've come out to you sooner, but I had no idea you were also gay. That would have made it easier for me."

"Join the club."

"What are you going to do about Bryan?"

"He's not bothered me as much since Kristy blew me off. Maybe he'll forget?"

Cashi twisted his mouth to the side. "Hate to tell you this but Bryan doesn't seem like the kind of guy to forget anything. He called me *four eyes* the entire way through middle school. He still sometimes says that when he sees me."

"Really? He's such an ass."

"Speaking of, tell me more about this Bryan blackmail situation."

I shrugged. "Not much else to tell. He hates me and Zack so much that he wants me to stay with Zack right now and if not, he'll leak the video of Kristy and I kissing."

"I don't get though why you have to be with Zack."

"I guess because I wasn't really attracted to Bryan. It made him feel crappy, so he wants Zack to feel that way too."

"Guys aren't as dumb as you think. They can tell when you don't want to be with them."

"I say it's because I'm waiting to have sex."

"That excuse will only last so long."

"I'm banking on that Bryan forgets about this blackmail scheme and I can eventually break up with Zack under the radar."

"Make sure you have a plan B in case he doesn't."

"I will. Thanks for listening to me," I said giving Cashi a huge hug.

Even if Kristy wasn't talking to me anymore, at least there was one more person in this world who could understand how conflicted and confused I was feeling. That would have to be enough for me until I figured out what to do next.

CHAPTER TWENTY-EIGHT

Weeks went by without Kristy giving me the time of day. I tried everything to get her to speak to me, even when I *accidentally* dropped my lunch bag in front of her in the cafeteria and expertly bent over to pick it up. That might have been the same day I was wearing a low-cut dress, but that didn't even work. Kristy's eyes were glued on Dylan who was chatting her up at her new lunch table.

I also became comfortable having Zack always by my side and I didn't hate it as much. I even looked forward to going over to his house after school to watch the latest episode of *She-Hulk* in his movie theater room. He hadn't tried anything more than kissing since I told him I was waiting.

I only had two more days left with my boot and crutches and then I was back to marching band, but I was still being forced to watch everyone rehearse so I could *learn* my part from the stands. As they finished up the last song of the night, I scrolled through my Instagram feed waiting for the evening to end so I could go home and finish the newest assignment from Mr. T.

Since Kristy and I weren't on speaking terms, our collaborative paper for Mr. T was disjointed and didn't make any sense, so much so we got a C. I've never gotten a C before in my life. I asked Mr. T how I could improve my grade and he suggested writing a story that explained what went wrong with our paper. *Boy did I have a story to tell him.*

I gathered up my belongings on the stands so I could get home as soon as possible to start on my story, when the band started playing another song. *Are you serious?* I thought rehearsal was finished for the night. Plus, this song wasn't a part of the routine. It sounded like *Yet To Come* from BTS, one of my favorite bands. And they weren't marching; the bells of their instruments were pointed towards ... me.

As the band wrapped up the song, Zack dropped his drum set on the ground and rushed off to the sidelines. When he reappeared, he was clutching at least a dozen pink roses. *This can't be good.* He jogged up to where I was sitting, kneeled on one knee, and said, "Shorty, will you go to homecoming with me?"

The entire marching band was awaiting my response; there was no way I could say no.

"Okay." I smiled as large as possible, hoping it looked real. I should've known this would happen sooner than later, but why did he have to make such a big spectacle of asking me? This wasn't the freaking prom.

"She said yes!" Zack screamed to the band and everyone, except Erin and Cashi, clapped. *Could Zack not be so excited? It wasn't like I said I'd marry him.*

Once everyone quieted down, Zack helped me up. "I can't wait! Let me know what color your dress is, and I'll get a matching corsage for you."

"It's going to be pink. No question about that."

There was only the question of whether it was him I wanted to go with but there was no backing out now. I'd been going back and forth the past couple of weeks, trying to figure out if I could dump Zack on the downlow. I thought Bryan wouldn't notice. But now, once again, I committed myself to something else with Zack. At this point, I had no other homecoming options, except for a couple of guys that would flirt with me when Zack wasn't around, and I really didn't want to go to my senior homecoming alone or with some other random guy.

At home I settled down on my bed, brainstorming how I'd respond to Mr. T's assignment. I wasn't sure how many details to give Mr. T. Plus things weren't as terrible and I didn't want Mr. T making them worse. Then I remembered my awful grade.

Screw it. I decided to detail out my whole account of what had happened but change the names to protect the innocent and guilty, aka Bryan. My grade depended on it. My fingers furiously flew over the keyboard. After an hour, I put in the finishing touches and typed *The End.* I could have Hannah review what I wrote but a better idea came to my mind. Mr. Ricardo told me if I ever needed someone to talk to, he was there for me. I didn't know how I felt about the whole talking thing, but maybe I could show him what I wrote, and he could let me know if it was good enough to raise my grade in Mr. T's class.

As I reread my work, my phone vibrated. I glanced at my phone and gasped.

> Phase 2 of making Shorty's life a nightmare.
> Break Zack's heart like you did mine. You
> and I are going to homecoming together.

What? How could that be? He was with Erin.

> What happened with Erin?

> She was annoying.

> Why me? You broke up with me.

> U didn't put out. Maybe I can turn you back to being straight.

My mouth dropped. No, no, no. My life had settled and I was in a reasonable routine. He couldn't snap his fingers and expect me to get back together with him and *put out*. That wasn't happening. This was too much.

I wanted to build a fort under my covers and never leave. Going to homecoming with Bryan would hurt Zack more than anything and he didn't deserve that. But what could I do? Bryan might show the video of Kristy and I to our whole school and even worse, to my parents. I didn't even have Kristy anymore to run to if anyone did find out. I could be shunned, ridiculed, and possibly kicked out of my house. But then I started to think about the alternative, having Bryan own every single aspect of my life. The thought of dating him again and having him possibly touch me turned my stomach. *Would it be so bad if everyone knew about me?* It had to be better than being stuck with someone blackmailing me to be with him.

Most of the lies that I had to tell recently were because of Bryan. I couldn't live like that anymore. Being scared of who I liked and who I really was. I also didn't want to continue my pattern of hurting people, especially now I knew the reason I never liked the guys I dated. No one deserved that, especially Zack.

I squinted through my teary eyes at what I had written. I was so done with hiding and Bryan's threats, so I made a split decision and changed all the names back to everyone involved. I took a screenshot of Bryan's texts and didn't return his message. Enough was enough. There would be consequences for not responding to Bryan but at this point I didn't care. I needed to tell Zack everything before Bryan got to him first.

CHAPTER TWENTY-NINE

"I need to talk," I said as I approached Mr. Ricardo after class the next day.

Mr. Ricardo looked up from reading a piece of paper on his desk. "Oh? About what?"

"Everything. Why I've been off my game, why I got an awful grade in Mr. T's collaborative writing project, and why I feel like I have no control over my life." I took a deep breath. "To be honest, I need some advice. Things are not going as planned." My voice broke as I spoke.

Earlier that day Hannah and Zack both kept asking me what was wrong, but I said I was fine. I didn't want to further involve them in my mess until I had a solid plan. I could tell neither of them believed me, but they let it alone.

At lunch I almost warned Kristy, who still sat with Dylan, what was about to go down, but when I neared her table, she shot me daggers, so I steered clear. Kristy's hand was on Dylan's arm, and he gazed at her with a smitten expression. *Did she move on already or was she doing that to hurt me?*

"I'm sorry to hear that. Do you want to talk after newspaper tonight?" Mr. Ricardo asked.

"Works for me. I better go before Mr. Paul calls me out." I hobbled out the door. Today was the last day that I had to wear this blasted boot. *Finally!*

Kristy saw me enter bio and averted her eyes as I sat next to her.

"I know you're listening to me, even if you don't show it. Bryan is being a douche again, so who knows what is going to happen but this time I'm going to defend myself. I wanted to warn you in case something blows up, like him sending the video of us out to everyone."

Kristy raised her eyes to meet mine. "What did he do now?"

That was the first time she had spoken to me in weeks. I tried to not get my hopes up. It had to mean she still cared, right?

"Don't worry about it. I also wanted to say I'm sorry. I've been awful but I'm going to try and find a way to make it up to you. I promise." I held her gaze. I thought I saw a glint of warmth, but it lingered for only a second.

"There isn't anything you can do. You made your choice. I get it. You want to do the easy thing and fake being straight. Well, I won't be there when you realize it's harder than you think." Kristy looked back down at the iPad.

"I don't want to lie anymore. I'm tired of not being happy."

I was about to expand more when Mr. Paul began talking. It was probably better that way.

After bio was over, I lightly touched Kristy's arm and pleaded, "Please, don't give up on me yet. I made the wrong choice at Zack's party, but I know what I need to do now."

"We'll see, Sam. If you're still with Zack, then no, we aren't talking," Kristy said pulling away and slipping out the door.

I gave an aggravated sigh. *She's not even using my nickname anymore.*

"I never heard back from you, Shorty. When are you breaking the news to Zack?" Bryan asked, slinging his arm around my shoulders.

Where did he come from? I didn't even hear him sneak up to me.

Bryan looked down at me. "What, are you not talking to me now? I could shout out your secret and show your parents that their sweet Shorty isn't as innocent as they thought. I have solid proof to back it up."

Do not engage. It would also make things worse. I could feel the sweat staining the underarms of my dress. Could I rewind time and never date him? I also couldn't figure out what to say back to him that would make him stop talking but I also didn't want to appease him. We were *not* going to homecoming together, that I knew for a fact.

"What's going on?" Hannah asked, coming up behind Bryan.

"Didn't Shorty tell you, I'm her new homecoming date."

Hannah paled.

I shook my head.

"What do you mean no? Yes, you are. If not, your life as you know it is over."

I shrugged his arm off me. "Go away Bryan."

"I'm only giving you one more chance to break up with Zack and then the takedown of Shorty will begin. I think you know what you need to do. See you at homecoming," Bryan said walking out of the classroom.

Hannah opened the door for me, and by the time I got to the hallway, Bryan thankfully was gone.

"I'm handling this mess and don't worry, I'm not going to homecoming with Bryan. I don't want to involve you because I saw what he did to you last time."

"What's he up to now? When did he and Erin break up?"

"He said he got tired of Erin, but now he's back to terrorizing me. He hasn't mentioned you yet, so maybe you're off the hook this time."

"But that's not fair! Things seem really good with you and Zack now; I wouldn't want him to ruin that."

I bit my bottom lip. I had told Hannah I'd started to like Zack more, to try and smooth over her worries about Kristy ignoring me. I didn't want to listen to her tell me once again to be true to myself. I already had to deal with Cashi giving me judgmental glares whenever I was around Zack.

"What're you going to do about Bryan?"

"I'll figure it out. I have newspaper now, but we'll talk," I said as I trudged down the hall to Mr. T's office. Not having crutches tomorrow would make leaving awkward situations a lot easier.

Before sitting, I opened the box I had placed in Mr. T's classroom to collect questions for my advice column. There were three pieces of paper. The first one I unfolded said, *Shorty is HOT!*

I rolled my eyes but gave a small smile. Wonder what guy that was from? But then my smile left my face. If I tell people I liked women, I might be the laughingstock instead of receiving notes such as this. I opened the next note. *Do what I say, or you will pay.*

I sucked in my breath. It was in Bryan's distinctive handwriting. What the hell was wrong with him? He was adding to my case against him. I slipped the note into my purse and looked at the last piece of paper. *What do you do if the person you like is with someone else, but you know they like you and not their boyfriend?*

Was this written by Kristy? It was typed so I couldn't analyze the handwriting. I added this note to my purse, already brainstorming how to answer.

During newspaper, Mr. Ricardo assigned me a feature

story on homecoming preparations and the dance itself, in addition to my advice column. I would cover everything from how Cashi picked the Storybook theme, to the preparations involved with the big event, including interviewing some of the attendees about where they bought their formal wear, and report on some of the more elaborate ways girls, or guys, were asked to the dance. Then I was supposed to report how the dance went, who won king and queen, and anything else I deemed important news.

"I can't wait to get started. Thanks for this opportunity." It was the piece of a lifetime.

More assignments were distributed, and I fiddled with my purse as I waited for Mr. Ricardo to be free. Finally, everyone begun to disperse, and Mr. Ricardo sat on a desk beside me.

"Do you want to go talk in the conference room in the head office?"

"Can it be more informal? Like in your classroom?" I asked, biting my lower lip.

"Uh, sure. We just have to keep the door open. I'll also let Mr. T know where we are going." Mr. Ricardo strode over to Mr. T, said a few words to him, and then came back to me.

"Okay, we're good to go."

I followed him to his classroom, and he motioned for me to sit in a chair next to his desk.

After we both were seated, he waited, studying me. "So, Sam, what's on your mind?"

My tongue felt thick, and my brain numb. I couldn't tell him the truth, could I? Where would that get me? Then I pictured Zack's face stricken from news of me going to homecoming with Bryan and Kristy's disappointed look. No. I had to tell someone.

"I think I'm a lesbian. And I fell for Kristy, the girl that came to newspaper staff that one time. Bryan found out and took a video of Kristy and me making out. Now he's threatening to send it to the whole school and my parents if I don't do what he says. He first told me I had to stay with Zack. And Kristy won't talk to me because I kept going out with Zack even though I like her," I blurted.

Mr. Ricardo's mouth dropped. "That's a lot to process."

My gaze flitted to the floor. "Yeah, sorry to drop this on you."

"I'm not going to lie to you, Sam. Mr. T, Mr. Paul, and I all thought something was going on, so it's not a complete shock but I didn't know it was this bad. We are trained to look out for bullying and the way Bryan acted the first day of school set off an internal alarm."

"Before, I'd been hoping it would stop, but last night things got worse." I cringed just thinking of the text.

He arched a brow. "How so?"

"Mr. T asked me to write why my collaborative project with Kristy was so awful, so I began that last night, all with fake names, but as I was finishing up, Bryan texted me that I had to break up with Zack." I intentionally left out the part about Bryan saying maybe I'd put out this time. I couldn't even say that aloud.

Mr. Ricardo gave a loud sigh. "That's terrible, Sam. He can't be doing this to you. We really need to go see Principal Jergens right now."

I put my hand over my mouth. "No. I'm not ready for that. I need to tell everyone my secret myself before Bryan does it for me but I'm terrified. Scared of how everyone will react, that Zack will hate me, afraid that my parents will kick me out of the house, and most of all, I'm worried that it's too late and I already lost Kristy."

Mr. Ricardo's face softened. "Those are all very valid fears for you to have, Sam. Coming out is super scary, especially when you aren't ready yet."

"Yeah. I think I'm getting close to being ready though. I'd

rather that than them hear it from Bryan."

"Can you tell me more about what Bryan's been doing?"

I had to hold back a yawn. This was taking a lot out of me. "I wrote a paper about everything, that might be better than me trying to explain it. Can you read it over to see what you think?"

"I'd be more than happy to. Email it over to me."

I opened my iPad and sent off my paper to Mr. Ricardo's school email address. "Thank you for being so nice to me. I know this isn't what you would want to be doing with your free evening."

"I'm happy to help out a student. I'm glad you finally asked for help. We can figure this out together."

I inhaled a deep breath. "Thanks. I'll check in with you tomorrow to see what you think of my paper. I think I'm going to talk with Zack now."

"Good luck, you're doing the right thing," Mr. Ricardo reassured me.

Then why did I feel like I wanted to vomit? I hoped this wouldn't hurt him too badly.

In my car I texted my parents that I would be home shortly, but newspaper was running late. I vowed to myself after all this mess was cleared up, I would stop lying to them about everything.

I drove through the wooded area and the wrought iron gate came into view. I pulled up, rolled my window down, and pushed a buzzer next to what looked like an intercom.

"Hello?" Zack said.

"It's Shorty. Can you let me in?"

"Sure. Did I forget you were coming here or something?"

I ignored him and pulled through the gate once it opened. I drove to the roundabout and put the car in park. This was going to suck but was long overdue. After giving myself a pep talk that this was for the best, I removed myself from my car and pressed his doorbell. A loud gong sounded. After a minute Zack—wearing gray sweatpants and a faded black Beatles T-shirt with the lettering cracking—opened the door, perplexed.

Before he had the chance to say anything, I spoke the words that no one ever wanted to hear, "We need to talk."

Zack's forehead creased. "We can go to my room."

I waved to his housekeeper, Rose, as I walked upstairs. She and I had become friendly the more time I spent at his place.

In his bedroom, we sat on his couch, and I positioned myself as far from him as possible. "I'm not sure how to say this so I'll start from the beginning. Remember how Kristy and I used to hang out all the time?"

"Yeah, but you guys got in a fight or something and aren't talking now."

I bit my lip. "To be honest, we were more than friends."

"Wait, what do you mean?"

I cracked my knuckles a few times before responding. The sweat pooled under my arms. *Rip the band-aid off, Shorty.* "We've made out a couple times and I really like her. But we got into a fight because she wanted me to tell you what happened and for me to break up with you."

Zack's face was rock still and he remained silent.

"I know, I'm awful. I really did like you, but not the way I should with an actual boyfriend. I didn't want to give up on us though but the harder I tried with you, the more I realized I liked girls." I rocked on the couch. I made myself physically stop moving and waited for his response.

"You could have told me. Let me guess, you aren't really saving yourself until marriage either?" Zack asked with a scowl.

I blushed. "Uh, no."

Zack narrowed his eyes. "Wait, did you have sex with Kristy?"

"No! Well, not yet. I mean, I've thought of it, and we got close, but no."

Zack crossed his arms. "Every time I tried touching you, you pulled back with disgust, like I was diseased or something. I thought you just didn't think I was hot enough or something. It was starting to mess with my mind."

"I'm really sorry." *This felt awful. I never meant to hurt him.*

"How did this happen?"

I gritted my teeth. I really didn't want to discuss all the details with him, and he probably actually didn't want to know everything. Maybe if I gave him the bare minimum that would satisfy his curiosity.

"We clicked with each other since I met her on the first day of school and we got closer Labor Day weekend at the beach," I mumbled.

Zack snapped his fingers. "I knew something was weird that weekend. You never answered my texts or calls and that's when you started to pull away from me."

I stared down at my fingers. "I'm sorry."

"Why didn't you tell me sooner?"

I really didn't want to share Bryan's blackmail. It seemed like a copout, so I just shrugged. "I should have. I was scared and confused."

"I thought you were a better person. I really liked you but after hearing this, I kinda hate you right now."

That stung. This was exactly what I didn't want to happen.

"One more question, where the hell does Bryan fit into this? I knew you guys were texting a lot. I thought it was because you still liked him but if what you're saying is actually true, then why were you texting with him?"

I had hoped Zack wouldn't ask me that but I guess I really had to tell him what was going on because I was done with the lies.

"He was blackmailing me. He overheard me explaining to Hannah my feelings for Kristy and threatened to tell my parents and the whole school I was a lesbian unless I stayed with you. He wanted me to break your heart like I hurt him. Then at one point he videoed Kristy and I making out. So that video is also hanging over my head."

Zack shook his head. "What? You're just telling me this part of the story now? Is that the real reason why you stayed with me?"

I twisted my mouth. "I didn't want to tell you because it sounded like an excuse."

"I can't believe he did that to you."

"It gets better," I said grabbing my phone from my purse. I showed him Bryan's latest text messages.

"Are you freaking kidding me? Who does he think he is?"

"There is no way I'm going to homecoming with him or having sex with him. I'm trying to tell everyone I can that I like women before he does."

Zack shook his head. "That's so messed up that's how you have to come out."

He raised his eyes to mine and his steely gaze hit me like lightening. "You still should've told me about being with Kristy way sooner; we could've figured Bryan's blackmail out together instead of you stringing me along for so long."

A tear slipped down my cheek. "I know. I'm sorry. I was embarrassed and knew I shouldn't be having feelings for someone else, especially a girl."

Zack crossed his arms. "You can't help who you are. But you could have told me when you figured it out so I wouldn't also have to get hurt."

"I know," I whispered.

He pushed himself up from the couch. "I need to get some air."

He flung open his bedroom door and slammed it shut. I

was stuck here all alone with only the *Lord of the Rings* and *Star Wars* posters to keep me company.

I pulled my phone out of my pocket and without thinking dialed Hannah.

She answered after the first ring. "Shorty, are you okay?"

Whenever someone says that to me, I automatically start crying and today was no different.

"Shorty! Where are you? I can come help you," Hannah said, her voice panicked.

I took a deep breath and said shakily, "No, don't do that. I'm at Zack's. I told him what went on with Kristy and he just stormed off. I know he hates me."

Hannah let out of a puff of air. "Ooof. I mean you had to know he would be pissed. Look at Tyler. He was mad and I wasn't even cheating."

"I know. But I didn't think it would feel this horrible. I really hurt him."

"He'll get over it, eventually. I'm sure it was just a shock."

"Yeah. What do I do? He just left me in his room. Do I leave? Or should I stay to see if he wants to talk more?"

Hannah was quiet for a minute. "I'd say just stay where you are. He knows where to find you. Play on Instagram or TikTok or something."

"Okay. Thanks for talking me down."

"Always, and you do the same for me."

I hung up and opened my Instagram app. Pics of happy couples appeared in my feed and I quickly shut it. *Nothing better than social media to remind you that you were sad, alone, and single.* I decided to try TikTok instead and a video of the newest dance trend was the first thing I saw. *Much better.*

After a couple of minutes of watching people dance way better than I ever dreamed of, Zack opened the door. I stuffed my phone in my pocket and looked at him timidly.

"I needed some time. I wasn't sure if you'd still be here or not."

"I didn't know what to do. I can go if you want."

Zack shrugged and didn't say anything.

I took a deep breath. "I'm so sorry. I never meant for this to happen. I honestly thought I liked you and had wanted to be your girlfriend for so long. I wrote Sam plus Zack equals love all over my middle school notebooks."

Zack's forehead wrinkled. "Really?" He sat next to me on the couch, but not as close as before. Our legs weren't even touching.

"Yeah. I've liked you as a person forever, but it was when all the other stuff involved with being a girlfriend happened that made me not so happy. And then Kristy and I kissed, and it all made sense why I never wanted to do more with any guy."

Zack ran his hands through his hair. "I don't hate you; I didn't really mean that. I was just taken off guard and hurt. I can't even imagine what you're going through."

"Thank you," I said. The girl that ended up with Zack was super lucky.

"Are you going to ask Kristy to homecoming?"

I sighed.

"I want to. But I think I really need to tell my parents before they find out from Bryan. That way Kristy can see I'm all in. No more hiding."

"Oh, man. That's going to be rough."

"It'll suck but might as well do it now before I chicken out."

"Good luck with that."

My phone buzzed. I checked the message and sucked in a deep breath.

"What is it?"

I turned my screen toward him, and he read my message

aloud.

> What brand of condoms do you like? Wait you wouldn't know. I'll bring a variety to homecoming.

"What the hell! He's such a dick. I'm going to end this right now." Zack reached for his Chuck Taylor shoes beside the couch.

"No. I don't want you to ruin your life. Can you help me though figure out the best way to get back at him?" I put my hand on his shoulder to not let him up from the couch.

"I'm sure if you told Principal Jergens everything that would fix it."

"Or make everything so much worse, and Bryan is my enemy for life."

"But you're telling everyone your secret now. What else could he do to make things worse?"

"Yeah, I guess. I'll have to think about it."

"Thanks for finally telling me about Kristy. I know it probably wasn't easy."

"Sorry it took so long." I stared at my hands. Even though I was finally glad I told Zack, I still felt uneasy. *Maybe I'd feel better once I talked to my parents and everything was out in the open.*

My phone vibrated again in my pocket. I pulled it out, saw who was calling, and jumped off the couch. "Crap, it's my mom. I better go home."

Zack also got up. "Good luck telling your parents."

"Thanks, and sorry again." I gave him one last look and slipped out of his bedroom door.

For the first time since breaking up with Tyler, my heart hurt. Zack was a great guy and I hoped I didn't upset him too much.

CHAPTER THIRTY

As soon as my crutches hit the linoleum floor in the hallway of our house, a sense of foreboding hit me. "Hello?" I called out.

I found my parents on the couch staring at me with a grave look on their faces. My heart dropped and I began to sweat. Did Bryan already talk to them? I really didn't want to have this conversation yet. I was still recovering from Zack's house.

"Honey, can you sit down for a second? We have a few questions," my mom said.

"Okay," I mumbled. I slumped onto the couch next to her. *This was going to be awful.*

"Where were you tonight? The school called us with troubling news, so I've been trying to get ahold of you. They also let us know you had left newspaper staff hours ago," my mom said, her forehead creased with worry.

"The school called?" I asked, my voice hollow. *What did Mr. Ricardo do?*

"You didn't answer my question. Where were you?" my mom said, her voice shrill.

I took a deep breath. *Might as well get this over with.* "I went to Zack's house to breakup with him. I'm sorry I didn't tell you, but I knew it would make you have a lot of questions and I wanted to get it over with."

My mom grabbed my hand. "I'm sorry, honey. Why did you break up with him?"

My eyes welled. I didn't want to come out this way, but I was already on a roll tonight. "Because I like someone else," I whispered, tears rolling down my cheeks. Every part of my body was sweating, but at the same time I felt numb and cold all over. A pit formed in my stomach, and I was trying not to vomit.

"Oh?" my mom asked.

"I like Kristy. I've liked her for a while but couldn't bring myself to break up with Zack or tell anyone because I was embarrassed and knew you would hate me." Tears fell onto my legs and made wet marks on my dress.

I avoided looking into their eyes. I didn't want to see their disappointment and shame. I felt my mom squeeze my hand, and I finally got the courage to raise my head to meet her brown eyes.

"Oh, Sam, you can always come to us. I won't lie, I'm upset but mainly because I know how hard life's going to be for you, but I know you can't change who are." She clutched my hand tighter.

"What? Really?" *Were they really being this cool or was I dreaming?*

"You guys are super religious. Youth group taught me being a homosexual is a major sin."

"But it's also Christian to be accepting of others," my mom explained.

"Why are you guys not more surprised? I thought you would be screaming or crying?" I eyed my mom suspiciously. *Did Bryan already get to them before me?*

"I was watching security footage from Labor Day and saw

Kristy give you a kiss in the break room," my dad stated. He rapidly blinked his eyes. He took off his wire-framed glasses and wiped them on his shirt, still avoiding any eye contact with me.

My mouth dropped. I had so many questions. "What? You knew this long and didn't say anything?"

"We hoped you'd come to us. We didn't know what to think, especially since you'd told us that you were dating Zack. I did keep asking about Kristy," my mom said.

"You do the same thing about Hannah and Zack, so I didn't think anything of it. Do you hate me?"

"Honey, how could you even think that? I can't pretend to know how you feel about Kristy because that isn't something I understand. If you have deep feelings for her, that isn't something to dismiss because it's different than what we feel or believe," my mom said. "I've always been concerned about how many guys you dated. I still can't keep all your ex-boyfriends straight, and you never seemed upset when you broke up with them. When your dad told me what he saw, it made a lot of sense. I just wish you felt like you could tell us."

"I'm sorry. I didn't want to be kicked out of the house like Kristy."

My mom gasped. "That's what happened to her?"

"More or less. She got caught with her girlfriend and her parents wouldn't accept she's pansexual."

My mom's eyes widened. "Sam, how could you think we would do that?"

I shrugged. "I don't know. I guess I assumed the worst. We've never really talked about LGBTQ issues, so I thought because of our religion, you were against it."

My mom encased my body in a tight hug. "Sam, we will always love you no matter what. This will be hard for all of us, but if it's how you feel, then we're in it together."

My dad grunted and I assumed he agreed. His eyes were

glued to the landscape painting hanging beside the television, still avoiding looking at me. He was never one for awkward conversations but at least he wasn't scolding me.

Relief and hope flooded my entire body. They weren't throwing me on the streets to fend for myself. Maybe I wouldn't have to pretend I liked guys anymore and could be myself?

"What about homecoming?" she asked.

"I'd like to go with Kristy, but homecoming doesn't seem very Kristy-like. I don't know if she even will give me the time of day anymore."

"If you care about her, it's worth a shot though, isn't it? And if she says no, at least you can say you tried."

I nodded. "Very true." I thought for a second. "But what about Grandma? What should I tell her?"

"That's up to you, sweetie. You can tell her if you want but you know she won't be shy at hiding any strong opinions."

"I'll have to think about it."

"Now that we have all that cleared up, we need to talk about something really serious," my mom stated.

"More serious than me liking women?"

"Yes. The reason the school called was because of a paper you wrote for one of your classes. The principal said in the paper you described that Bryan is blackmailing you. Honey, is that true?"

"Um." I reddened.

Mom placed her hand on my arm. "Sam, you can tell us."

"Bryan has a video of Kristy and me kissing. He first used it to make me stay with Zack but now he's saying if I don't go to homecoming with him, he's going to leak the video to you and the school."

"What exactly did he say?" My dad met my gaze for the first time all evening.

I was so done lying and covering things up that weren't even my fault. I grabbed my phone and pulled up my texts. Bryan's were right at the top. I handed my phone to my dad.

He quickly read the screen and his eyes, laced with concern, rose to meet mine. His jaw tightened. "Who the hell does this Bryan think he is? He can't be sending messages like this. I'm calling the police!"

"The police? No, don't do that!" Panic rose inside me. "I was thinking about telling Principal Jergens tomorrow about them, but what if Bryan makes my life worse?"

"I would never let that happen. No one messes with us, especially some punk who probably hasn't worked a single day in his life," my dad grumbled.

"Thank you, Dad!" I cried running into his arms.

He awkwardly patted my back. "You're welcome. At least that Kristy is a hard worker."

That was about as good as I was going to get from him, and I was okay with that.

"Honey, Principal Jergens needs to see those text messages. We have a meeting with him tomorrow morning to talk further through this issue. He was very concerned about your paper and wanted to know more details. After seeing those messages, I'm sure he's going to ask if we'll press charges."

"You have a meeting with him? I don't want to press charges; I just want it to stop!"

This was spiraling fast. Bryan was terrible, but pressing charges was not something I knew was even on the table. *How could Mr. Ricardo break my trust and go to the principal?*

"We could file a restraining order if you feel scared, Sam. Any judge that reads those messages would grant that immediately," my dad said.

"I'll think about it. Can I go to my room now? I need some time to process everything."

"If you end up having more to talk about or need us, please, honey, let me know," my mom said, rubbing my arm.

"Okay, I promise." I stood, then headed down the hall. I closed the door to my room and collapsed on my bed. *What just happened?* I buried my face into my pillow. My whole body felt tired and heavy. Did I break up with my boyfriend and come out to my parents in less than an hour time span? I'd basically done what I thought was impossible. No wonder I was exhausted but there was one last item on my list I had to accomplish. I picked up my phone and stared at it. I needed someone that would truly understand how momentous of an occasion today was for me.

I opened a blank message and typed in Kristy's name.

> I broke up with Zack and came out to my parents. Alive to tell the tale.

While I was waiting for a response, I replied to the million messages from Hannah, stating the same thing I texted Kristy. I also shot off a quick text to Cashi thanking him for his advice about telling my parents and I let him know it went way better than expected. Hannah replied almost instantaneously asking how I was. As I was replying, a text from Kristy came in.

> How'd it go?

That was a good sign!

> Much better than I expected. Zack and my parents don't hate me. Can we talk after school tomorrow?

It took longer than I'd like for her to reply.

> You're not going to cancel on me for Zack?

I grimaced. If only I could go back in time and tell myself that lying to Kristy wasn't worth it and she was really the one I desired.

No. I promise. No more lies.

Okay.

That was something. It still didn't sound like she completely trusted me but I'm sure it would take time.

CHAPTER THIRTY-ONE

The next day I wasn't sure what to expect at school or how I would feel about myself. I made myself get up super early, giving myself time to take my boot off. Turns out, they are incredibly easy to take off yourself. All the extra time in the morning let me slip out the door before I had to see either of my parents. I was hoping they wouldn't take back how accepting they were last night.

I pulled into my spot and for once Zack wasn't waiting for me. I slung my pink backpack over my shoulder and shut the door. It felt freeing not to have to worry about my crutches and boot. I put one foot in front of the other. I'd almost forgotten what it was like to walk normally. I'd never take that for granted again, that was for sure.

As Kristy came into homeroom, she raised her eyes to meet mine. I gave a tentative smile, and she returned it with a small side-grin.

She slid into her chair. "No crutches or boot?"

"They're gone for good, unless I somehow manage to re-injure myself."

There was a moment of silence between us. I picked at my nails.

Should I say something first or let her? I didn't want to seem too desperate.

Finally, Kristy broke the tension. "That was really brave of you to come out to Zack and your parents on the same day."

"I hadn't meant to do it all at once, I was forced to."

Kristy pulled back, her eyes wide. "What do you mean?"

The bell rung, signaling it was time to go to creative writing. "I'll tell you later when there aren't so many people around."

We picked up our stuff and headed out the door.

"How did Zack take it?" Kristy asked as we walked down the hall.

"I mean, not great. But I guess that's expected. I was cheating on him, and that was a super shitty thing for me to do."

"Hopefully he won't be like Bryan and take up a vendetta against the both of us."

I shook my head. "I doubt it. He might just take some time to get over it though."

"That's good to know. You don't need another ex with a grudge. Where are you going to sit at lunch today?"

I gazed over at her. "I was planning to stay at the same table. Do you want to join us?"

"You're still going to sit with Zack?" Kristy asked, her eyes narrowing.

"I'm assuming he'll be okay if I still sit there for the time being. I don't know where else I'd go."

"The guys I sit with are actually pretty cool," Kristy said, running her hand through her hair.

I eyed Kristy curiously. "I think they all have a crush on you."

A small patch of red appeared on Kristy's neck. "Erin's

gone from your table, right?" she replied, ignoring my statement.

"She better be!"

"I'll think about it."

That was better than nothing. I guess it would take time for her to trust me again.

As soon as we entered Mr. T's classroom, he motioned for me to come to his desk. "Sam, before you say anything, Mr. Ricardo told me about the paper and we both had a late-night meeting with the administration. We're both ethically bound to share your paper because of the nature of what you wrote. I'm sorry but we could've lost our job if we didn't."

"What's going to happen to Bryan?" I whispered, not wanting the class to hear what had happened.

"I'm not sure, just tell your side of the story. The meeting with your parents is in a few minutes, so a substitute teacher will be coming in soon to run class for today."

"I need to tell Kristy quick though what's going on before she hears it from anyone." I took a peek back at Kristy. Her forehead was scrunched, and her eyes were focused on us.

"You have about ten minutes before the substitute teacher shows up. I'll tell everyone to work with their writing partner during that time."

"Thank you!" I rushed back to my seat.

"What was all that about?"

I turned around and leaned in close to her desk. "Look, I don't have much time. Remember how I kept telling you I wasn't ready to break up with Zack? Most of that was because Bryan was threatening to tell my parents and the school that I'm a lesbian. When he got that video of us making out, it only made the blackmail worse. He sent me these texts last night." I showed her the texts.

She scanned them, her eyes widening. "Sam, why didn't

you tell me? This makes way more sense. I thought you were ashamed of me."

"I didn't want to involve anyone else in my mess. I was trying to take care of it myself, but I guess I did an awful job of that." I hung my head.

"This is a huge deal. I can't believe he threatened you like that!" Kristy's hands clenched into fists.

"I know. Zack had never been my endgame, but I didn't know what to do because I wasn't ready for people to find out who I truly wanted but now I am. I'm tired of hiding and sick of being forced to do what Bryan says."

"Are you going to Principal Jergens?"

"My parents and I have a meeting with the school administration in a couple minutes. I wanted to let you know before you found out from someone else." I was done lying to Kristy, even if she didn't want to be with me anymore.

"Thanks for telling me, I wish it was sooner. Things could have ended up differently," Kristy said, her eyes downcast.

"I hoped you'd consider dating me, for real this time but I get it. You can't trust me," I replied, giving her a half-hearted smile.

Kristy opened her mouth to speak.

The loudspeaker announced, "Sam Daniels, please report to the principal's office. I repeat, Sam Daniels please report to the principal's office."

The class, in unison said, "Ohhhh!"

Ignoring the peanut gallery, I straightened. "Guess I better go." I tossed my backpack over my shoulder and headed out the door. I needed to get this over with so I could move on with my life.

CHAPTER THIRTY-TWO

The meeting with Principal Jergens, Mr. T, Mr. Ricardo, and my parents went way better than I expected. I'm pretty sure I sweated out all the water I gushed down right before going into the conference room, but I didn't care. What mattered more was I told them the truth about everything and no one flinched. They were more horrified by what had happened to me.

At the end of the meeting, Principal Jergens promised me that bullying of any kind was not tolerated at Dale. They would make Bryan delete all copies of the video and he would be suspended for an undefined amount of time.

After my parents and I left the conference room, my mom pulled me in for a long hug. "Honey, I'm so proud of you."

"Then why do I feel like crap? I might have ruined someone's life." My voice shook. Getting suspended might affect Bryan's college football scholarship and even his future career.

My mom broke the hug. "Never feel bad for speaking the truth. He's the one that ruined his life by treating you this way.

There are consequences for every action." She rubbed my arm reassuringly. "You did the right thing."

I swallowed hard. "Thanks, Mom."

"And he'll never do this again to you," my dad said.

I had never heard him use such a menacing tone. I gave him a smile. "You guys better get going though, I know you have to get to work."

"Are you going to be okay?" my mom asked.

"I'm better than I was before, that's for sure. Can I go over to Kristy's tonight to talk more with her?"

"That's no problem, honey, just no closed doors!" my mom said.

My dad started blinking rapidly and walked away.

I involuntarily blushed. "Mom, no. We aren't together like that, at least not yet. I mean, romantically. I'm not even sure if she's going to forgive me."

If things weren't awkward enough telling them Kristy and I made out, now my mom was already thinking a step ahead.

"Give her some time, I'm sure she'll come around," my mom replied, lightly rubbing my shoulder.

I hoped she was right.

I scooted out of the principal's office to try and make it to lunch. I scanned to find my usual table. Zack was already there, gazing off into the distance. Hannah and Tyler were engrossed in each other. Kristy was nowhere to be seen.

I walked to my table. "Can I still sit here?"

Zack gave me a vacant stare. "Yeah. I guess."

As soon as I sat down next to Zack, Principal Jergens appeared at the cafeteria doorway with a stern look. He panned the room and when he found his target, he walked with a purpose toward him and placed his hand on Bryan's shoulder.

"Mr. Rickter, you need to come with me right this instant," Principal Jergens stated.

Bryan's mouth dropped. "What for? What did I do?" he asked, jutting out his chest.

"Just come with me Mr. Rickter. You'll find out soon enough," Principal Jergens said, his mouth taunt.

Bryan whipped his head around and looked directly into my eyes and shouted, "Shorty, you lesbo, you're dead!"

The entire cafeteria went a buzz. I lost count of how many eyes were stuck on me. My stomach dropped. *I needed to think of something fast.*

The old Shorty would have grabbed Zack and made out with him like my life depended on it. But no, that wasn't me anymore. I was tired of hiding. Instead, I waved at everyone and shrugged with a small smile and opened my lunch bag.

Guess my secret was out, but I didn't care as much as I'd imagined. Maybe if I didn't act like it was a big deal, people wouldn't either?

"Making off-color comments about your classmate isn't going to help your case. Come with me now before I call the police," Mr. Jergens said loudly to Bryan.

Bryan's face reddened, and he was about to say more but must have thought better of it. He reluctantly followed Mr. Jergens, with his head down, out of the cafeteria.

The cafeteria still hummed with chatter.

"What was that?" Hannah asked me, her eyes wide.

I sat straighter. "I reported Bryan's threats to Principal Jergens."

Tyler gave me a high five. "Zack told me what Bryan did to you. About time someone reported that asshole!"

"Turns out you aren't the only one he was messing with," Zack said, frowning.

"What do you mean?"

"I talked to Erin after you left last night because I had no idea she and Bryan broke up, so I wanted to check on her. She was pretty upset. Apparently, Bryan was treating her bad, so she broke up with him."

As much as I didn't like Erin, no one deserved someone like Bryan hurting them. That made me even more secure on my decision to tell Principal Jergens everything. Erin rejecting Bryan was also probably what put him over the edge. I bet he went back to seek revenge on someone that was an easy target, me.

"Really? He implied he was the one that broke up with her. I wonder how many other girls he has hurt over the years. I'm so happy he's getting suspended. I hope it's for a long time," I said.

"Is this seat taken?" Kristy asked, coming up beside me.

"Oh, uh, no," I replied, blushing.

This was a welcome surprise.

I snuck a glance at Zack. His face clouded over as he inspected his ham and cheese sandwich. The tension at the table as Kristy sat could have been felt a mile away. Sitting at the same lunch table with your ex was brutal. No wonder I kept faking it until the last day of school with Paul. Maybe having Kristy crash the table wasn't the best idea.

"You changed your mind," I whispered in her ear.

"Yea. You looked pretty miserable here. I just had to take care of something at my other lunch table first," she replied, avoiding my eyes. *What did that mean?*

Tyler's eyes shot between Kristy and Zack. He opened his mouth when Zack lightly shook his head.

"Come on, man. We have to tell her about Dylan," Tyler responded.

"Tell who what?" I asked.

Zack looked up from his lunch. "You should hear it from Kristy not us."

"Hear what?" I was full of so many questions.

Kristy froze in her seat. "I told Dylan not to say anything to you guys!"

"Don't be mad at him. Erin told me. She knows everything that happens at Dale, especially when it has to do with her ex," Zack replied.

"What am I missing?" I gritted my teeth.

"I thought you were purposely not breaking up with Zack because you either still wanted to be with him or were ashamed of me. I was really pissed," Kristy explained chewing on her lip.

"I mean I knew that. You stopped talking to me for a couple of weeks," I replied, scratching my head.

"I got so mad that I had Dylan over and we got drunk together. And I did something stupid with him," Kristy responded, her eyes clouded with regret.

I gasped. My brain felt disoriented. That made no sense. She had been with Dylan?

"I'm sorry, Sam. You were still with Zack and if he was around, no offense Zack, I'd always be an afterthought to you," Kristy said, her auburn hair falling in her face as she hung her head.

"Are you still with him?" I whispered.

"No. It was a one-time thing and a mistake. He's hot, but I'm not emotionally attracted to him like I am with you. I can't stop thinking about you. But I guess he thought it could be more because he freaked out when I told him today I was coming back to this table. That's what I was dealing with."

I froze in place. My stomach turned over and I felt myself start to get angry. Is this what jealousy felt like? *I needed to reign it in. I wasn't with Kristy at the time, and she thought I chose Zack. She could do what she wanted.*

I gave her the world's worst smile. "Okay."

She clearly saw through it. "Can you still come over

tonight? We can talk about it more," Kristy said, her voice insistent.

I sharply inhaled and slightly nodded.

After a moment of silence, Zack cleared his throat. "Was the reason you were called to the main office this morning because of Bryan?"

"Yep. They brought my parents in to talk about Bryan's blackmail."

"Does that mean you told your parents about you?"

"I had to. After I came home from your house, they cornered me because the school called them about the paper I wrote. They weren't as shocked as I thought. Apparently, as my dad was looking at security footage from the store, he saw Kristy and I kissing on Labor Day." As soon as this came out of my mouth, I realized my mistake. No one needed to know I had been cheating on Zack with Kristy that long but on the other hand, I was tired of the lies.

"Oh, wow. That's brutal." Tyler stole a worried glance at Zack.

I couldn't tell if he meant it was brutal in the way my parents found out, or if it was brutal that I brought this up.

Zack crumbled his bag of *Lay's* chips in his hands but hadn't eaten a single chip. Suddenly, he grabbed the remains of his barely touched lunch and his backpack. "I can't do this," he said as he walked away.

My heart thudded and my stomach clenched. How could I do this to him? He didn't deserve to be hurt and why did I even mention the store? Not lying was one thing but flaunting that I was cheating with Kristy behind his back was another.

After Zack left Tyler said, "Shorty, I don't care if you like girls, it makes a ton of sense, but Zack seems pretty messed up over it. Maybe you guys should sit somewhere else until this blows over?"

"Good idea, we'll do that tomorrow, right, Sam?" Kristy said nudging me.

It only made sense to not sit with Zack, but it still hurt. I wouldn't be sitting with my best friend anymore. Did that mean Kristy and I would have our own lunch table together? Was there even an available table for us? The thought of a two-person lunch table made me want to break out in hives but at least I wouldn't be sitting all by myself.

Before anymore awkwardness could occur, the bell rang, and it was time for Mr. Ricardo's class. *Great. More time with Zack.*

Kristy and I walked together for a bit and when it was time for her to go to her next class, we stood in the hallway staring at each other.

"Still good to come over tonight?" she asked, her forehead creasing.

I nodded and walked towards Mr. Ricardo's class without saying anything. I was a ball full of emotions and thought it was better if I waited to say anything more until tonight. Way too much just happened.

As soon as I entered the classroom, I gave Mr. Ricardo a pissed off look. He motioned for me to come to his desk. I walked over and put my hands on my hips.

"You have every right to be mad at me, but I had to report the paper. I hope you understand," Mr. Ricardo stated.

"Mr. T explained why. I wouldn't have wanted to get you in trouble, but a little heads-up would have been great."

"It all happened so fast. I'm sorry. As soon as I read your paper, I knew I had to report it. I took an oath by being a teacher and that oath was to protect all my students. I hadn't been doing that with you and I literally had proof in my hand that you were in danger. I had to do something; I might have gotten fired if I didn't."

"I guess that makes sense. I didn't think that involving you could hurt your job."

"It hasn't, but could you imagine if something really did happen to you, and I could have prevented it?"

"Okay, mister voice of reason. I told Zack and my parents last night."

"How did they take it?"

"My parents already knew actually. I'm still living with them so that's a big win. Zack's upset but I guess that's expected."

"I'm glad your experience coming out wasn't as bad as you thought it might be. Just so you know, Bryan's had to sign a statement saying he deleted the video he was using as blackmail. Mr. and Mrs. Rickter were mortified by what Bryan did. Even if there were multiple copies of that video on Bryan's computer at home, I have a feeling Bryan's dad will find it and delete any evidence to save face for his family."

I gasped. "Wait, for real?"

"Yes. It wasn't only you that reported him, another girl came in during lunch while Bryan was being questioned and told Principal Jergens about her experience. After word got around about you, I guess other girls felt like they could speak up."

I was floored. "Our own *Me Too* movement I guess?"

"All thanks to you. Do you want to write an article in the paper about what happened, so people can learn the truth?"

My eyes widened. "Really?"

Mr. Ricardo nodded. "I'm sure you haven't had much time to work on the homecoming article. This is bigger news, and the student body deserves to hear it from the source, rather than some fictionalized version that's bound to be passed around."

"Actually, I just came up with another idea while you were talking."

I told him my thoughts.

"That sounds great. I can't wait to see the final product."

The rest of class, Zack completely ignored me and when the bell rang, he ran out without a word. Even Bryan's friends didn't have a single thing to say to me.

Instead of being the object of ridicule, were people ignoring me?

Hannah and I walked to Mr. Paul's class, and I filled her in about Mr. Ricardo's conversation.

"I'm so proud of you for reporting Bryan," Hannah said, rushing to hug me.

"Thank you, and thanks for always supporting me."

I also told Hannah about another girl going forward about Bryan.

"I got lucky that he didn't pressure me to go further when I was at his beach house."

"It sounds like he has really gone off the deep end now."

In bio, since Hannah lost her lab partner, Mr. Paul assigned her to work with Kristy and me for the rest of the semester.

"Really?" I asked incredulously when I was standing in front of Mr. Paul's desk. He had called the three of us up to tell us the news.

"Yes. I don't want to accidentally pair Miss Greer with another deviant so I thought it was best to put her where she wants to go. Does this work for you?"

Hannah smiled. "Yes! Thank you so much."

"You're nicer than I thought," I said and clasped my hand over my mouth when I realized what I said.

"Oops, sorry," I said, blushing.

Mr. Paul laughed. "No apology necessary. I do try and act like a stickler, especially at the beginning of a new semester, so everyone knows I mean business, but I'm not heartless. There was something off about Mr. Rickter. Miss Greer, I'm sorry for pairing you with him in the first place."

"I did enjoy when you gave him detention," I said smiling.

"The entire time he stared off into space with a furious look on his face as if he was devising an evil plan," Mr. Paul said.

"Yeah, to ruin my life," I said rolling my eyes.

"Next time tell someone sooner," Mr. Paul recommended.

"There better not be a next time."

CHAPTER THIRTY-THREE

"You came," Kristy stated, as she opened the front door to her aunt's house. She wore tight black leggings and a gray workout tank. Her hair was in a small ponytail, and whatever strands that didn't fit were clipped tight to her head with multiple barrettes.

"I said I would. I'm trying to keep my promises. Are you about to work out?" I gestured to her attire.

"I put this on in case you didn't show so I could run off my frustrations."

Kristy's aunt said hi from the living room couch; her eyes never left the TV screen. I followed Kristy down the steps. We sat on opposite ends of the retro multi-colored couch.

"So," I said, looking at her. "Where should we start?"

"I shouldn't have been with Dylan, it was a mistake. I just couldn't get past that you wouldn't break up with Zack. It didn't make any sense to me, and I knew there had to be a reason, but I didn't think Bryan was blackmailing you."

"I hadn't realized it would make a difference. It was another excuse. And I was scared if he found out I told anyone, he really would tell my parents."

"Sam, it's not an excuse. No one wants to be outed by another person. You should be able to do it on your own time, not being bullied into doing it."

"That ship has sailed but you know what, I'm glad I told people. Now I don't feel like I'm hiding anymore."

Kristy was silent for a moment. "I shouldn't have pressured you so much either about breaking up with Zack. I'm sorry. I knew what I wanted and didn't want to have to wait around until you were ready. I was more worried about that pic of you with Zack, but now I realize I should've trusted you when you said nothing happened."

"We made out but that's it. It's also when I realized I really am a lesbian. I took that picture for Bryan to show him I was doing what he asked."

"That's when things went really wrong. After I saw that picture, a couple days later I invited Dylan over. I didn't want to be alone because I was afraid I'd text Talia in a moment of weakness, and Dylan's pretty chill. And then we drank too much of my aunt's tequila, and one thing led to another. We didn't go the whole way; I stopped it before we got too far along. I'm sorry," Kristy said gazing at me, her eyes heavy with sadness.

I took a deep breath. "I mean, it sucks, but we weren't together so it's not like you were cheating on me or anything, not like I was doing with Zack. Was it any good?" I asked. As soon as I asked that question, I realized I didn't really want to hear the answer.

"We can't have this kind of conversation. Friends talk about that. I can't talk about that with someone I want to be with."

I blushed. "You still want to be with me? Even after everything?"

"Sam, ever since I stepped into Dale High I've wanted you and not just because you're hot. You make life interesting and

I like being around you. I know what I did with Dylan was stupid and I hope you still want to be with me." She looked expectantly at me.

She wasn't with Dylan to hurt me, she did it as a reaction to seeing a picture of me with Zack. I really missed her, and I wanted to start this journey of being a part of the LGBTQ community alongside her.

"Of course, I do. I did some pretty awful things, too. I shouldn't have lied to you and told you from the beginning about Bryan's threats, then you might not of done stuff with Dylan. *Ew*. Dylan. He was with Erin too!"

"And so were Bryan and Tyler, your ex-boyfriends," Kristy said, giving me a smirk.

It was weird to think that there would be no more boyfriends for me, only girlfriends from this point forward.

"What if we start over again?"

I stuck out my hand. "Hi, I'm Sam but you can call me Shorty. You're pretty sexy, especially in those tight running clothes."

Kristy laughed. "Hi, I'm Kristy, and you're not too bad looking yourself with that short pink dress."

She caught my eye, and I gave her an inviting smile. She took the hint and scooted closer to me.

"I've missed you." I ran my hand through her hair. She still smelled of lavender. It was good to see some things didn't change.

"I've missed you, too. It was so hard for me to ignore you, but it was the only way I could protect myself."

"You don't have to do that anymore," I whispered. I leaned close to her, and Kristy closed the distance, her lips brushing my own. The kiss grew deeper and deeper with each second. What started out as a couple of minutes, it ended up being an hour long make out session. Making up for lost time I supposed. Seventeen years of it

Kristy eventually pulled away. "Okay, I need a breather or I'm not going to stop." Hair spilled from her side ponytail.

I patted my hair to feel what mine was like.

"Your hair is a hot mess, but don't worry, you still look amazing." Kristy gave me a coy smile.

"Back at you."

As I straightened my dress, Kristy asked, "I have to ask, what made you write that paper?"

I thought about her question for a second. "The moment Bryan sent me the text ordering me to break up with Zack to go to homecoming with him. That's when I knew he'd never stop. I was tired of him controlling my life."

"If that prick was still around, I'd go punch him in the face."

"That's part of the reason I didn't tell you. I didn't want you to have to get involved."

"But honestly, communication is what makes relationships work. And if I knew what you were dealing with, I could have helped," Kristy replied, putting her hand on my leg.

"I know, I'm sorry. From now on you'll know everything, the good and the bad."

"At least we have each other now to balance it all out," Kristy said smiling.

She laid on the couch and pulled me next to her.

I nestled beside her, my head resting on her chest, and I closed my eyes.

Everything felt right and I never wanted to leave this spot.

"Why did you forgive me?" I asked after a bit.

"How could I not? When I found out from Bryan you had lied to me about being with Zack, I was devastated and didn't trust you at all. But the more I thought about it and the more time went on, I realized you were also hurting yourself by not doing what you really wanted."

"Yeah, you can say that again."

"You breaking up with Zack and coming out, that took guts, especially now that I know you were also dealing with Bryan's blackmail. You took a risk and now I need to do that too and trust you. As a great advice column writer said, *The riskiest things are sometimes the best.*"

"You read my advice column!" I felt like I was in an alternative reality. I had my dream girl, and she also was supportive of my writing.

"Of course I did. Sorry I bailed on it, but you've been doing a great job without me, although I still haven't seen an answer to my question."

"I was right, I knew that one was from you. Well, my answer is, you have to be patient until the person you like comes to their senses."

"I'm glad it didn't take all year."

I laughed. "But I need your help with the advice column. I won't always have the answers. Please come back."

Kristy said of course she would help me. She glanced at me. "What're you thinking about? You have a weird look on your face."

"I realized since everyone knows I like girls, I can tell everyone who I'm with and why I'm with them, including my parents. Who would have thought? It's really freeing to think about."

"That's the dream right there," Kristy said, kissing my forehead.

"Nothing about you and I makes sense to me on paper, but you know what, that doesn't matter anymore. It's about how I feel when I'm with you, and I can't even describe it without feeling cheesy and cliché," I said, raising my face to kiss Kristy on the lips.

She kissed me back. "I feel the same way and I'm glad you came to that conclusion on your own. I won't lie to you, some days it won't be easy. People are going to say crap about us, and it's going to make you mad. But if we talk to each other when we get scared or upset, it will work out."

"And I have you to show me the ropes!"

"No one I would rather show them to," Kristy said pulling me closer.

"But before we have to face the world, let's lie here a little longer," I said snuggling into her chest.

"Deal!"

CHAPTER THIRTY-FOUR

"Sam! Kristy just pulled up!" my mom called urgently. "Are you ready?"

Crap! I was still applying bright pink lipstick in the bathroom. I pursed my lips, hurriedly finished up, and stuffed the bottle in my wristlet. My reflection stared back at me as I moved to look at the full-length mirror on the back of the bathroom door. After hours at the mall, Hannah and I had found a light pink dress with spaghetti thin straps that fit me like a glove. So much so it kept riding up. I pulled it down so my mom wouldn't complain too much.

I gave myself a smile and took in the moment. When I bought the dress, I still thought I was going with Zack, and was going through the motions. *Was this really happening? Was I going to homecoming with a girl, especially one as hot as Kristy?*

"Sam!" my mom hollered again.

"Coming!" I yelled back.

It was go time and that smile I gave was the first genuine one I had ever had thinking about an upcoming date.

I ran into my room, slipped on my matching pink wedges,

and pulled down my dress one more time. My stomach was a mess, but this time it wasn't from dread, more like nervous energy. I wasn't sure how the school would react to us dating but I was trying to not care. Learning to have Kristy's blasé attitude was hard but I was trying my best.

Going to homecoming with Kristy had been my endgame but I wasn't sure of her view because I knew it really wasn't her jam. It really took me by surprise that a couple days after we reconnected, she popped the question during our first official date out at a pizza shop near my parents' store. We'd split a veggie lovers pizza that she insisted on paying for. Her reasoning was that I helped her get the job, and she wanted to treat me. I'd never thought about it before then, but how did girls figure out who paid for dates each time? Was it usually halfsies or did we switch off? There was so much to learn.

Then partway through dinner, Kristy had asked, "I know I'm a little late to the game, but do you want to go to homecoming with me?"

I had frozen in my seat. *Did I hear her correctly?* "Wait, really? I thought that'd be something you'd hate."

"I know it's something you'd like. It could be fun. I'm not going to pass up a chance to dance really close to you," Kristy said, her eyes sparkling.

"Yes! I'd love to go with you. This is so exciting!" I had said, jumping out of my seat to give her a hug.

I smiled, recalling that memory. As I emerged from my room in my homecoming attire, Kristy stood at the entryway to our house wearing a sexy all-black pantsuit. Her auburn hair was slicked back, and her burgundy lipstick popped to match. When her eyes connected with mine, her mouth opened, and she almost dropped the pink corsage she held.

"You look amazing," she said, her eyes wide.

"So do you! You can really rock that pantsuit," I replied with a huge smile.

She laughed. "I don't think I've owned a dress since I was like twelve, so thanks for being cool if I didn't wear one."

My mom's eyes followed us back and forth during our interaction.

"You look very handsome, Kristy. Is that the right thing to say?" my mom asked, chewing on her lip.

"That works, Mrs. Daniels," Kristy said, giving her an encouraging smile.

"Let's get some pictures before you leave!" my mom said. She called out for my dad because she never could figure out how to take good pictures on her cellphone.

Kristy and I stood next to each other near the piano and smiled at each other while my dad showed my mom what to do.

Kristy slipped my corsage over my wrist and the color of the pink rose matched my dress almost perfectly.

"I still feel bad I didn't get you one!"

"Shorty, I hate flowers. I'm glad you didn't get me one. It means you actually listened to me. That's how I know you really care," Kristy said, her cheeks glowing.

"Get closer to each other!" my mom instructed.

I put my arm around Kristy and pulled her closer. I wouldn't go against my mom's wishes.

My mom snapped a few pictures. After my dad showed her again how to not cut off our heads, we finally got one that was Instagram worthy. I posted it with the hashtag #homecoming2022 #loveislove #lovewins. Immediately the hearts appeared, and I smiled. Who knew me coming out to the school would be the opposite of what I thought would happen?

After everything went down with Bryan, instead of my normal advice column, I wrote a letter to myself with advice I wished I knew before this whole fiasco with Bryan ever began. That it was okay to be true to yourself, even if it wasn't what you thought was the easy or normal thing. To not ignore all of the signs and feelings you felt. I gave myself guidance on how to not care what people thought anymore. At the end, I officially came out as a lesbian and announced that I was planning to go to homecoming as Kristy's date. My hands shook as I typed out the entire piece but if someone was going to judge me for being with Kristy, why should I care if I was happy?

Mr. T and Mr. Ricardo loved it so much they ran it on the front-page and it was a hit. People were shipping Kristy and I left and right. This newfound fame didn't make going to homecoming any easier though. My stomach was still all knotted. *What if everyone laughed at us once they saw us together?* Seeing reactions online was one thing, being in front of everyone on a date was on a whole new level.

"Shorty, ready to go?" Kristy asked, her eyes never leaving mine.

I nodded and swallowed hard.

My mom hugged me goodbye and told me to be home by midnight. My dad gave me a small side hug and grumbled. "Have fun."

Kristy and I scooted out the door. "Phew, glad that's over! Your chariot awaits my lady," she said while moving her arm in front of her Jeep.

I nervously laughed as she opened the car door. I slid inside and took a deep breath.

Once she was at the driver's side, she eyed me. "You okay? We don't have to do this."

My forehead creased. "No, we do. I'll probably be fine once we get there. Thinking about it beforehand is the worst."

Kristy placed her hand on the side of my face. "And I'll be there with you. If it sucks, we leave. We don't owe it to anyone to be there."

"You're right. Nothing is making us stay. I don't want to

miss this because I'm too scared of what might happen," I said, leaning over to kiss Kristy on the lips. "Let's go before I change my mind!"

Kristy nodded. "Good call. Let's leave before your mom decides to come take another awkward picture of us."

We both laughed and talked about my parents' efforts to be normal on the way.

At school, I let Kristy borrow my parking pass, so our spot was closer to the entrance. I didn't want to kill my feet with these heels before we ever entered the dance.

I was about to open the car door when Kristy reached over and stopped my hand.

"Before we go in I want to ask you something."

I turned towards her, tilting my head.

"Shorty, will you officially be my girlfriend?" Kristy asked, looking intently at me.

My heart warmed as I gazed into her emerald, green eyes. Not missing a beat, I kissed her. "Yes."

Unlike with Zack, this time I had no misgivings or doubts. My grandma always told me to go with my gut when it came to love and until this moment, I had no clue what she had been referring to. Now, it all made sense.

We kissed a bit more until Kristy moved away. "Trust me, I'd like to continue this, but we should go inside. I don't want you to miss anything."

I smoothed out my hair and reached for the car door. Kristy ran ahead of me to open the doors to the entrance of the school.

"You're pulling out all the stops!" I said, flashing her another smile. *Was I ever going to get used to being this happy?*

"Anything for you, Shorty," Kristy said, returning my smile. "Okay to hold your hand?" she asked, her eyes questioning.

"Yes!" I took hold of her hand. And that's how we entered

the gym where we immediately were greeted with an oversized pink banner covered in rainbow glitter that read, *Happily Ever After Dance*.

I turned to Kristy, tears forming in my eyes. The banner was truer than anyone could ever realize. I leaned and lightly kissed her on the lips. As I pulled away, cheers and clapping echoed around the gym. I turned incredulously to our audience.

"Go, Shorty!" a cry called out. How could this really be my life right now? I thought everyone would hate me, that I was destined to be a table of one forever. I should've given my classmates more credit.

I threw up my hands. "Time to dance!"

Our spectators cheered as Olivia Rodrigo's *good 4 u* blared throughout the space.

"I love this song!" I said, grabbing Kristy by the hand to the dance floor. My body took hold, and I was bouncing up and down as much as possible in my wedges.

As I danced, I took in the atmosphere. Cashi's Storybook theme came together even better than he imagined. A silver glitter cardboard cutout castle was a large part of the makeshift stage. An open oversized book that started out with *Once Upon a Time* in fancy lettering was the backdrop for homecoming pictures. A couple making out were trying to hide in the sparkling trees of the enchanted forest. To top off the theme, teachers wore various storybook costumes. Mr. Ricardo wore a black suit with a name tag that read *Prince Charming*, and Mr. Paul had a fake falcon attached to his left shoulder. I guess he didn't realize there was a difference between Storybook costumes and the Renaissance Faire, but I gave him an A for effort.

Cashi found us with his date, Reggie.

"Hey! Way to make an entrance, Shorty!" Cashi said, reaching in for a hug.

Once I had confided to Cashi that Kristy and I were going to homecoming together, it prompted him to bring a guy, Reggie, he'd been casually talking to from Tinder.

After our hug broke, I saw Kristy and Reggie in an animated conversation. Reggie's dark complexion and bushy black hair complimented his mango orange dress shirt and silver tie.

"Cashi, Kristy and I went to Archfield together," Reggie said, clapping his hands together. "Girl, I've missed you! Archfield is so boring without you around," Reggie said, frowning.

Kristy chuckled. "Not going to lie, I don't miss that place at all, except for you and a few other people, but I see you found someone outside of Archfield to spend some time with like I suggested."

Reggie waggled his eyebrows. "I see you have too."

"Reggie and I hung out when we could because we both felt like we didn't belong."

"Yea, you know it. Being the only openly gay black guy in a school full of white straight ass kids sucks," Reggie said, pursing his lips.

"Why do you still go there?"

He shrugged. "The education is solid. It helped me get into Harvard."

My eyes widened. "That's a good reason. I didn't even bother trying to go to any ivy league. That's amazing!"

Another catchy tune began to play, and Reggie said, "Come on, enough talk. Let's dance."

We all nodded in agreement. Kristy hooked her arms around my shoulders, and we danced a bit too close to each other, but I dared anyone to say anything.

After a couple of songs, I couldn't take my shoes anymore and told Kristy I'd be back. I really didn't want to re-injure myself. She nodded and continued to dance alongside Reggie and Cashi.

I hobbled over to the corner, alongside the line of chairs, where there was inevitably a couple of lone individuals. I bent down to remove my shoes and as I was coming back up, Zack appeared before me. I started out of my seat and gave a small yelp.

"Sorry, I didn't mean to scare you," he said, turning red.

"You're fine, I didn't even hear you coming!" I said twisting my lips to the side. He looked really good in his baby-blue dress shirt and navy-blue shiny tie. We hadn't talked much after Kristy and I left his lunch table to sit with Cashi and his friends.

Zack wiped his hands on his black dress pants and sat in the empty seat beside me. "I wanted to say hi and see how you're doing."

I gave him a half-hearted smile. "Thanks, I'm good. Things have been weird, but slowly starting to be my new normal. But what about you? Hannah said you and Zoe are back together."

Zack gave a tentative smile. "We are, she's over there now with Tyler and Hannah," he said pointing across the room.

Zoe gave a small wave and went back to dancing with Hannah and Tyler. Zoe looked amazing in her red dress and long, curly black hair.

"You're happy then?"

"I am. Zoe's awesome. I didn't realize how well we worked together," Zack said shrugging.

A pang of regret hit me. I'd been the reason he broke up with Zoe. I hadn't fully thought of the consequences when I started flirting with him.

I frowned. "I'm sorry. I didn't mean for all this to happen."

"Shorty, you can't blame yourself. I really liked you. I

always had. If you and I hadn't gotten together, I still might be wondering if Zoe was right for me. Because you and I didn't work out, now I'm a hundred percent sure she is," Zack said, staring straight at me.

I looked at him through moist eyes.

"You're so nice," I said, looking away from him.

"I'm not that nice. Just stating the facts. Oh, and I read your article. That took some serious guts."

I grimaced. "How do you not hate me after seeing that?"

"It's the opposite. I had no clue all of that was going through your head. I can't even imagine not being able to be me," Zack said knitting his brows.

"It sucked. I'm glad I finally don't have to lie all the time. Speaking of which, I should probably get back to Kristy. She's probably thinking I sprained my other ankle or something," I said, eyes glancing at the dance floor.

"Do you and Kristy want to dance with all of us? Hannah probably misses you and I don't want to get between you guys," Zack said blinking.

I shook my head. "Thanks for the invitation, but I think it's probably better if we all do our own thing for now. Hannah and I promised each other to text after the dance. Thanks for talking with me though." He gave me a small head nod and I walked on the dance floor towards Kristy as *Born This Way* by Lady Gaga began blaring over the speakers.

Kristy wore a coy smile. "I couldn't resist," she said, bringing me close.

As we swayed together and I breathed in her lavender scent, a content smile rested on my face. Never in a million years did I think my senior year would turn out this way but sometimes the best laid plans go awry for a reason. I knew it wasn't going to be easy being a lesbian, but I took the hardest and most important step, admitting to myself and then to the world, who I really was and so far, the world hadn't turned me away. It was time to make new and improved plans for the rest of my senior year and my life. But before I got ahead of myself, I took a deep breath and decided to live for each moment, especially the current one with the amazing girl I held in my arms.

ACKNOWLEDGMENTS

I honestly never thought I'd be writing the acknowledgement section for a book I've published. This is beyond a dream to be able to thank the countless people that have supported me and my creative writing throughout the years.

A huge thank you to my wonderful team at Creative James Media; you've been so amazing to work with. Jean Lowd, even from the first time we virtually met, I've been so incredibly impressed with you. I don't know how you do it all! Thank you for believing in me and my story. To Rachel Burchett, my amazing editor, you really have an eye for detail and know the YA market so well; thank you and Jean for helping me make my book what it is today. Stephanie from Alt 19, I love the cover. Thank you for your creativeness and perfectly capturing Shorty and Kristy. To all the authors in our CJM family, thank you for all your kind words and for guiding me through this publishing process! Kate Martin, if it wasn't for you, I would have never thought querying CJM was an option. You were with me every step of the way and for that I'm eternally grateful. Robin Alvarez, I'm so happy we have become such good friends through CJM. Thank you for all of your support.

Thank you to Brianna Wyble, my editor before I signed onto Creative James Media. Your ideas took this book to a level I had never thought I would achieve. Thank you for all your time and effort spent helping me accomplish what I thought was impossible! Charley, I can't believe we only know each other through Twitter. You've beta read this book for me multiple times and have always been there, telling me not to give up. I am so grateful for you and our virtual friendship. Becka Caffery, thank you for beta reading my book and creating our YA twitter group! Danielle and Abi, thank you both for being great beta readers and writing friends. Molly Fennig, thank you for your edits to my querying letter, my manuscript, and introducing me to the wonderful world of writing Twitter. Stacia Friedman, you're the first writer I met in real life; thanks for all the guidance and advice throughout the years. Big thank you to the super supportive 2023 Debut Stars, @debuts23, group. I always love our chats so much. Also thank you to the @2023Debuts group and all the other writers I've met on Twitter.

Everyone's support during the querying process, pitch events, and publishing process has been phenomenal. Thank you to my street team members for all your hard work promoting this book!

Thank you to my SAGA group. You've been so supportive of who I am as a person, and I'm very excited you want this book to be in your queer library!

Rachel Caulfield, my friend that's been always there for me and even offered to help staff my author events! My hurricane club, Alexis Furlong, Helene Pospischil, and Sophie Shrader. You've always supported my writing and been there for me during the highs and the lows of the querying process. Alexis, thanks also for beta reading this book and always offering to be a reader of my work.

Heather Rossell, to my friend that I consider to be like a sister. You can't wait to read my writing and that means so much to me. Thank you for reading this book twice! Your edits and insights are always so helpful. I couldn't have done this without you.

Thank you to my in-laws, Cathy and Tony Billas and the sisters-in-laws and brothers-in-laws that I gained, Alison, Ross,

Chris, and Summer, and all the aunts and uncles. All of you mean so much to me and have been supporters of my writing since I've become a part of the family, telling me to not give up.

Thank you to my Grandma Roberts, who always tells me to keep going. To my aunts and uncles and my amazing cousins and their families. You all have always believed in me, and we've had some crazy times together! I will always be baby Diane, and that's fine by me.

To my parents, Jane and Steve Poff, thank you for all of your support and loving me no matter what. You've always taught me not to give up on my dreams. Thanks for keeping all the stories that I wrote and illustrated, even my very first book I wrote when I was six, *Up the House*. What a gem that was!

To my baby Luke; I never thought you would be here. Now that you are, I'm excited to have you read my writing someday. I love you so very much.

Lastly, thank you to my amazing husband, Matt Billas. I literally couldn't have done this without you. You've been along this journey every step of the way. I had been in a writing lull until we started dating and then the words finally started flowing. Thank you for always being my first beta reader and helping me improve my writing. You truly are my other half. Love you, always and forever.

LGBTQ+ RESOURCES

https://www.thetrevorproject.org 1-866-488-7386
https://pflag.org/needsupport
https://www.stompoutbullying.org/lgbtq-bullying
https://www.cdc.gov/lgbthealth/youth-resources.htm

You are valid, you are special, you are you. Love deserves to win.

ABOUT THE AUTHOR

Diane Billas lives in the suburbs of Philadelphia, Pennsylvania with her husband and son. When she's not writing she can be found reading multiple books at once, performing the French horn or piano, or dreaming of the next country she's going to visit.

Does Love Always Win? is her debut novel which is drawn from Diane's personal experiences as a queer individual who has struggled throughout life being comfortable identifying and expressing herself. Diane wrote the book she wished was available to her when she was in high school. Diane can be found at dianebillas.com, on Twitter at @dianebillas, on Instagram at @dianebillaswrites, on TikTok at @dianebillas, or at her Facebook author page @dianebillas.

www.ingramcontent.com/pod-product-compliance
Lightning Source LLC
Chambersburg PA
CBHW021218220726
48287CB00015B/1689